THE LAST BREATH

Also by Danny Lopez

The Last Girl

THE LAST BREATH

A DEXTER VEGA MYSTERY

DANNY LOPEZ

OCEANVIEW PUBLISHING
SARASOTA, FLORIDA

ISBN 978-1-60809-297-0

Published in the United States of America by Oceanview Publishing
Sarasota, Florida

www.oceanviewpub.com

10 9 8 7 6 5 4 3 2 1

PRINTED IN THE UNITED STATES OF AMERICA

To all who enjoy the beach

THE
LAST
BREATH

CHAPTER 1

I WAS DRINKING with Rachel Mann at Charley Copek's new brewery, the soon-to-be-famous Blind Pass Brewing just off Stickney Point Bridge, east of Siesta Key. What we'd planned as a fun summer evening in the brewery's new tasting room was a bust. The gang of Seminole Indians from Lee County that Copek had hired to build the chickee hut left early without finishing the job. The parking lot was a mess of dry Palmetto palm fronds and lumber. So Copek put us in a corner of the antiseptic warehouse where we sat on a pair of white plastic Walmart chairs surrounded by big stainless-steel vats full of Charley's famous Siesta IPA.

At least the beer was free.

Despite a nice buzz, I was miserable. Money had come in, and it had gone out. For the last few weeks I'd been fishing in an empty pond. I was broke.

"If I don't get a gig soon," I complained, seeking a little sympathy from Rachel, "I'm gonna have to start liquidating my record collection."

"You know what your problem is?" She pointed at me with her glass. It was obvious Rachel had had it with my whining. She was full of herself since she'd hooked up with her old girlfriend, Dana, the guitar player for the Funky Donkeys, a Goth with an attitude who had a day job with the Sarasota Medical Examiner's Office. She was feeling mighty powerful under the influence of Copek's magic brew. "You don't know how to function in a freelance economy," she said. "You get money, you spend money."

"I got expenses."

She shook her head, took a long drink of beer. "I've been doing this all my life, Dexter. When you're not getting a paycheck every two weeks, you gotta build a slush for the dry spells. When it rains it pours, buddy. But when it don't—"

I raised my eyes, gave her a little grin. "My life's a goddamn desert."

She drained her glass, tilting her head all the way back. "Welcome to another Dexter Vega pity party."

It was true. Rachel had me pegged. She'd been trying to help me ever since I was laid off from the paper, telling me how to freelance, save my money, nagging me about that kind of shit. I guess I wasn't listening.

She ambled over to the keg Copek had set out for us in a big tub of ice, refilled her glass.

"Look here," she said, leaning against the keg. "If you hate it here so much, why don't you leave? Do a national search. There's gotta be something somewhere."

I shook my head and stared down at my beer. I complained about Florida, but I didn't want to leave. Sure, I had my issues with Sarasota. The town and I were like an old couple constantly quarreling about noise ordinances, or the expensive restaurants downtown, or all the new condo buildings that were sprouting like weeds around the bay.

But Sarasota was home.

And despite being a sleepy coastal town where nothing happened—things *were* happening. I just had to look at Charley Copek—bald with a long red beard, a huge barrel chest, and a belly to match, looked like a goddamn Viking. Two years ago, he was selling storm windows and brewing malt liquor in the garage of his home in Gulf Gate. Now he was a big shot in our local microbrew scene and was drawing a paycheck for himself doing exactly what he loved in little sleepy Sarasota.

If he could do it, so could I.

But hanging out behind the scenes at Blind Pass Brewing sounded more glamorous than it was. The place stank of bleach and yeast, and the fluorescents made us look dead. And Charley wasn't even drinking with us. He was holed inside his little office crunching numbers and freaking out about his unfinished webpage.

"Life's expensive no matter where you live," I said doing what I did best: make excuses. "I had to fix the sewer line and the AC. It's like everything breaks when you're broke."

"You should rent."

"In this town? I couldn't afford a place like mine for what I pay in the mortgage."

"True."

"I swear . . ."

Rachel took her seat, poured half her beer into my glass. "You know what my Uncle Herbert used to say?"

"You really had an Uncle Herbert?"

"Either shit or get off the pot," she said.

Yeah, I got the message loud and clear. When I had money, I sat around and loafed like a college dropout. When the money ran out, I panicked. It happened every time. Rachel was right. I had to take action. And I had to take it now.

I slept on it.

* * *

The following morning, despite a mild hangover, I did what Rachel's Uncle Herbert suggested. I sat at my desk and stared at the screen of my laptop. I had two items on my to-do list: pitch story ideas to possible clients and write copy for Charley Copek's website. But that was a freebie—sort of. And I'd been stuck from the moment he got me drunk with that delicious new IPA with a twist of grapefruit and honey. He said if I wrote him a catchy slogan for Blind Pass Brewing and a few seductive paragraphs that would give people a sense of our low-key lifestyle in Siesta Beach, he'd give me a case whenever I wanted.

But I was blocked.

Short and brief wasn't my thing. I tried a few phrases, turned them every which way. Dull. Dull. Dull.

My mind wandered. I glanced out the window. The old house that had occupied the lot catty-corner from my place since the early twenties was bulldozed a few months ago. A developer had cleared the land and was getting ready to start work on yet another condo building. I had attended the city council meetings with some of my neighbors arguing against the project, citing the history and character of our little downtown neighborhood. But the developer got his way. In Sarasota, they always did.

Surveyors had staked out the land prepping for a nine-story monstrosity that would cast a permanent shadow on my little cracker house. Pre-construction prices were a steal at $750K for a one-bedroom unit with a view of the parking lot of another condo on Ringling Boulevard.

The land was marked with little orange flags. At the corner of the lot was a big sign with a fancy logo for *"The Majestic," by Dieter & Waxler. Luxury downtown living with exquisite views of Sarasota Bay. Sold exclusively by Alex J. Trainor, Real Estate.* Across the sign like a strip of yellow police crime scene tape with big block letters, it read: *90 Percent Sold!*

The shit made me sick. It didn't even have a foundation and it was almost sold out.

I turned my eyes back to the computer screen. I had nothing. Just a few sleepy sentences that lacked punch.

But then magic struck. I sent Copek an email suggesting he hold a contest to see who can come up with the best slogan for the beer. Make a party out of it. The winner gets a case of Siesta Key IPA.

I was off the hook, at least temporarily. Now I just needed to write a couple of paragraphs about our beachy lifestyle. Problem was, I lived less than five miles from Siesta Beach but hadn't been there in months. What was a beach lifestyle like anyway?

I set that project aside. I needed to focus on getting work that paid. I switched gears, got busy pitching editors. Problem was, I was in the wrong profession at the wrong time. No one paid writers anymore. Everyone wanted free articles or an exchange of services. Eight hundred words for a burger—as if.

But there was something else bugging me: my daughter, Zoe. Last Sunday we'd been on the phone making plans for her next visit, and the whole conversation had gotten away from me. I was all riled up because my ex-wife had hooked up with some oil tycoon in Houston, and they were living high on the hog. They were going to Paris for a week. I had to offer Zoe something awesome.

By the time we hung up the phone, I'd had a few tequilas and had promised her a week at an all-inclusive in Punta Cana, Dominican Republic.

Cheap—but not so cheap.

I followed Rachel's suggestion. I went through all my old emails and made a list of clients. Then I wrote out a few story ideas and sent them out to everyone on the list.

Three days later I got nothing. Not even a *thank you for thinking of us.*

Finally, I swallowed my pride and called the editor of *Sarasota City Magazine* to pitch a story on people who adopt racing greyhounds for pets in order to save them from the slaughterhouse.

"I'm terribly sorry, Dexter," she said in her usual superior tone. "We just put the summer issue to bed. Why don't we talk in August and come up with something truly fabulous for the fall."

"My summer's looking pretty sad," I admitted. "You need any editing, restaurant reviews? Anything?"

"It's summer. You know how it is."

Summer in Sarasota: hot and humid and wet and very dead. Businesses closed, restaurants reduced their hours. Tourists and snowbirds, that's what we lived for. When it wasn't "season," we didn't exist.

"Listen," she said breaking the static. "I'm sure we'll have something when season picks up."

"That's November."

"I wish I could—wait a sec. I have an idea. It's not writing, but I think it might be right up your alley."

"Go on."

"Last weekend I was at a fund-raising event at the Ritz-Carlton and I was talking to Bob Fleming. Do you know Bob?"

"I don't think so."

"Oh, a dear of a man. Real sweet—and very wealthy. He used to manage a hedge fund in New York. Anyway, apparently his son passed away in a bizarre accident."

"I'm sorry to hear that."

"Yes. Well, it turns out Bob's not happy with the police report."

"How do you mean?"

"Well, he said something about hiring a private investigator to look into what really happened."

"I'm not a detective," I said. "I'm not licensed."

"The case is closed. He's got the police report. Hold on a sec." There was a brief pause. I could hear the clacking of her manicured fingernails on a computer keyboard. Then she was back. "Sorry about that. Okay. Where was I?"

"This guy Fleming wants someone to look into his son's death."

"Oh, yes. Bob. He's older, well into his seventies, I believe. And not in the best shape, but a real sweet guy. You'd like him. Anyway, I think he just wants proper closure. It was his only son."

"So what happened?"

"It was in the paper."

I glanced at the stack of unread *Sarasota Herald* newspapers next to my recycling bin. "I don't read the paper. Ethical reasons."

She laughed at that, then said, "He drowned while kayaking on the Intracoastal."

"What's so bizarre about that?"

"He was fit, twenty-seven. Calm waters . . ."

"So? It can happen."

"Apparently it did," she said quickly. "Look, I can give you Bob's number and maybe you two can come to an arrangement. You get a little paid work, and he finds the closure he's seeking."

"Yeah, a win-win," I said reluctantly. It sounded simple enough. But the truth jabbed at my gut: nothing's ever simple.

CHAPTER 2

BOB FLEMING AGREED to see me right away. I put on a pressed shirt and drove out to his mansion in the Sanderling Club, a vintage, mega-exclusive gated community on Siesta Key where every property is worth millions. And if that wasn't enough, you still had to pay over three thousand bucks a month in homeowner fees, plus a 20K club membership. In return, you got a pleasant and safe neighborhood that felt like old Florida with Gulf views, a lagoon at the back, and a small private beach between Point of Rocks and Turtle Beach. No riff-raff, no tourists, no traffic, no hassle. It was paradise—as intended—with just a dash of snob.

Fleming's place was on the Gulf side of the road, just past the community beach and the cool-looking fifties cabanas. There was nothing tropical about the house. It was a large, two-story traditional Georgian Revival with a red brick facade and white columns at the entrance. It looked as if it had been plucked out of McLean, Virginia, and dropped on the side of the ocean. In the driveway was a crisp white Maserati Grand Turismo. Sweet.

A small, elderly Latino lady in a maid's uniform opened the door and led me into a living room that screamed conservative Republican: tall ceiling with elaborate crown moldings, the standard red brick fireplace surrounded by a pair of ghastly flower-patterned Chippendale sofas, a love seat, and two hard-back chairs on a Persian rug that covered most of the hardwood floor in that part of the room. On the other side was another, more comfortable-looking furniture arrangement, which also seemed to be the one that got more use. And just past it were pane windows and two sets of French doors that led out to a screened, covered patio, the pool, and then the deep aqua of the Gulf of Mexico as a backyard.

"Dexter Vega." A pudgy man in khaki pants and a light blue Polo shirt with the collar turned up came into the living room from a doorway at the opposite end from the fireplace. He looked to be in his late sixties, and he fit the house perfectly: trim whitish-blond hair, sad blue eyes, and a red nose and heavy jowls. He looked like the kind of man who'd never suffered a day in his life. I could tell he was a drinker. And now that he'd gotten old, the good life was taking a toll on him.

His handshake was firm, but his flesh soft. He introduced himself as if everyone in the world knew who he was. "Bob Fleming." Then he took a deep breath, straightened his back, and added, "I appreciate you coming on such short notice."

He didn't invite me to sit. Instead, he stared at the scar in my ear for a moment longer than was polite, took my arm, and led me to the foot of the stairs. A large formal painting of a family hung on a wall beside the stairs. It had its own special light that was attached to the top of the elaborate gold leaf frame illuminating the canvas.

He pointed at the young Bob Fleming in the painting: slim, blond, smiling. Sitting next to him was a pretty blond lady in a long, dark dress and a nicely groomed preppy child about ten years old. The painting was a trophy, a picture of success.

"Liam was my only child," he said. "My wife says I'm delusional thinking that it was something more than an accident, but I'm just not convinced."

"Why's that?"

"In here." He tapped his chest with a stubby index finger, his gold Rolex catching a glint from the light atop the painting. "It just feels wrong."

"No, your wife," I said. "Why does she think you're delusional?"

"Liam's my son from my first marriage. She doesn't have any children."

"But she knew Liam."

"Of course. But he was at the University of Florida when I met and married Brandy."

"Did they get along?"

His glassy blue eyes searched my face, probably trying to decide whether I was kidding. "The point, Mr. Vega, is that Liam was a competitive swimmer in high school. He went out on his kayak just about every day. It doesn't seem right that he drowned. Not like that. Not in that backwater. The Intracoastal is dead calm."

I didn't know what he wanted me to give him. If the cops had looked into it, and they had declared it was an accident, then that was probably what it was.

Fleming tapped my arm and gestured to the living room. "What do you say we have a drink?"

I followed him. "I don't know that I can do any better than the cops. And I'd hate to set you up for disappointment."

He led me to a small bar situated between the kitchen and the dining room and opening up to the living room. I could hear the maid doing something in the kitchen. "Marta," Fleming called, "two glasses with ice."

I heard the ice dispenser doing its thing somewhere in the kitchen. Fleming grabbed a bottle of Grey Goose and removed the cap. The maid came with the glasses on a tray and set it on the counter. Fleming gave her a quick smile and she went back into the kitchen.

He poured two glasses of vodka and handed me one. "Look." He took a short sip and rubbed his red nose with the back of his hand before setting the glass back on the counter. "I'm not looking for someone to blame. I just . . . I just want to know what the hell happened out there."

I glanced at my drink. I hated vodka. I set it on the counter. Fleming stared at me suspiciously.

A part of me didn't want to take the job. What I saw was a rich, lonely man trying to force a narrative that wasn't there—as if his son was not capable of having an accident. Or maybe he just wanted to prolong his mourning. Either way, it just felt wrong. On the other hand, it seemed simple enough. And it meant a payday. I kept thinking of Zoe and me having a blast in Punta Cana.

"So you're basically looking for a second opinion," I said.

He handed me my drink again, grabbed his own. "Something like that." He took a long sip and walked across the living room to the foyer at the foot of the stairs, looked up at the painting. I could tell he wanted me to know we were on the same page, a young and innocent Liam Fleming staring down at us from the large canvas.

"I can do that," I said. "We just have to come up with the terms."

"Money's not a problem."

"Yeah, well, it's more than that. I mean, when do we decide the job's done?"

His eyes grew wide and he pointed at me with his glass. "You tell me."

"If I look into this and come up with a conclusion, even if it concurs with the police report, we call it a done deal."

"Well," he said reluctantly, "what shall we consider a proper conclusion?"

He had a point. "Evidence," I said. "My job is to give you evidence that tells what happened. But if I feel I've exhausted all the angles, I'm done."

He let a few seconds pass before nodding. "Fair enough."

We were about to shake hands when a young woman in a stylish tennis dress skipped down the stairs. She had long black hair tied in a tight ponytail and a designer tan—skin as brown as mine but smooth and even. At first, I thought she was in her late twenties, but when she reached us, I could see she was older, maybe mid-thirties.

"Ah, here's Brandy." Fleming seemed to brighten. "My wife."

Brandy smiled like a model. She was petite and attractive in a manufactured way: personal trainer, spa every couple days, bright pink fingernails that matched her lipstick. Perhaps an occasional Botox shot in her brow. But I could tell that even if she removed her makeup and was caught late one morning with a hangover, she'd still look good. She was Bob Fleming's little trophy.

I introduced myself, glanced at the painting of the family. The woman in the frame was heavier, blond.

Brandy leaned against her husband, laced her arm around his. "What's going on, dear?"

"Mr. Vega's going to look into Liam's accident for me."

Brandy rolled her eyes and pursed her lips.

"I'm just going to check things out," I said quickly, trying to diffuse whatever storm I felt brewing between these two. "Make sure the cops did their job."

"Honestly," she said and shook her head so I got a pleasant whiff of perfume that smelled of money. She stared at him, a slight frown over her dark eyes. "It's not as if it's going to bring Liam back, Bob."

"Brandy," he said. "I need to do this."

"I don't think it's healthy to go on like this," she said sharply. "You're obsessed."

Bob Fleming seemed to physically retreat at her displeasure.

I said, "It's only been a little over a week since the accident. I don't—"

"Please," Brandy interrupted me and ran her hand up Bob's back and caressed his neck. "Don't take his side. You don't know him. He'll dwell on Liam's death for months. He's just going to keep suffering. He's torturing himself with this."

"It's true," Bob said and kissed the top of Brandy's head. "But I need closure, sweetheart. I need this."

Brandy glared at me then turned to Bob. "Do what you want, dear. But six months from now when you're lying in bed in a drunken stupor crying for Liam, don't tell me I didn't warn you."

After that little verbal slap, she kissed the old man on the cheek and skipped across the living room and disappeared into a hallway.

Bob cleared his throat and grinned uncomfortably. "She's always watching out for me." Then he brought the glass to his lips, and I watched his Adam's apple go up and down like a bouncy ball as he consumed the liquor.

"Lucky guy," I said so we could get back to business. I wasn't a psychologist and I wasn't one to judge, but it was clear that big hedge fund millionaire Bob Fleming was weak at the knees for his hard-ass wife.

"She thinks I'm wasting my money," he said.

"Yeah, about that," I said. "This is a peculiar case. I mean it's difficult to put a price on the work."

"You have a fee?"

"No, not really," I said and caught sight of his Rolex again. I thought of a week in Punta Cana, Zoe—all inclusive. "Maybe three grand—"

"In advance?"

"That would be best. And if there's any expenses—"

"Of course," he said and pulled out his wallet.

I thought he was going to give me the cash right there and then, but instead, he gave me a business card for Thomas Pearlman,

Esquire, attorney at law. "Tom's your point man. He'll pay you for the first week. He also has a copy of the police report for you."

Bob didn't see me out. He moved toward the bar for a refill of Grey Goose. I went out the front door the same way I came in. Just as I reached my car, I heard Brandy call my name.

She was coming from around the side of the house. "Are you really doing this?" she said when she caught up with me, her hands perched on the sides of her slender waist.

"Doing what?" We stood face-to-face between my old Subaru and that fine, 160-thousand-dollar Maserati.

"Taking his money just like that, prolonging his misery. He drinks enough as it is."

"I'm sorry. But he hired me to do a job. Someone has to pay for my time."

"Now you listen to me," she snapped and waved one of those perfectly manicured fingernails at my face, her voice sharp and full of poison. "I won't let you take advantage of him. You understand me? So handle with care, buster."

With that she turned around and skipped back to the house. When she jumped up the step to the front door, her miniskirt bounced up and floated down. I could swear she wasn't wearing any panties.

CHAPTER 3

ON MY DRIVE home, I called Pearlman. I expected the runaround, having to set up an appointment and all that crap that usually accompanies anything involving lawyers, but his secretary said to come right over.

The office was in the sixth floor of the Orange Blossom Tower, a tastefully redone old building on the corner of Main Street and Palm Avenue in downtown Sarasota. The reception was all dark wood and smelled of Murphy's Oil and tobacco. There were four high-back black leather chairs in front of a wide desk where Pearlman's secretary sat. Behind her, the wood-paneled walls were decorated with old black-and-white photographs of Sarasota history: fishermen, the circus, parades.

The secretary's name was Vivian McCutcheon—it was etched in gold, all caps Helvetica on the nameplate on her desk. She was young and polite and professional. She had medium brown hair combed to the side and wore a navy-blue skirt suit and medium heels. When I entered, she stood and asked me to sit in one of the four chairs.

After a little small talk about the terribly hot summer, she disappeared behind a set of large double doors and reappeared a few seconds later, closing the door very gently. She offered me two manila envelopes. "This is the file on Liam Fleming," she said, pointing to the larger of the two. "And this is your weekly fee. In advance, as agreed with Mr. Fleming."

I smiled and nodded at the double doors. "What about him?"

"Mr. Pearlman?"

"I'd really like to ask him a few questions about the—"

"Mr. Pearlman is extremely busy." She glanced at her wristwatch. "At the moment, he's on his way to the airport."

I looked at the envelope with the file on Liam Fleming. "Did he handle Mr. Fleming's son's case?"

"There was no case," she said and her eyes dropped to the floor. "It was an accident."

"When do you expect Mr. Pearlman back?"

"Thursday morning."

"Can I see him then?"

"Mr. Pearlman doesn't see anyone."

"What about his clients?"

"He only has one."

"Mr. Fleming."

"That is correct," she said and gripped the back of the chair in front of her. Her eyes darted nervously about the room.

I glanced at the envelopes.

"There's an extra five hundred for expenses," she said quickly. "Please keep proper records and turn in your receipts at the end of the week."

"It's all very neat," I said.

"Mr. Fleming likes things properly handled. I will have another envelope for you next week if the case should need further . . . looking into."

I held up the envelope with Liam's police file. "And if I have any questions about the case?"

"Call the office."

"You mean, call you."

"That is correct." She bit her lip and stole a quick glance at my ear. "It all goes through me."

"Is that how the cops investigated this thing?"

She frowned. "Mr. Vega, this *thing*, as you call it, is the tragic death of a human being—of Mr. Fleming's son. The man is crestfallen."

* * *

I left Pearlman's office and walked around the corner to Caragiulos. I took a seat at the bar, ordered a Big Top Circus City IPA on draft and looked over the police report.

It was all pretty cut and dry. The kid was twenty-seven years old. His body was found early in the morning by a woman after it got snagged on her dock off Kensey Lane in Osprey on the other side of the Intracoastal, south of Little Sarasota Bay. Toxicology report showed THC in the blood. So he probably smoked a little weed. I didn't imagine it would impede his ability as a kayaker.

I used my phone to Google the Flemings, both father and son. Hedge fund Fleming retired six years ago after twenty-seven years of managing other people's money in a private fund that was still in existence, and which, as far as I could tell, had never made much of a profit. Still, his compensation and retirement bonus was at least three times the yearly budget of the City of Sarasota. The man wasn't just loaded. He was mega-loaded.

Liam Fleming graduated from some prep school in upstate New York. He was on the soccer team and the swim team. He attended the University of Florida in Gainesville where he graduated with a degree in business. He then moved to Sarasota. His father came down a year later from New York City, after he retired.

I ordered another beer. There are two types of mourners, as far as I know. The ones who clam up and keep their pain inside, and the ones who talk. It's like therapy. But Bob Fleming was neither. He didn't tell me what a great kid Liam was, or how much he missed him, or how unfair the whole thing was. Instead he sent me to his lawyer's office to pick up the police report—a cold, analytical description of the scene. Maybe that's what the old man was after.

I wasn't the best father. My daughter, Zoe, lived with her mother in Houston. We spoke on the phone every so often. I never knew what to say. But deep down in my heart, I wanted more. I wanted to connect, feel that familial love that connected us as father and daughter. All parents want that. Maybe that was what Bob wanted, to know more about his son.

Either way, there was no point in wasting any more time. From what I could gather, the best place to start looking was with Liam Fleming.

I drove down to his address on Midnight Pass Road at the south end of Siesta Key, just across the road from Turtle Beach. And maybe it was just a coincidence, but it was just down the road from the Sanderling Club where his father lived.

I parked on the shell driveway behind a blue Volkswagen Golf with a surfboard on the roof rack. Next to it was a late-model silver Range Rover with one of those *Coexist* stickers on the back. The house was an old cottage from the early seventies covered in moldy vinyl siding, cheap aluminum jalousie windows, and a tin roof. Still, it was on a huge lot dense with sea grape and scrub oak and mangroves. On both sides were multimillion-dollar mansions. The backyard was the Intracoastal Waterway.

No one answered when I knocked on the door. I don't know what I was expecting. I checked the mailbox. It was empty except for a weekly pamphlet with special deals and coupons for local businesses. I walked slowly around the house to the back where there was a patio with a nice set of rattan furniture and a couple of plastic

Adirondack chairs arranged around a fire pit. At the edge of the mangrove forest was a narrow dock that led out to the Intracoastal.

I sifted through an ashtray. A lot of cigarette butts and a couple of roaches. The ground was littered with a dozen empty beer cans, JDub's and Darwin's and Corona, and Blind Pass Brewing's Siesta IPA. I peeked through the back windows. The lanai was empty except for a few oars, a paddleboard, and two surfboards. No kayak. Beyond the lanai was the living room where something moved.

I knocked on the back door, hard. Tried the handle. Locked.

"Hey!" I called and moved to the next window where I got a better view of the living room. Something crashed inside, like a pan falling on a hard surface. A figure ran past. I knocked on the window. Then followed quickly around the side of the house. A man in suit pants and a blue Oxford shirt appeared from the front, came walking straight toward me, quick.

"Hey," I said. "I'm a friend of—"

He hooked me high on the gut—like a flash. No warning.

I lost my air. Fell on my knees, gasped for air. Then I got it on the back of the head. Pain. Everything went dark.

CHAPTER 4

I WOKE TO a stereo blasting CCR's *Proud Mary*. My head throbbed from the base of my neck to my brow. I staggered to my feet, leaned against the side of the house for support. My knees were weak, head dizzy, nauseous. I rubbed the back of my neck. The pain felt as if someone were pressing a hot iron against the back of my skull. I took a few deep breaths and slowly made my way to the front of the house. The sun was at an angle, blinding. I'd been out an hour. Maybe less.

I shielded my eyes from the sun with my hand. The silver Range Rover was gone. In its place was a cream-colored 1980s Toyota Land Cruiser that looked pretty beat up. A man wearing shorts that sat low on his waist and reached down to his knees and no shirt hopped out of the driver's seat. He looked like a surfer with shoulder-length blond hair, well built, trim and tan. A tight Puka shell necklace around his neck. Tied to the roof rack of his SUV was a red plastic kayak.

"Whazzup, brah?" he greeted me with an upbeat nasally tone but didn't pause his work, moving around the truck, untying the bungees from the roof rack.

"Nothing." I grunted and walked to where he was parked, leaned on the front of his car. The hood was hot, stank of burnt oil.

The surfer snapped a couple more bungees. "Liam around?"

"No."

He finished with the cords and pulled the kayak off the roof and set it on the ground next to the Land Cruiser. "What about Jaybird?"

"I . . . no, I don't think so."

He paused, shifted his weight to one leg and looked at me for the first time. "Who're you?"

"Dexter Vega. Friend of the family."

He showed me his pretty white teeth. "No shit."

I nodded. "Who're you?"

"Keith, man. I brought back the kayak."

"Liam's kayak?"

He nodded and tossed his long blond hair to the side. "Just spent a freakin' awesome week in Ten Thousand Islands with my kids. Nothing else like it anywhere in the country. I don't think a whole lot of people appreciate it the way they should. Outrageous place, brah."

"So you don't know?"

"Know what?"

"About Liam."

He stared at me, waiting.

"He's dead."

He kept his eyes on me for a moment. Then he chuckled. "No way. You're bullshitting me, brah."

I shook my head. "Drowned. Last Friday." I pointed to the back of the house.

"You serious?"

I nodded.

"What the fuck?" He ran his hand over his golden hair and turned away. "Liam, man. What happened?"

"They said it was an accident."

"Who's *they*?"

"The cops."

"The cops . . ." He said it with distaste, like he was spitting something out. "Liam, man. Dead." He leaned against the truck. "That's some shit."

"Did you know him well?"

"Yeah, kinda. Like everyone else."

"His father said he was a pretty good swimmer."

"Like a fucking shark, brah."

"It doesn't make any sense."

"Shit's bogus."

I moved to the side of the car and leaned against the side mirror. I needed it for balance. Everything was off, tilted, turning. "So how did you meet . . . Liam?"

He pointed with his thumb over his shoulder at the place behind Midnight Pass Road. "Turtle Beach, brah. We hung out."

I pointed to the kayak. Red plastic with a nice back on the seat. "And you borrowed his kayak?"

"Right on." He glanced at the kayak, then picked it up and walked past me and along the side path to the back of the house. I followed him, my legs wobbly, my right arm out, hand touching the house in case I faltered.

He set the kayak on the ground, leaning against the back wall next to the door to the lanai. Then he turned and looked around the patio and nodded. "Man, we had some good times back here." He winked at me. "Smoked a lot of ganja."

"Can I ask you something?"

He turned to face me.

"You think anyone would want to hurt him?"

"Liam?" He snorted and tossed his head back a little. "Fuck no. Liam was boss, brah. Like with everyone. I can't imagine—" Then he paused and stared at me like he'd just figured something out. "You think someone killed him?"

"No." I forced a smile. "I'm just checking."

He shook his head and started back to the front of the house.

I followed. "It's just that he was a good swimmer, right? They say he was out kayaking on the Intracoastal," I said. "I don't really see how that could happen. I mean how does that happen? Water's calm. He's on a kayak."

"Dunno, brah. But I guess shit happens." He gathered the bungees from the roof rack and tossed them across the front seat to the passenger side of the SUV.

I tried to focus, think of questions, of what I needed, but it was all getting away from me too quickly. The back of my head throbbed, throwing me off. I just wanted to close my eyes and sleep it off.

"Was he living on his father's dime?"

Keith laughed. "No way, brah. Liam was indy all the way. Besides, those two didn't get along."

"Really?"

He seemed to consider this for a moment. Then he said, "It's not as if he talked shit about him or nothin', but you could just tell, you know?" He moved his hands in front of him as if he were caressing a bowling a ball. "Like there was a vibe. You just knew . . ."

"I understand."

Keith tossed his head to the side, squinted at me. "Yeah, just a vibe, brah. Like he had a chip on his shoulder about the old man."

"Did you ever meet him?"

"The old man? Can't say I had the pleasure."

He opened the door to his truck. The sign on the door read: *Sun n' Surf Adventure Kayak Rental.*

"Wait a second." I pointed at the sign on the door. "Why'd you borrow Liam's kayak if you . . ."

He stepped back and glanced at the sign, then ran his hand over his golden locks. "That's business, brah. I had a friend working my gig while I was away. Matter fact, gotta book and pick up my boards."

"Is there anything else you could tell me about him?"

He lowered his head, moved his bare foot lightly over the crushed shells. "I dunno. Liam, man. He was . . . he was cool." He raised his eyes at me and smiled, tapped his chest with the side of his fist. "Open hearted. Like with everyone."

He hopped in the Land Cruiser and shut the door. He stared ahead for a moment. Then he said, "All the good ones die young."

He started the engine. John Fogerty's voice screamed out of the speakers. He backed out onto Midnight Pass Road, then lowered the volume on the stereo and leaned across the passenger side. "Yo, brah, can you do me a solid? If you see Jaybird, tell him to swing by Turtle Beach tomorrow so we can toast Liam. Give him a proper good-bye."

"Who's Jaybird?"

"Jaybird, brah. Everyone knows Jaybird. Dude leads the drum circle at Siesta Beach."

CHAPTER 5

THE SIESTA BEACH drum circle happened every Sunday at sunset. What had started as a casual gathering of beach bums and hippies over twenty years ago was now a huge beach party with a bunch of rules about participating, reserving a place, or entering the circle, and taking photos. Just as with everything else in this town, the fun had been sucked out of something nice.

Today was Tuesday. I wasn't sure what I would find. I pulled up to a space in the middle of the Siesta Public Beach parking lot. The sun had not yet reached the horizon but was already painting the distant storm clouds gold and stretching shadows over the powder white sand across the beach. I could hear faint drumming in the distance, sporadic, disorganized.

I was still fuzzy in the head as I walked along the wide stretch of beach. It was insufferably hot. People were still out, mostly couples and older people walking for exercise, wading in the shallows, lying on towels. A flock of seagulls stood together, all of them facing the same direction like soldiers.

Farther to the north, a dozen drummers formed a crescent facing the sun and ocean to the west. In front of them, a handful of dancers hopped and swayed and gyrated to the disjointed rhythms. It was nothing like the giant Sunday drum circle. This gathering was just a small contingent of diehard hippies doing their thing. Felt nice. Like in the old days.

People paused to watch, many holding their beach chairs and umbrellas, then moved on toward the parking lot.

There was at least an hour before sunset. And at the moment, the sun was half-hidden behind heavy storm clouds. It was raining to the north of us.

Men and women danced around like flower children, free-flowing hair, light cotton skirts and beads, waving and playing with hoola-hoops like they were at a Grateful Dead concert. A couple of young guys danced in place, their eyes closed. A mild breeze blew. I got a sweet whiff of marijuana.

I watched a young woman dancing alone. She had a nice tan and dark long hair and wore a colorful Indian skirt and a bikini top. She moved close to the drummers, smiling at them and gesturing as if her movements were having a conversation with their drumming.

My head still throbbed from that vicious blow. And the drumming wasn't helping. I tried hard to focus, take inventory of everything Keith had told me. And the silver Range Rover that had been parked in the driveway. I had to remember that. I had to remember a lot of things. But what I really wanted was to walk away and go home, lie down in the air-conditioning and sleep.

The young woman I had been keeping an eye on stopped dancing and approached one of the drummers. They talked for a couple of minutes, laughed. She touched his scruffy goatee and then walked off to the side of the circle where a few bags and shoes lay in a pile on the sand. She opened a cooler and pulled out a plastic bottle of water.

I walked around the circle to where she was. "Nice dancing."

She looked at me while she drank. "Thanks." She closed the bottle and put it in a hemp bag, then tossed the bag on the pile with the others. "It's the drumming. You really feel it, you know?" She made a gesture with her hands, like butterflies floating up to the sky. "It lifts the spirit, clears the mind, yeah?"

"That's awesome," I said.

She nodded toward the drum circle. "You should get in there. Let your spirit soar, man."

"Thanks, but it's not my thing," I said, leaning forward so she could hear me. "You know Jaybird?"

She laughed. "Yeah, man. Everyone knows Jaybird."

I looked past her at the drummers. "Is he here?"

She pointed to a skinny guy with a hawk nose and blond dread-locks that reached down to his waist. "Right there at the center wailing on that djembe drum."

Jaybird looked like the poster boy for an aging hippie: torn shorts, an oversized wife-beater with the fading image of Bob Marley, and a big bead necklace that bounced on his chest as he smacked the hourglass-shaped drum like he was summoning the spirits. Every now and then he moved his head to the left and right as if to better hear his drumming, then smiled at himself. Yeah, he was in his own world. A grown boy and his drum—for real.

The young woman I'd been talking with tossed her head to the side and sauntered back to the center of the circle where she extended her arms out and twirled like a child. I pressed the bridge of my nose, trying to relieve the pressure in my head. The sun peeked between the clouds, rays spread out like the hand of God. The drumming became stronger, louder, faster.

It was fucking torture.

The crowd of spectators grew. People leaving the beach and a whole wave of folks there to catch the sunset joined the spectacle. I moved away, feeling light-headed.

Jaybird turned and said something to the drummer sitting beside him. He stopped drumming. A moment later he slung his instrument over his shoulder, waved to another drummer, high-fived another, and made his way out of the circle on the opposite side of my position, heading away from the water.

I caught up to him just as he reached the path that led to the parking lot. "Jaybird."

He turned around, but kept walking backwards, a curious smile on his face. "All right. What's goin' on, brother?"

"Can I talk to you a sec?"

He pointed behind him, thumb over his shoulder. "I'm runnin' kinda late, man."

"It's about Liam Fleming."

"You a cop?"

"Does it matter?"

He stopped walking. I caught up to him. His smile dropped and his little red eyes moved up and down, suspiciously. He saw my ear, pointed to the side of my head. "Oh, gnarly, man. What happened?"

I touched the scar, a souvenir from my trip to Mexico City. "Someone used it as an ashtray."

"No fucking way."

I nodded. "Listen—"

"That's fucked up, man."

"Listen, about Liam—"

He shook his head. "I already told you what I knew."

"What are you talking about?"

"Liam, man."

"I don't understand. Tell me from the beginning."

Jaybird took a long breath and tossed his dreads to the side. He pointed at me with his index finger and thumb together like he was holding a joint. "There's no beginning, man. Liam just vanished, like a ghost. Poof. Then you all show up asking questions."

"Jaybird," I said. "Liam's dead."

He looked at me as if trying to figure out if I was pulling his leg. "I know, man." Then he backed away and shook his head. "And I told you all I know."

"I'm not a cop," I said. "I know nothing."

He glanced back at the drum circle. The sun was just turning orange. And in his reddish eyes I saw this odd disconnect, like fear and sorrow and this flash of lucidity that seemed to record the gravity of the moment.

"I thought he'd hooked up with some chick," he said quickly.

"Then the cops showed up asking questions?"

"A cop," he said. "Dressed like a fucking banker. I told him what I knew." He shook his head, dreads dangling around his shoulders. The clarity, that moment of comprehension was gone. He started walking toward the road again, his head down.

I followed.

"This is fucked up," he mumbled to himself. "Liam."

"Jaybird."

"I still can't believe he's dead."

"I'm sorry," I said. "Can you tell me about him?"

"I don't know, man. What can I say?" He turned around, and in a tone that seemed to teeter between anger and sadness, he said, "He was a class act. Got along with everyone. Like if you saw him, you'd think he was a square, you know, like some rich daddy's boy. But he was cool, man. A good fucking friend."

He turned quickly and started again toward the road.

"What did he do for a living? Did he have a job?"

We reached the sidewalk, and he started north on Beach Road toward the business district of Siesta Village. I grabbed his arm and stopped him, turned him around. "Help me out here," I said.

He glanced at my hand gripping his bicep, then at me. "Why you asking me all these questions, man? The dude's dead. Let him rest in fucking peace."

"I'm looking into this as a favor to his father."

"That's a laugh."

"Why? Tell me about it."

"The usual shit, man." Jaybird waved and started walking again. "Old man was too busy getting rich to play ball with his son. Liam still carried the grudge."

"Can you stop walking for a moment?"

"Gotta get to work."

"You have a job?"

"Dude."

"I'm sorry."

The walk was making me nauseous. My head was about to explode, bricks pounding against it one after another. "I just want to know more about Liam," I said. "Who were his friends?"

A girl on the other side of Beach Road waved. "Yo, Jaybird, whassup?"

He waved but kept walking. I struggled to keep up. "Listen," I said and offered him my business card. "Please. Call me? Can you call me tomorrow?"

He took the card and shoved it in his back pocket without looking at it. We stopped where the road curved and became Ocean Boulevard. The heart of Siesta Village, half a dozen blocks of bars and restaurants and boutiques. Beach Road continued straight north and disappeared into the fine powdery sand.

On the corner by the beach access next to the Terrace condominium building, an older man with a scruffy gray beard was having a heated conversation with a teenager who stood with one bare foot on a long skateboard. Next to them was a red, white, and blue sign: *Keep Beach Road Public.*

"Yo, Cap'n Cody," Jaybird called to him and held his index finger and thumb pressed together to his lips. "Come by later, man. We'll light one up."

The old man nodded, glanced at me, and turned back to the teen-ager, gestured at the kid's longboard.

"Jaybird . . ." I said.

He ignored me, checked both sides of the street. "Gotta clock in, man. Don't want to piss off The Man."

He adjusted the strap of the drum over his shoulder and crossed the street toward the Siesta Beach Resort.

"Hey," I called after him, "where do you work?"

"The Old Salty Dog."

* * *

When I got home I took some Motrin, broke up some ice, wrapped it in a kitchen towel, and held it over the bump on the back of my head. I didn't even feed the cat or put on any music. I just lay back on the couch and closed my eyes. I'd heard sleeping was bad for a concussion, but I was so damn tired. I had to close my eyes, told myself just a few minutes.

CHAPTER 6

My phone woke me up. "Yeah?"

"Dude, it's Jaybird."

It took me a moment to come out of the daze of sleep.

"Yo, dude. You there?"

I looked at my phone. "It's four in the morning!"

"Yeah, no shit, man. I just got home. Someone's been here. They've gone through the house, man. It's a fucking mess."

"So? Call the cops."

"Oh yeah, sure thing. I thought since you were on the case maybe you wanted to check it out."

I sat up. "What are you talking about?"

"Liam's place, man. Someone came in and ransacked the place."

"You're at Liam's?"

"Yeah, man. This is where I crash. I told you. Rent free."

"You didn't tell me that."

"Well, I'm telling you now, man."

"I'll be there in ten minutes. Don't touch anything."

* * *

When I got to Liam's place, Jaybird was sitting on an old rattan couch in the small living room browsing through the pages of *Curl* magazine, a can of Siesta IPA on the side table. When I walked in, he tossed the magazine on the wooden cable spool that doubled as a coffee table and chuckled like a little kid caught in the act. "Hot chicks can surf, man."

"What happened?" I was thinking of the man I'd encountered the previous day—the man who pummeled me. I hadn't tried the front door. I'd talked with Keith, the surfer-kayaker who said he'd been at Ten Thousand Islands, then I went to find Jaybird. Stupid move. But I'd been so out of it from the blow to the back of my head. I wasn't thinking straight. My bad.

"No idea, man," Jaybird said. "I wasn't here. When I came home, I saw the place was all messed up. Then I called you."

The drawers to a small desk were open, papers pulled out. A bunch of CDs lay on the floor in front of a shitty stereo component. On the corner a bureau had been rifled, contents tossed aside: a box with a Monopoly game, a few paperback novels, kitchen utensils, two detailed maps that looked like sea charts—all of it strewn on the floor. On the cable spool coffee table, there was a stack of real estate and surfing magazines and a purple plastic bong—all of it undisturbed.

"Did they take anything?"

Jaybird took a long drink of his beer. "There's nothing to take, man. Look for yourself. Maybe the TV or the stereo?"

But the old tube-style television and the cheap stereo were there. Untouched.

"So nothing of value?"

He shook his head, his dreadlocks dangling like golden ropes. "The house was like, always open to friends. That's how Liam was, man. Everyone was welcome. Anytime, all the time."

I sat on the couch next to Jaybird and ran my hand over my unkempt hair. I didn't even know where to start. I had rushed out of my house half asleep. Hadn't given this a lot of thought. But something had to be going on. Not that Liam's death was foul play, but something was not right—especially after yesterday.

Jaybird pushed himself off the couch and walked to the other side of the room and leaned against the kitchen counter. He bit his thumbnail as he looked over the mess. "Man, I'm gonna have to clean all this shit up."

"You get out of work at four?" I said.

He raised his eyes at me, smiled. "Nah. We all went over to Tessa's place to party. Fucking Felipe got so drunk he kept trying to put the moves on Lisa, the new waitress at The Dog. He kept saying things like, 'Come here my little-little.'" He laughed. "Dude ended up passed out in front of the neighbor's apartment."

"Who's Tessa?"

"Bartender at The Dog, man. Cool chick. Liam used to date her a while back."

"You need to tell me more about Liam. Tell me everything. Tell me about his work, who his friends were."

Jaybird shook his head and looked at me with a sideways glance. "What's your game, man?"

"I'm just trying to find out if someone . . . I don't know."

"Like, killed him?"

"Yeah, something like that." I stood and came around to where he stood by the kitchen. "When I was here yesterday, some guys were in the house, probably the same people who messed the place up."

"But you're a cop, man."

"I'm not a cop. I told you. I'm working for Liam's father. But that's not the point. Those men must have been looking for something. You have any idea what?"

"What?"

"What they were looking for!"

"Chill, dude." He stepped back and pulled at one of his dread-locks. "How the fuck would I know what someone else is looking for? I don't even know who they are."

"But you must know something."

He bowed his head. "Dude, I don't know." His voice was low, fragile. "Liam was my friend, man. Dude never hurt anyone. The last of the good guys."

"I'm not a cop," I said. "Trust me, Jaybird. I want to find the people who hurt him."

"They didn't hurt him. They killed him."

"Who?"

"I don't fucking know, man." He waved his hand in an arc. "You said it."

"What about drugs?"

"What about them?"

"I don't know. Drug dealers are criminals, right? Maybe . . ."

"Nah, man. We just smoked a little weed. Dude was into health and nature. Know what I mean? He worked out, swam, went kayaking, was learning to surf. That's the shit that got him high. Nature. That's the shit—"

I raised my hand to stop him. "Can you think of anything those men might've been looking for? Anything at all?"

"What men?"

I sighed. "The men who wrecked the damn place!"

"Oh, right. Shit. No, man. No clue."

This was going nowhere. Jaybird was like a goddamn child. I moved to the kitchen. "You got any coffee?"

"Yeah, man, somewhere in that mess. Next to the toaster."

The kitchen looked just like the rest of the house. Dirty dishes piled on the sink and counter, spaghetti sauce splattered over the stove, empty beer cans, and an open bag of Cheetos, an empty pizza box. The place reeked of sour milk and rotting fruit.

"This is disgusting," I said as I rinsed out the coffeemaker. "How can you live like this?"

Jaybird didn't answer. He was sitting on the couch huddled forward. I heard the gurgling of the water in the bong as Jaybird took in a long drag. Seconds later I got the sweet scent of burnt weed. I turned back to the kitchen and prepped the coffeemaker.

There was more gurgling, then Jaybird coughed.

I rinsed out two cups and poured two coffees. When I walked back into the living room, Jaybird was lying on the couch, snoring.

I stood leaning against the wall, watching him, wondering how I might get some information from him. Eight times out of ten, the victim knows the criminal. I didn't suspect Jaybird.

At least not yet.

I sat on the recliner across from the sofa where Jaybird had fallen asleep and sipped my coffee. I watched him for a while. He was out. Didn't even twitch.

I couldn't figure it. Jaybird was filthy. He lived, looked, and smelled like a homeless person. What did he have in common with Liam Fleming?

No. That was presumptuous of me. I didn't know Liam. But from what Jaybird said, he kept the house open to his friends. That meant anyone. My mind made a few circles. All I could think of was drugs. Rich kid lives the life of a beach bum, smoked weed, and floated around in a kayak all day. He had to get his dope from someone. And maybe that someone was owed some cash. Maybe that someone just knew there was money in the house. But would that lead to murder?

The men I'd encountered at the house yesterday knew exactly what they were doing. That one guy, he came directly at me, didn't talk or try to negotiate or make excuses. And he knew exactly where to punch.

They had to be looking for something, and when I showed up, they knocked me out of the way. That's not the work of a street dealer selling dime bags. That's the work of a professional . . . hit man?

No. My imagination was running wild with this. I sipped my coffee. Jaybird didn't move, dreadlocks spread out over the cushion.

I sifted through the papers on the top of the cable spool. There were a few *National Geographics* from the seventies, half a dozen surfing magazines, the stub from an electric bill, a Publix receipt for three six-packs of beer, and at least a dozen real estate publications.

I grabbed my cup and walked around the house. It had only one bedroom. I was pretty sure it was Liam's. The furniture wasn't fancy but it seemed organized: a double bed—unmade—a desk and a dresser. There was no computer, but there were cables to power a laptop and connect a printer that sat on the floor next to the desk, and a small trash can.

I set my coffee cup on the desk, opened the drawers, and flipped through the papers. All domestic stuff: bills, receipts, one for a new AC wall unit from Home Depot, a few soy sauce packets like the ones you get when you order Chinese takeout, a pair of sunglasses, pens. I crouched and sifted through the trash bin. More of the same.

On the dresser, I found a pile of clothes, a few real estate flyers, and a stack of *Sarasota City* magazines. I flipped through the issues. I found a recent one with an article I'd written about a newly redecorated house. It looked like an ad. But it had paid. I had no room to complain.

I turned the pages. Near the end was an ad for luxury real estate. One of the properties was circled with a red marker. It was a small lot in north Siesta Key.

I walked to the other side of the room and sat on the bedside and checked the drawer on the night side table. A John le Carré novel, an empty glass, a small jar of melatonin from Trader Joe's, a roach clip, a small Swiss Army knife, Trojan condoms, and a few photos, faded and a little frayed at the edges. One was of a man and a woman that I quickly recognized as a young Bob Fleming and his first wife, Liam's mother. The other photo was of her with a boy, maybe seven years old, probably Liam. They were sitting in an outdoor restaurant. It looked like it could be Florida, somewhere that seemed to say vacation. The other photo must have been of the same time, but it was the kid, Liam, making a sandcastle on a beach that could pass for Siesta Beach. His mother was lying on a towel to the side. She looked good. Young and pretty and happy. The last photo was more recent. It was crisp and clean and showed a young man smiling at the camera. Again, I imagined it was Liam. He was good-looking, dirty-blond hair, a nice smile, friendly eyes. It was taken in a bar. He was holding a beer and pointing at the camera. In the background, falling off the light and out of focus, people sat at the bar drinking and minding their own business. There was nothing written on the back of any of the photos.

I checked the closet and under the bed. Nothing. I looked around one last time. On the wall over the bed were a couple of surfing posters. On the other wall next to the desk was a detailed map of Siesta Key. Someone had taken a red marker and circled a few spots at the north end of the key near the beach and at the south end: Midnight Pass.

I grabbed my coffee and walked back to the living room, wondering where Jaybird slept because there was no other room or bed. But when I saw him laid out on the couch, I realized he probably just crashed wherever he fell asleep. There was a small pile of clothes on the corner behind a dinette between the kitchen and the living room. Next to it was his drum.

I nudged Jaybird's shoulder with my foot. He let out a loud snore and turned on his side, away from me. A big brown cockroach appeared at the top of the couch and ran across his hair and face and disappeared under the blanket that covered the bottom cushion.

Jaybird didn't move.

I took a long drink of coffee and set my cup on the counter, then made my way past the bathroom to the lanai where the two surfboards were propped against the wall. The paddleboard was on its side with a few oars stacked next to it. The rest of the room was empty.

I threw the latch on the door and walked outside. It was dawn. The sky was a deep blue except to the east where it had a light, translucent quality. It was hot and humid, but there was a freshness in the air that almost made it pleasant. I made my way to the end of the rickety dock. The mosquitoes and no-see-ums were out in force. The sound of my hands slapping my neck and arms was the only thing disturbing an otherwise quiet morning.

On the mangroves across the Intracoastal, dozens of egrets perched quietly together. A great blue heron walked in slow motion in the shallow below, hunting for its breakfast.

When I walked back toward the house, I noticed the red plastic kayak Keith had brought back. It had molded seats and a deck hatch.

I grabbed an oar from the lanai and carried the kayak to the end of the dock. It was cumbersome because of the narrow dock. I flicked off my shoes, pulled off my socks, eased the kayak onto to the water, and got on. I pushed off with the oar and rowed gently out. The water was calm and clear and shallow enough—less than three or four feet. I could see the mud and grass below.

I rowed easily to the south, suffering the no-see-ums and mosquitoes. Pretty soon I was sweating, my shirt sticking to my skin. I stopped rowing and rested the paddle across my lap. The tide barely moved the kayak. I didn't see how someone could tip over, much less drown.

To my left, the sun was tinting the eastern horizon a light pink and blue like a fine, well-polished jewel. Overhead an osprey floated like a kite. In the distance, I could hear an engine, a motorboat revving, someone getting ready to go out fishing.

It was almost impossible for me to tell exactly where I was relative to the roads. To my right the condominiums disappeared as I came alongside Midnight Pass. To this day, Midnight Pass was a point of contention with the people of Sarasota. In the early eighties, the county and the Corps of Engineers closed the pass that led out to the Gulf in order to save a few beachfront houses that were being washed away by erosion just south of Turtle Beach. Despite closing the pass, a couple houses washed away. They never reopened the pass.

I saw a couple on paddleboards ahead of me. I picked up my oar and rowed toward them.

"Morning," I said as I came up from behind.

They stopped paddling. They looked like husband and wife, both in their fifties, trim, healthy-looking.

"It's a nice one, hey?" the man said.

"Sure is," I said. "You know how deep it is around here?"

"Not very," the man said. "Four feet."

"It depends," the woman said. "It's more like six feet when it's high tide."

The man looked at her. "It doesn't get that deep."

"It does," the woman said to him. "Maybe not right here, but there are places where it gets deeper."

"Yeah, except for the channel at the center, it's all pretty shallow," the man said.

The woman pursed her lips and turned to me. "It's not bad, but it's not consistent. There are a couple of deep places once you pass Blackburn Point Bridge. And then the channel. That's a good twelve to twenty feet deep."

"It's for the boats," the man said.

"I'm sure he knows that," the woman said to the man.

"You don't know that," he said to her.

"Well, thanks," I said and paddled back a little.

"Sure thing," the man said.

"Down that way you have some great mangrove islands. They get covered in birds this time of the morning," the woman said. "Egrets and herons and cormorants."

"Thanks," I said and kept rowing backwards, away from them. They watched me move. I was pretty sure they were curious about my awkward handling of the kayak. The woman said something to the man. He said something back and then they started paddling south.

I rowed back to the house. Pulling the kayak out of the water onto the dock was not easy. When I finally managed to get it out, my legs were soaked. I sat on the dock and put my socks and shoes on. Then I carried the kayak to the patio and set it leaning against the back wall of the house. I walked into the lanai and placed the oar with the others and marched into the living room.

Jaybird was gone.

CHAPTER 7

I POURED MYSELF a fresh cup of coffee and paced around Liam's house for about forty-five minutes, opening and closing drawers, rifling through papers, bills, and staring at the map on his bedroom wall and the places he had circled: a house on Beach Road, a lot near Siesta Village, and empty lots around Midnight Pass. I hoped to see some kind of pattern, but it could mean anything: places where he'd gotten drunk, friends' houses, real estate he was interested in, or just places he liked. I made a note of it. No one marks up a map with a red Sharpie for no reason.

I checked the fridge. A few boxes of Chinese food, jelly, bread, leftovers of something foul, a small package of expired ham, and a six-pack and a half of Copek's Siesta IPA.

I poured myself another cup of coffee and sat on the recliner, staring at the old rattan couch where Jaybird had been sleeping. What was his deal? And what did he have in common with Liam?

My mind wandered as it usually does, and pretty soon I was thinking of the men who knocked me out yesterday. It happened so damn fast. I had a flash of the man's face: clean-shaven, grinning. His shoes. Boat shoes. Topsiders. And that's it.

One thing I was pretty sure of was that Bob Fleming was right about Liam's death not being an accident. Something must have happened. A strong swimmer drowning in four or five feet of water.

And the Intracoastal was dead calm. How the hell do you even fall off a kayak in that kind of water?

I tried to imagine that day—a day just like this one. Sunset, maybe nighttime. Liam putting on a bathing suit, Jaybird sprawled on the couch, snoring. Liam carrying the kayak to the little rickety dock, lowering the kayak into the water and rowing out in the crystal calm water.

Then what?

I finished my coffee, got in my Subaru, and looked over the police report. Nothing jumped out at me. The body was discovered Friday morning almost two weeks ago just south of here, at an address on Kensey Lane in Osprey.

I opened Google Maps on my phone and traced what I imagined had been Liam's final trip, from his house to the address on the police report. It wasn't far. Might take fifteen minutes from here to there by kayak, probably less. In that short period, the man lost his life.

But how?

The medical examiner's report estimated time of death sometime between ten p.m. and two a.m. Thursday night–Friday morning. The cause of death was asphyxia due to drowning. The decedent showed no indication of trauma of any kind. He had marks on the skin of his left shoulder and on the left side of the torso consistent with scrapes from the barnacles of the pilings of the dock where the body was recovered.

According to responding Sheriff's Deputy Lester Norton, the victim had gone out on a kayak Thursday evening. A woman by the name of Tina Parker discovered the body and called 911. Norton responded to the call, arriving at the house at 7:41 a.m. Parker led him to the back of the house where the deputy found the body facedown underwater, caught between the pilings of the wooden dock of the residence of Tina Parker.

The report was written by Detective Fenton Kendel, investigating officer who was called to the scene and arrived at 8:18 a.m. It was all pretty cut and dried and to the point.

I could understand Bob Fleming being suspicious of the report because the victim was his son. But the report raised no questions whatsoever for me. The only thing that kept me here, trying to figure this out, was the two men from yesterday. And from what I had seen in the house, I had the nagging suspicion they had stolen a laptop computer from Liam's bedroom.

I sat in the car staring at the front of the house, trying to process. Sweat beads built on my brow and upper lip, mosquitoes and no-see-ums buzzing around my face. After a while, I started the car, put up the windows, and turned on the AC.

I needed to talk to Jaybird. I needed to know about Liam's work, if he had an office, the name of his company, an address, what he did for a living. And about the computer. I figured I could sit in the messy house and wait for Jaybird. Or move on. Do my damn job. Besides, I was starving.

* * *

I went through the drive-through of the McDonald's on the Trail at Stickney point, got a breakfast burrito and a large coffee, and drove down to Osprey. Tina Parker, the homeowner, lived in a beige pseudo-Mediterranean two-story house at the end of Kensey Lane, a narrow dirt road. It wasn't exclusive and it wasn't big, but the backyard ended at the Intracoastal giving the property its value.

Tina Parker opened the door and stood with her arms crossed over her chest. She looked to be in her seventies, skinny, her white hair in rollers. And she didn't look happy about me knocking on her door so early in the morning.

The first words out of her mouth were, "Not interested."

"I'm not selling anything," I said. "I'm just—"

"I'm a Christian and I'm very happy with my religion and my church," she said and reached back to close the door.

"I'm not a Jehovah's Witness, ma'am. I just have some questions about the body you found a couple weeks ago," I said quickly, taking a step forward.

"What about it?" she said sharply.

She watched me like a hawk as I explained how I'd been hired by Bob Fleming to check into the death of his son.

"I told the detective everything I knew," she said. "Why would I tell you any different?"

"I just want to see and understand what happened. Mr. Fleming is distraught about the loss of his son. He's in terrible shape. He's looking for closure."

Tina glanced to the side suspiciously. Then she turned her little dark eyes on me and barked, "I'm a very private person. Why did this have to happen to me?"

"Well," I said. "At least it wasn't your son who died."

She frowned and seemed to chew on that for a moment. Her eyes softened a little.

"If you could just give me five minutes," I said quickly trying to take advantage of the moment, "and show me where you found the body, I'll be on my way. Promise."

She was reluctant. Didn't let me in the house. Instead, she led me around the side of the house without saying anything more. We walked around the caged pool to the narrow dock that jutted out between the mangroves to the Intracoastal. It was a wide section of blackish water with a few small mangrove islands. We were directly across the north end of Casey Key and a little south of Midnight Pass. Siesta Key was to the north. A Robalo motorboat, about thirty feet, made its way along the center of the canal, heading south toward Venice, which was the next outlet to the Gulf.

I looked down at the dark water. "So it was here?"

She pointed to my side. "He was lying facedown in the water right there between the pilings. Got caught in there, I suppose."

"It's not very deep," I said.

"It's low tide," she said.

I looked back at her house. "And you saw him from your patio over there?"

She looked back at the house. "No. I was upstairs in my room." She pointed to a window on the second floor. "I was looking out at the birds. In the morning, the mangroves get crowded with egrets and herons. Then I saw something red at my dock. I didn't know what it was. I went downstairs and had a coffee and then walked out on the dock. I thought it was trash."

"Must have been quite a shock."

Her face tightened. "You're telling me."

"And then you called the cops."

"That's right."

"You went back into the house?"

"No, I called from my cell phone. I stayed right here."

"Did you see anything else?"

"Anything else like what?"

"I don't know, his kayak, or other people."

"It was seven thirty in the morning. There was nothing out here."

"No fishermen going out?"

"Well, maybe a boat or two went past. But the channel is over there." She pointed to the middle of the Intracoastal. "Not too far, maybe twenty, thirty yards. You can run aground if you don't stay at the center of it."

The tide was moving south. It was just as the police report said: Liam Fleming must have fallen from his kayak farther north, drowned and floated down to this place.

"And you're sure it was seven thirty?" I asked.

She nodded. "I wake up at five forty-five every morning. I took some time, maybe half an hour to enjoy my view, look at the birds. Then it took me about half an hour to get my coffee and come out here."

"That would make it six forty-five."

She frowned and her eyes narrowed. "I had a bowel movement," she snapped. "You done yet, mister?"

* * *

It was clear Liam had drowned somewhere between his house and Tina Parker's dock in Osprey. I couldn't imagine that anything new would resurface. And cops, even if they realized they missed something in their investigation, would never admit it. Especially Fenton Kendel. He was old school. A Florida cracker with roots that went deeper than a banyan tree. He'd been with the Sarasota Sheriff's office for thirtysomething years. Fenton Kendel didn't make mistakes.

Still, I had to at least go through the motions. I drove north to the Sarasota County Sheriff's office downtown.

I hated the place. The Sarasota Police Station was in a new modern building. It was clean, plush, kind of like a Holiday Inn Express. The Sheriff's office, on the other hand, was an institutional shithole, puke yellow walls with depressing fluorescent lighting. Even the lobby felt like a prison. Those who had been picked up for petty crime and misdemeanors, their families, children, loitered or moved along the halls like zombies, heading to the courthouse or to pay a fine they couldn't afford. They were mostly black or Hispanic and a handful of white folks—all in the unemployed or minimum wage category. And everywhere, the deputies in their dark green uniforms walked around like superheroes. This was their home. Everyone else was an unwelcomed guest.

The place reeked of attitude.

The desk sergeant, a big burly redneck with a bald head who looked over the small room from his perch a few feet above the rest of us, was his usual unhelpful self. He stared at me with suspicious eyes. To the deputies, we were all criminals.

"Kendel's out," the desk sergeant said without even calling up-stairs to check. I guess he knew everything. And I didn't know shit.

I pulled out the police report and found the responding deputy's name. "What about Deputy Lester Norton?"

It took about half an hour for Deputy Norton to come down and see me. He was young, looked like a teenager—squeaky clean with a military-style buzz cut and a forceful frown and a couple of red pimples marking his cheeks. His bright gray eyes bounced back and forth to the sides, taking in everything that was happening around us.

There was no place to sit in the lobby, and he didn't invite me up to his office. I nodded to the front. "Can we talk outside?"

He led the way out to Ringling Boulevard where the noon sun was blazing down on the concrete. We moved to the side where there was a sliver of shade, our backs against the wall of the building.

"I have a couple of questions about Liam Fleming," I said. "I guess you were first on the scene."

He nodded, his eyes catching mine then bouncing past me to the street and then to the sidewalk and back at me.

"I'm a friend of the family's," I explained. "I was just curious about how you found him."

"It's all in the report," he said.

"Yeah, I read it. But I was wondering about how you found the body."

"It was facedown underwater," he said.

"So you walked up to the dock?"

"That is correct, sir."

I sucked in a little air. This guy was like a robot. I said, "What about the woman, Tina Parker?"

"Mrs. Parker stayed behind."

"By the pool cage?"

"That is correct. She remained inside the pool cage."

"And then you walked out to the end of the dock."

"That is correct, sir."

"Okay. And you saw nothing suspicious as to how the body was snagged on the dock or how it was floating."

Deputy Norton bit his lower lip. His eyes danced all over me like he was watching a fly buzzing around my face. "It's all in the report, sir. The body was floating facedown on a slight diagonal. His left side was caught against two pilings. There was no sign of trauma of any kind."

"Yeah, I read that in the report," I said. "But you couldn't know about the trauma right then, right?"

"That is correct, sir."

"The medical examiner said he drowned Thursday night or early Friday morning."

"That is correct, sir." Deputy Norton waved to another deputy who was crossing the road and called, "Softball on Saturday. Don't forget!"

"Okay," I said. "One question. What happened to the kayak?"

"The kayak was not recovered."

"But it should have floated somewhere, right?"

His eyes narrowed slightly, and for the first time they stopped moving. "That is likely. But it was not at or near the scene where the body was recovered."

"Where was it?"

"It was never found."

"Did you look for it?"

"No, sir."

"Why not?"

He took a long breath and sighed. "We don't have the time to search the length of the Intracoastal for a kayak. It could have floated all the way to Venice for all we know. Or someone could have picked it up."

"So how did you know he was out kayaking when he drowned?"

"From the evidence," he said quickly and hooked his thumbs on the sides of his belt.

"But you can't be sure that's exactly what happened, right?"

"Yes, I am. He must have fallen off the kayak. All the evidence points to that."

"No, it doesn't," I said. "Not if there's no kayak."

"The witness told Detective Kendel he saw him out on the kayak that morning."

"You have a witness?"

"Yessir, I believe so."

"It's not in the report."

"Detective Kendel wrote the report."

"Yes. But it's not in there. I have a copy of it. I've read it like five times. There is no mention of a witness."

He clenched his jaw. "I am pretty sure it is in the report. If it's not, it must've been an oversight."

"Really?" I said.

He gave me a quizzical look as if daring me to cross him.

I said, "So who's the witness?"

"You'll have to ask Detective Kendel about that, sir."

"But you must have his name and address somewhere."

"That is correct, sir."

"Can I have it?"

"You would have to speak with Detective Kendel."

"And when can I find Kendel?"

He glanced at his wristwatch. "Comes in after three p.m."

"A witness, and it's not in the report," I said. "That's quite the oversight, don't you think?"

"It happens sometimes," Norton said and glanced up the sidewalk. "Is there anything else, sir?"

"I don't know," I said. "Is there anything else you omitted from the report?"

He frowned, looked pissed. Then he did an about-face and marched away, his arms swinging wide at his sides.

A witness, I thought. *A fucking witness.* And it was not in the report. That was way too much for me.

CHAPTER 8

I WAS SUSPICIOUS. Very. And I was also a little rattled by how this simple open-and-shut case by the Sarasota Sheriff's Office had quickly turned into something so damn complicated. Detective Fenton Kendel was a stand-up guy. I trusted him. He was thorough and ethical and had more experience than the whole law enforcement community in Sarasota put together. I couldn't imagine him leaving out something as important as a witness' statement and information—by mistake or on purpose.

I drove home. Mimi, my tired old gray tabby, met me at the door. Her bowl was empty. I fed her and gave her fresh water, but she just stood there on the polished hardwood, staring up at me as if I'd missed something important.

"What," I said, "would you like some hot sauce?"

She blinked a couple of times, stared.

"Whatever," I said and opened the fridge. "You're getting too moody for me, girl. I don't know what you want anymore."

I served myself a hefty portion of leftover rice and beans and zapped it in the microwave for a couple of minutes. I added a few pickled jalapeños from a can, grabbed a Big Top Trapeze Monk wit ale, and sat at my desk in the living room where my MacBook had been sitting idle for too long.

I opened a document, named it Fleming, and typed a few notes—what I knew and what I wanted to know. It all came down to two things. Number one: Talk to Detective Kendel, find out who the witness is and interview the witness.

Number two: Keith had said Liam had his own business. I had to find out about that, see what kind of money he made, who he might've crossed.

I also had to take Jaybird out of his environment, take him somewhere where he could focus so he could answer my questions. And Keith. Maybe he knew what kind of kayak Liam had gone out on that night. I could compare notes and look for any discrepancies. Eventually, something would point to a motive: drugs, money, or love. Or perhaps all three, although I was pretty sure I could scratch out love. Those two men I'd met at Liam's place yesterday didn't seem like the romantic type.

I pushed my chair back and ate my slop of rice and beans. I was getting so tired of this food. Right there and then I made a promise to myself that once I cracked this case, I'd allow myself to splurge— drive out to Oneco Meats off old Highway 301 and get myself a giant rib eye steak and grill it over charcoal to a perfect pink and juicy center.

I finished my lunch and called the Sheriff's office and asked for Detective Kendel.

No dice.

I set my dirty plate in the sink and filled it with water, grabbed another can of Big Top from the fridge, and turned on the old Scott amp. I placed side two of Clarence "Gatemouth" Brown's *Bogalusa Boogie Man* on the Thorens turntable and sat back on the couch and let time do its thing.

At three thirty p.m., I called the Sheriff's office again, but I was told Detective Kendel hadn't come in yet. I asked for Deputy Norton. He was out on patrol.

I didn't like it.

I wanted to go back to Siesta Key, find Jaybird, drill him with questions. But I also wanted the dope on the kayak witness. I couldn't be in two places at once. I paced across the small living room. Mimi hopped off the couch, stretched, and made a dainty walk to her food bowl and finally began to chow.

I kept moving, trying to figure out my next move. From the side window, I could see weeds in my yard almost two feet tall. We'd had so much rain in the last month everything was overgrown. On the corner on the other side of the street, the big sign was as loud as ever: *"The Majestic" by Dieter & Waxler. Luxury downtown living with exquisite views of Sarasota Bay. Sold exclusively by Alex J. Trainor, Real Estate.*

Still 90 percent sold.

I could already imagine the wealthy condo owners looking down at my little old house and complaining that I wasn't taking care of my yard. That the place looked abandoned—driving down property values.

When the record ended, I tried Detective Kendel again. *Nada.*

An hour later, I still couldn't get ahold of Kendel or Norton. I felt cooped up, going stir crazy. Like Tom Petty says, the waiting is the hardest part.

Yeah, I'll never win an award for patience. I drove back to Siesta Key, took the north bridge. It was a nice drive with the manicured gardens and the big houses and the overgrown sea grapes and scrub oak. Just after the bridge there was a large sign on the front yard of a house: *Keep Beach Road Public.*

As I came up to the Village, I slowed down. The business district had changed quite a bit in the last few years. The road had been re-surfaced with brick-paved crosswalks, and a few new condos—four and five stories tall—rose up in the distance toward the beach. The vibe in Siesta had changed—the place felt closed in, like an outdoor mall. Siesta was losing its funkiness. Back in the day, when I first came to Siesta Key for spring break, it was just a quaint old Florida beach town. Now it was too nice, too clean—too corporate.

I thought of Jaybird and the hippies at the drum circle. They still had the vibe. Maybe they were right—holding on to the past. I couldn't believe I was getting nostalgic over Siesta. It was just five miles from my house and I rarely came here anymore. It was almost impossible to find parking or a table at one of the outdoor bars: the Daiquiri Deck or the Siesta Key Oyster Bar.

I followed Ocean Boulevard to Beach Road and headed south. After a string of low-rise condos on my right, the parking lot of the public beach appeared flat and hot and crowded with cars. If I stretched my neck up, I could see a sliver of ocean.

At the light, about a mile past the public beach, the road turned into Midnight Pass Road. I passed the small Crescent business district and continued on the narrow two-lane road, past the entrance to the Sanderling Club on my right, past the beachfront trailer park, and the entrance to Turtle Beach. At the short driveway to Liam's cottage, I turned left.

The blue VW Golf with the surfboard on the roof rack was still there gathering dust. The door to the cottage was unlocked, just as I'd left it. I walked in and called for Jaybird.

No answer.

"Hello?" I called a little louder. "Jaybird!"

Not a sound.

I walked across the living room and past the lanai to the patio. I was thinking of what Deputy Norton had said: a neighbor saw him on a kayak. There were mansions on both sides of the cottage, but the foliage, scrub oak, tall sea grape trees, and mangroves blocked the view.

I went out to the dock and looked back at the neighbors' houses. I could see part of the windows on the house to the south, to the right of Liam's place. It didn't have a very clear view because of the mangroves. But still, they could've seen him once he was out on the Intracoastal.

The house to the north was locked up and shuttered for the summer. The mangrove islands on the Intracoastal blocked most of the view of the house from the mainland.

After checking the bedroom and the bathroom, I drove north about a hundred feet and took a left onto Turtle Beach Road, which curved to the left onto Blind Pass Road. To my right was parking and the beach, to my left the boat launch and the lagoon that led out to the Intracoastal.

I parked and walked to the beach. I always found it curious that Turtle Beach had this brown coarse sand and that only a mile or two farther up was Siesta and its fine white sand. Siesta had the distinction of being the number one beach in the USA. Even had its own reality show on MTV. We were famous.

I looked up and down the long stretch of sand and water from the ugly yellow condo in the south to the trailer park to the north and beyond to the beach at the Sanderling Club. The sun was still high in the sky. A few families and older couples sat under colorful umbrellas. A young man and a teenage girl played on a paddleboard by the water, and three little kids were busy building a large sandcastle that looked like a blob with two tilting towers. Down near the first condo, a heavyset man in overalls and no shirt was fishing from the shore.

No Jaybird. And no Keith.

I walked back and crossed Blind Pass Road to the parking lot where three trucks with trailers were parked. On the shore of the lagoon, under the Australian pines next to the boat ramp, was Keith's Toyota Land Cruiser, a small trailer hitched to the back with two kayaks and a few paddleboards stacked on what looked like a homemade aluminum rack.

In the lagoon, just past the boat ramp, Keith was up to his thighs in the water, keeping steady a large paddleboard for a woman who was struggling to get on.

I walked across the parking lot and sat at the picnic table by the water. Keith was leaning forward holding the board for the woman. When she finally climbed on, he made his way around the side and placed his hand on her thigh and handed her the long paddle. Three other girls and two men were standing on their boards farther out in the lagoon, watching, waiting.

Keith gave the board a gentle shove and it glided slowly forward toward the center of the lagoon. "Right on!" he yelled. "Stay on your knees until you get a feel for it. And keep your eyes on the horizon, yeah? Don't look down."

He waved at the others in the group before wading back to the shore.

"How's it going?" I said.

He smiled and gestured toward the water with a flip of his hand. "She'll get the hang of it."

"You seen Jaybird around?"

He shook his head, his golden hair caressing his tan shoulders. "Not today, brah."

"You don't remember me."

He squinted and his pale blue eyes moved from side to side as he took on my features, the scar in my ear. "The Daiquiri Deck?"

"Yesterday," I said. "Liam's house."

He threw his head back. "Right on." He picked up a long paddle, and we started toward his Land Cruiser. "That's some sad shit about Liam."

"You brought his kayak back, right?"

"Yeah, the red Eddyline."

"So he must've had another one."

"Yeah." He chuckled. "The blue whale."

"It seems the cops never found it."

He set the paddle on top of a board on the trailer and turned, leaning back on a kayak and crossing his arms over his chest. "It was junk. He picked it up on Craigslist a few months ago."

"But the cops never found it."

He tossed his hair back with a wave of his hand. "You just said that, brah."

"I know. It's just weird. You would think the kayak would've turned up. The only reason the cops say it was a kayak accident was because a neighbor told them he'd seen Liam out there on a kayak that night."

He squinted and pursed his lips like maybe he was giving it some serious thought.

"You know the neighbors?" I asked.

He snorted. "They don't talk to the likes of us, brah."

On the outside, Keith seemed like a total burnout, but he ran a business. Maybe the Puka shell necklace and all the brah surfer talk was an act. Or maybe I was assuming too much.

"Yesterday you said Liam worked for himself," I said.

"Right on."

"What kind of work did he do?"

"He had some business. The Corporation."

"You know the name?"

"That's it."

"What's it?"

"The Corporation. That's what he called it. Even said it with a deep voice like he was being serious." He laughed and mimicked his dead friend making a deep voice and speaking slowly, "The-Cor-por-a-tion."

"You have any idea what kind of work he did, an address, anything?"

He shook his head and pulled his bangs away from his eyes with the tips of his fingers. "Nah, brah. Maybe if you talked to his partner—"

"He had a partner?"

"Yeah, he did. One day I saw him shoving papers in his little black briefcase and mumbled something 'bout having to take them to his partner." He let out a short nasal laugh and shifted his weight to one leg. "Liam was like that, brah. One moment he was all chill, and the next he was mega-serious about work. We teased him about it all the time. Called him Trump and shit."

"What about his partner?"

He bowed his head, then tossed it up like a horse so his hair fanned out and landed neatly at the back of his head. "He never talked business. He'd just split. The rest of us would just party on, smoking the ganja and shit 'til he came back."

"When you say the rest of us?"

"The regulars, brah—Jaybird, me, Candy, Omar, Tessa, Cap'n Cody, Felipe."

I stared at his squinty eyes, the thin crow's feet, the freckles. For the first time, I could see he was older, maybe in his late thirties, early forties. It seemed odd that they wouldn't talk business, or about whatever they did when they weren't smoking dope and drinking beer.

"You think somethin's up," Keith said and pointed at me with a lazy finger. "Like maybe someone did it on purpose?"

"It just doesn't sit right with me."

"Far out." He tossed his head to the side and glanced at the sky. "A murder mystery right here on the fucking key!"

"Don't talk like that."

"But you just—"

"No," I said. "Maybe. But if it's true, I don't want anyone knowing we're on to them."

"Yeah, I can dig that, brah."

"I need to talk to Jaybird."

"You think he did it?"

"No. But he might help me find some answers."

"Yeah, that crazy Jaybird. He knew Liam better than most, for sure."

"You know where I can find him?"

"Gotta be somewhere on the key, brah." He laughed a brief snort. "That dude never leaves the island."

CHAPTER 9

I DIDN'T WANT to chase Jaybird's shadow. I figured I'd find him later at the sunset drum circle or the Salty Dog. So instead, I went to the place where I was sure to get something solid: Bob Fleming.

The guard at the gate of the Sanderling Club called in my arrival, and a minute later, allowed me to pass into the rich man's paradise. The white Maserati wasn't in the driveway. I drove right up to the front door where Bob Fleming was waiting for me. His face was crimson—more so than the first time I'd met him, his eyes razor-thin slits. He was barefoot and wore cargo shorts and a lively Tommy Bahama flowered shirt. He held on to the doorknob with one hand. In the other he had a short tumbler with what I was sure was vodka on the rocks.

"Mr. Vega," he said, his words slurring just enough to let me know he'd been hitting the booze for a while. "This is a surprise. I was just . . . just getting ready to appreciate the sunset."

Across the living room, through the French doors and the caged pool, I could see the Gulf. It was still a few hours until sunset, but the storm clouds in the distance gave the sky a dramatic flair that made it feel later than it was.

I followed him to the middle of the living room, a place that looked as unlived-in as a model house in one of those new developments east of Interstate 75.

"You all right?" I said.

"My son's dead," he said harshly. "How do you think I'm doing?"

"I know," I said. "We talked about this."

He rubbed his red nose and waved his glass, motioning to the pane windows that faced the pool and the ocean.

"Paradise," he said with a slight tone of disgust. "Paradise . . . took my son."

I placed my hand on his shoulder. "Maybe you should sit down."

He eyed me carefully, maybe trying to figure out what the hell was going on. Then he wobbled to the windows and the French doors and looked out at the violent sky.

"Mr. Fleming," I said getting right down to business. "Can you tell me about Liam's work?"

"What do you mean?" he said without turning away from the window.

"What did he do for a living?"

He shrugged and took a short drink from his glass. "He was in business for himself."

When he didn't volunteer anything more, I asked, "What kind of business?"

Finally, he turned and took a few weak steps to where I stood. "Apparently, he was into acquisitions. Real estate."

"He was a realtor or an investor? What?"

He huffed and cleared his throat but said nothing.

I said, "What can you tell me about his work?"

He poked me in the chest with the hand that held the glass. "He bought real estate. The kind that costs a lot of money."

I took a deep breath and moved to the side of the sofa and leaned against the sidearm. "Mr. Fleming, I don't know if someone hurt your son or if it was an accident. But the more I look into this, the stranger it seems to get. I have some suspicions. But I could be wrong."

"Tell me what you know."

"It's not a lot," I said. "But yesterday at his place, a pair of thugs nailed me pretty good."

The old man took a couple of steps forward and sat across from me on a large cushy chair. "Go on."

"I went to check out Liam's place and stumbled into a couple of men who wasted no time in knocking the wind out of me. No greeting."

"Well, that's proof right there," he barked.

"No. That only proves that two men broke into his house."

"Did you tell the police?"

"No," I said. "But that's another little bit that bothers me. The responding officer said the detective spoke to a witness who saw Liam in the kayak that night."

Fleming drained his glass and moved it around so the ice clinked like a bell. "And?"

"And it's not in the police report your lawyer gave me."

Fleming bowed his head, shoulders slouched.

"Liam seemed to have a lot of friends, but no one knows what he did for a living," I said and leaned toward him. "I thought maybe you could shed some light on that."

Fleming huffed. Then he set his glass down on the side table next to his chair and pushed himself up with some difficulty. "Let's have a drink."

"Sure," I said. "But I'd rather have an answer."

He grabbed his glass, and I followed him to the bar in the side nook between the fancy dining room and the living room. He poured two glasses of Grey Goose and carried them into the kitchen where he dispensed a couple of ice cubes into the drinks from a large stainless-steel Subzero refrigerator.

"Sit," he said, and set my glass on the granite kitchen island. I took a stool and grabbed the glass and took in the smell of the liquor. I wet my lips with the vodka and set the glass down. He took a nice long swallow and leaned his head back and sniffed at the air like he'd recognized a smell from his childhood.

Then he sat across from me, his shoulders hunched, and finally gave me the skinny on his son. "When I first moved down here a few years ago, I helped Liam start a company. We formed—he formed—a corporation in order to invest in real estate. It was good timing. The economy was still weak and the real estate market was in shambles. There were foreclosures and short sales in every block."

"I was here," I said. "I remember those days."

"My God." He grinned at his glass. "It was a fabulous time to buy."

"It was a terrible time for a lot of people," I said. I couldn't help myself. My wife lost her job. We got divorced. I almost lost my house.

"Yeah," he said. "But not for us. Not for Liam."

He paused and took another drink and set his glass on the counter and looked away. I followed his gaze. I thought maybe his wife was about to walk in, but there was nobody there. He tapped the side of his head with his index finger. "Liam was smart. He seemed to have a plan. So I helped him."

"Then what happened?"

He sighed. "He kept buying. All he did was buy. There were good deals out there. Still are. But he kept coming to me for money."

"But he never sold," I said.

He shook his head real slow. "Never. Not a single property."

"Why?"

"I don't know."

"What was he investing in? Land? Houses?"

"Everything. His company must own dozens of places. I don't really know. He said he was interested in the long-term investment. It wasn't the right time to sell."

"And you financed the whole thing."

He stared down at his hands, his finger resting on the rim of the glass. "I wanted to help him."

"You just wrote him checks without asking to see an overview of his investments or business plan or even a property title or anything?"

Fleming took a deep long breath and let the air out slowly. His whole body seemed to deflate like an old balloon. The alcohol on his breath floated across the counter like a storm cloud.

"I was trying to make up for lost time," he said.

"What do you mean?"

He seemed to hesitate for a moment, looking past me at the back wall of the kitchen then refocusing on me. He spoke in a flat monotone. "I always felt my responsibility as a father was to provide for my family. And I did that in spades. I was . . . I was so busy making money, I missed Liam growing up. Because of that, we were never close. I think—I know—he resented me for it. And for the death of his mother."

"What happened?"

"An aneurysm."

"You can't blame yourself for that," I said.

"Liam was at boarding school at the time. I called and told him over the phone. I didn't . . . I didn't bring him home."

Now I had to take a drink. Memories of my father, of the police officer pointing at him, gesturing for him to get down. My father getting on his knees, hands reaching for the back of his head. My face pressed against the window of the car, watching him. The loud explosion of the patrolman's weapon just as my father turned his eyes to me—just as our gazes connected for an instant before he fell face-first into the dark asphalt of that deserted stretch of Texas highway.

"We were mending," he said. "When he came to me for financial help, I thought it would bring us closer. I was willing to do anything, give him anything."

"But it must be millions of dollars of real estate."

He slouched so far forward I thought he'd curl into a ball and bounce away.

"Who's inheriting the properties?" I said.

"I don't know," he said somberly. "Everything's in the name of the company."

"So you lose your investment."

"I don't care about the money." His hand turned into a fist. "I have plenty of that. Besides, it was not an investment. It was a gift."

He was obviously a very wealthy man. But everyone cares about money. Especially the very wealthy. They probably care more about their money than anyone else. And when there are millions at stake . . . "Does he have a lawyer?"

"Joaquin del Pino."

"You're kidding me."

He nodded. "The guy from TV."

"Justice for All, del Pino," I said with a hiss. That son of a bitch was everywhere.

Fleming pointed a finger at me and stood. He stumbled back but held on to the counter to keep his balance.

I followed him to the living room where he sat on the sofa, leaning back, the drink resting atop his stomach. I sat on the cushion chair, holding my drink with both hands. I said, "Mr. Fleming, I know this must be difficult for you—"

"What the hell?" he barked. "You don't know me."

"There are things I need to know."

"My son is dead."

"And the money you gave him is gone with him."

"I told you, money is irrelevant." His voice was loud, growling with an edge like a knife. He sat up, leaned forward, and set his glass on the coffee table in front of him. "I set it up for him to go to law school. Yale. I pulled strings, called in favors. He was set. Instead, he came down to Florida. He wasted his life with these good-for-nothing beach bums he called friends. What the hell kind of a life is that?"

"I don't know," I said. "Maybe he was happy."

"Bullshit. That's just liberal brainwashing." He poked his chest with his thumb. "I was footing the bill."

So the money was important after all. Or at least he thought he was buying his son's love. "Do you think," I said, "it was bringing you closer?"

"I don't know." He cleared his throat. His jowls trembled. "At least I got to see him. We'd meet someplace off the key and have lunch or dinner every few weeks. We talked real estate, mostly. He'd tell me about a property he was closing on or how baby boomers were going to change the face of Sarasota."

"And you cut him a check for whatever he wanted."

He shook his head. "My lawyer did that."

"Pearlman." I leaned back and looked at the drink in my hand. I took a taste. The ice had watered the vodka enough to make it acceptable. But two little sips already had me levitating. The room felt hot. "What was he planning on doing with the properties?"

"I don't know. I think he was looking at the market twenty, thirty years from now." He leaned forward. His face twisted and his red eyes welled up with a couple of small sad tears. "He was my son," he said slowly. "I loved him."

"I'm sorry," I said—and I was. He looked broken. But I was pretty sure it had to do with more than the death of his son. Something was eating away at him. Maybe it was remorse for how he acquired his wealth. Hedge fund managers and the CEOs of multinational corporations—I always thought of them as heartless. But maybe they were human, had feelings, loved just like the rest of us. At least Bob Fleming did. Maybe in his old age he'd come to realize that all his wealth meant nothing. He was a tired old man, alone with an uptight trophy wife. And all his money couldn't buy his son's love. Certainly, couldn't bring him back from the dead. No. All the money in the world couldn't do that.

But then again, maybe I had it all wrong. Maybe he was broke. Maybe he had funneled so much money into his son's business he was going to have to downsize, live on Social Security.

Or maybe he was just a sad old alcoholic.

The light outside had changed. The sky was warming up, turning gold and pink. It was time for me to find Jaybird, give him another shot at explaining Liam's life. I set my drink on the coffee table and stood. A rush of dizziness hit me like a wave, then settled.

"One more thing," I said before walking out. "What was the name of his company?"

Fleming glanced at me, his eyes small and red. "Beach City Holdings."

CHAPTER 10

I LEFT FLEMING'S house and drove north on Midnight Pass. The two small sips of vodka had me buzzing. And our little meeting troubled me in more ways than one. I felt sorry for the guy. But I was also a little afraid of him. I didn't know how rich he was. But he must be rich enough not to give a damn about anyone and anything. He seemed very pleased with himself for swooping in and taking people's homes when the banks foreclosed on their faulty loans. Maybe that's what it took to be rich: an I-don't-give-a-shit-about-anyone attitude.

And del Pino. That fucker was everywhere. I'd always thought of him as a greedy accident chaser, but in the past, he'd proven himself ethical. I had to give him some credit for that. At least now I had some leads. It was too late to try del Pino at his office, so I pulled into the parking lot at Siesta Public Beach and drove around for fifteen minutes until I found a spot just as the sun was beginning to tint the sky with a warm haze.

I took my shoes and socks off, rolled my pant hems up to my calves, and walked in the soft hot sand to the small drum circle. Only three hippies were waling on their instruments while two girls danced, skipping and fluttering their arms like they'd just dropped acid. In the periphery, a handful of curious older people paused to check out the show, then moved on.

Jaybird wasn't there.

I made my way behind the drummers hoping I might find him lying in the sand, sleeping. The soft smell of patchouli and marijuana waved over me. Past the drummers and to the side of the dancers, I recognized the girl from the night before. She was wearing a pink bikini and was twirling a hoola hoop with her arm.

I walked over. "How's it going?"

She looked me up and down, suspiciously. No smile. No hippie love. Just a defensive stance. I guess she felt I was invading her space.

"I'm a friend of Jaybird's. We met yesterday."

She moved her long wavy hair away from her sweaty face and frowned. "No, we didn't."

I pointed to the side of the circle. "We were over there. You pointed out Jaybird for me."

No reaction. She was either on something, or had been so high yesterday that now she didn't remember me.

"Never mind," I said. "Is Jaybird around?"

She shook her head and looked at the drummers.

I followed her gaze. Long shadows stretched across the sand.

She moved her arm in a long arch. "They're drumming for Neptune, man."

"Cool."

She curled her upper lip—a look I'd seen many times—and rolled her eyes like a disgruntled teenager. She probably thought I was trying to pick her up. I just smiled and walked away, sat on the sand in the periphery, and watched the show.

The inconsistent rhythm of the drummers reminded me of an event when Zoe was four years old. My ex, Nancy, and I were already suffering our troubles. I was pretty sure we were headed for divorce. We attended a show at Zoe's day care. Each kid had made a homemade instrument. Zoe used a large aluminum pot and a wooden spoon because Nancy and I had been too busy, too focused on our own bullshit that we hadn't been involved. Most of the other kids had made string instruments out of boxes and horns out of tubes, decorated with tempera paint and papier maché. Some of them looked real nice with straps and ribbons hanging from them like festival decorations.

The concert was a beautiful disaster—an all-out free-for-all cacophony that stabbed at the eardrums. But the faces on those little kids were priceless. They loved every second of their jam. Every single one of them was a John Coltrane or a John Bonham or an Angus Young. And Zoe was right there with them, crouched over that pot in the corner waling on it as though life itself depended on how hard and fast she could hit the damn thing.

I wondered what she would make of the drum circle.

* * *

The dense tropical clouds floating over the horizon made for a long and spectacular sunset. When the sky turned red and the clouds glowed orange, the drummers went nuts, reaching an intense crescendo. The dancers hopped and waved and cried out with joy. I could only imagine Neptune having a laugh somewhere under the sea.

When things finally slowed, and two of the drummers paused and lit up cigarettes or joints and drank water or beer or whatever they found in a big red cooler, I approached.

"Hey, man," I said turning on my best hipster. "You seen Jaybird?"

"Not today, dude."

"Any idea where he might be?"

He laughed. "Probably getting high somewhere."

The other drummer who was standing to the side said, "You check out Turtle Beach?"

"Yeah, I just came from there."

The other drummer glanced at his friend. "Maybe he's up by the pier on Beach Road."

"Nah," the first one said shaking his head. "Dude's probably at work."

It was a long hot walk back to the parking lot. I sat in my car for a moment, cranked the AC while I put on my socks and shoes. The clouds to the east, somewhere where the swamp turned to suburbs, were dark and heavy with the occasional flash of lightning.

I drove north on Beach Road, turned at the curve where the road changed to Ocean Boulevard, and entered the Village. The whole business district was lit up like a party despite it being just an average weekday in July. The Siesta Key Oyster Bar was packed. Even with my windows up I could hear the musician on the little stage on the porch of the restaurant strumming his guitar and singing "Margaritaville." A big sign attached to the railing read: *Keep Beach Road Public*. Next to it on a black board, it said: *Tonight: Live Music by Cap'n Cody*.

I got lucky and found a parking spot right in front of the Old Salty Dog. The restaurant was a Siesta Key institution. It had been there since forever, but really, it was pretty much like the other restaurants in the key: outside seating on wooden picnic tables, a palm thatch roof, flat-screen TVs. But inside it was dark and a little funky. Like a little pub in Ocho Rios, Jamaica.

I walked past the hostess, turned left and up a couple of steps to the bar. It had a long wooden counter and stools where three scruffy older men sat drinking together. They looked like fishermen without a boat. At a small table, two red-faced tourists drank tall, fancy colorful drinks. They were still wearing bathing suits, flip-flops, and pastel Florida t-shirts.

I took a stool. The bartender had her back to me. I was tracing the outline of her bare shoulder when she turned around, caught my eye, and smiled. Then her eyes grew wide and she pushed her head forward as if to get a better look at me. "Dexter?"

I smiled, but for the life of me, I couldn't place her. She was young, late twenties, her hair pulled back in a ponytail. And pretty. Very.

"You don't remember me, do you?" She leaned forward on the counter. "Tessa Davidson. From the *Sarasota Herald*. I was the education reporter for like six months. They sent me home with the first round of layoffs. That weekend a big group of us went out for drinks at the Gator Club with the photographers."

Nope. I didn't remember her. But I had a vague memory of a drunken night at the Gator Club. We were all angry. Most of the photo staff had been canned. We knew it was the beginning of the end, yet none of us wanted to admit it. We just got drunk and complained. I was still married. I remembered calling my wife and arguing. She wasn't happy that I was out after work, drunk, commiserating with my newspaper friends. She never liked them— probably because she wasn't one of them.

But what mattered now was Tessa. Jaybird had said she'd dated Liam. She could help me with the case. I nodded like a sappy old friend and said, "Yeah, that was one crazy night."

She laughed, then crinkled her nose. "We got pretty hammered, huh?"

"Looks like you've moved up in the world."

She glanced up and down the bar and shrugged. "It's okay. It helps pay the bills. I also freelance on the side. Mostly blogs, you know?"

"I hear you."

"So what can I get you?"

I leaned forward and studied the drafts at the end of the bar. I recognized a Cigar City tap. "Is that the Maduro or Tocobaga?"

"Maduro," she said, "a nice brown ale."

I nodded. She smiled at me and went to pour.

I hadn't been to a bar in Siesta Village in ages. It was refreshing to be out in a different place. And the vibe at the bar of the Salty Dog was totally different than at the outside tables. The walls were a deep blood-red, and the tables polished wood. I figured most people who came to the Village didn't come to sit in a dark bar. They wanted the palm-thatched roof, the salt and humidity of the beach, big colorful fruity drinks. They wanted Margaritaville.

Tessa came back and set the glass of Maduro in front of me. "It's on me," she said.

"Really?"

"Yeah, for old times. You want a food menu?"

I glanced at the entrance to the bar area. On the wall by the steps were old photos of the restaurant when Siesta was low key and funky. There were no palm-thatched roofs then. Beyond the steps, past another section of the dining room, was the kitchen. "Is Jaybird working tonight?"

"You know Jaybird?"

"Yeah."

She leaned forward. "He was supposed to come in at eleven and work a double, but never showed. The manager's pretty pissed."

"We are talking about Jaybird, right?"

She laughed. "He's actually pretty good about coming to work."

I took a long sip of the ale. Pretty powerful stuff. Those Ybor City folks knew how to brew a good beer. "He told me about an after-work party last night. Maybe he had a little too much."

Tessa tilted her head to the side. "That was at my place," she said. "But he was only there for an hour."

"He told me he was there until four."

"Right. I was asleep by three."

A man walked up to the bar, looked left and right, then took a seat a couple of places from me. Tessa looked at him and back at me. "Be right back."

I watched her work, taking the man's order, handing him a food menu, then popping open a Corona and topping it with a lime wedge before setting it in front of him. I glanced at the entrance and tried to imagine the kitchen where Jaybird was supposed to be.

Tessa came back. "So how do you know Jaybird?"

"From around the beach." I had to tread carefully.

"He's a character, huh?"

I nodded. "He was helping me with something."

She laughed. "Help from Jaybird?"

"What do you mean?"

"It's usually the other way around," she said. "Everyone's always helping Jaybird out. He's gotta owe me at least five hundred bucks by now. Not to mention all the nights he's crashed at my place or the rides I've given him to the south end of the key."

That was my cue. "To Liam's place?"

Tessa's expression fell. Her smile turned into a taught line. "Yeah," she said quickly, her eyes dancing around me. "You knew Liam?"

"Not really," I said, "but I'm trying to find out more about him."

"Order," a waitress called from the end of the bar, leaned forward on the counter, and looked our way.

Tessa grinned, pushed herself away from the bar, and proceeded to take care of business. She looked at the drink order and poured two Budweisers, pulled out a container of something bluish from under the counter, and poured it into the blender. She moved quickly, taking long sure steps back and forth along the bar as she added rum and another liquor from a bottle I didn't recognize, ice and orange juice. The blender made a racket as the blades crushed the ice. The scruffy fishermen on the other side of the bar looked over for a second, then went back to the basketball game on TV.

Tessa prepped two tall goblets with a sliver of pineapple, a red maraschino cherry, and a little paper umbrella. Then she turned off the blender and poured the frothy blue drink into the glasses and placed them on the tray.

When the waitress left with her order, Tessa came back to where I sat—only she didn't lean in all friendly like before. She just stood squarely in front of me and crossed her arms over her chest and said, "So what about Liam?"

It was time to go fishing. "You knew him?"

"Everyone on the key knew him."

"Weird, because I'm trying to find out about him and no one seems to know anything."

"Anything about what?" she said.

"About him. About his business. About what exactly happened the night he died."

"You working on a story?"

I grinned. "Laid off."

"So you're a cop now?"

I laughed. "Far from it. But the cops did close the case. Said it was an accident."

She leaned forward, her hands resting on the bar. "So why are you looking into it then?"

"Liam's dad."

"What about him?"

"He thinks it wasn't an accident."

She drew back. "Oh?"

I took a sip of my Maduro. "You seem defensive," I said.

She stole a quick glance toward the scruffy fishermen at the end of the bar and then fixed her big brown eyes on mine. "I dated Liam for a while. We were together for almost a year. But this thing . . . him dying. It really . . . it's really messed up. I still can't believe it happened. I keep thinking he's going to walk up those steps with his charming smile and say, 'Hey, Tessa, how about a Pony Ride Margarita?'"

"What's that?"

"One of our silly fruity drinks."

"He drank that?"

"No. It was our ongoing joke."

I could see the hurt in her eyes. She'd gone from happy bartender to take-no-bullshit woman in less than a second. "His dad doesn't believe there was an accident," I said.

"His dad," she said mockingly. "I can only imagine he'd be happy to see him gone."

"You can't be serious. It's his father."

"Those two hated each other."

"Yeah, Jaybird said something about that. But then the old man is paying me good money to find out who might be behind his death. If—and this is a big if—indeed there was foul play—"

"Miss." The man of the tourist couple at the table behind me held up his empty glass. "Please?"

Tessa forced a quick smile and went to work the blender and make another one of those colorful drinks. When she came back, she whispered, "So what do you think happened?"

"I have no idea." I drained the rest of my Maduro. "But something's going on. The cops never found the kayak. They said they talked to a witness who saw Liam kayaking that night but then kept it out of the report."

"Order." A waitress was at the station. She didn't look happy that Tessa wasn't hustling. During the summer, when things were slow, you had to do the best you could with the few customers you had. Every tip mattered.

An older couple walked in. They were drenched, laughing. The woman took a napkin from the bar and wiped her face. The man pulled out the two stools to my left and sat, then leaned to the side and elbowed me. "Two blocks, and we got soaked," he said in a light British accent.

"It's coming down hard, eh?"

"Unbelievable," he said. "It's like a bloody typhoon."

Tessa came back to the bar and took their order. She gave me a look and pointed to my glass.

"Sure." I looked sideways at the couple and back at Tessa. Maybe this was not the place to talk about Liam's case. But the time was right.

She went off to the far side of the bar to make the drinks. A small group of young people came in, laughing, all of them drenched. They stood around looking at the room. One of the men pointed to the bar and they all came and crowded the area between the British couple and the old fishermen.

They ordered drinks. One of the men kissed one of the women. They were all dressed for the sun—shorts and t-shirts and tiny dresses, flip-flops and hats.

When Tessa came back to me, she apologized and winked. "So, where were we?"

"The cops never found a kayak. I was wondering—"

"Miss," one of the young men said and held up his hand like he was in school. "Can we get another round?"

Tessa looked at me. "They drink fast."

I grabbed my beer and made my way to the terrace. The rain was coming down hard, a typical summer storm. Across Ocean Boulevard, and a little to the east away from the beach, a Sheriff's deputy cruiser was parked. No lights.

I walked back into the bar and took my place. A couple of minutes later, Tessa came back.

"I'm going to take off," I said. "But you and I need to talk."

"Sure."

"Tomorrow?"

"Yeah, but not too early. I'm here until one, and I have a piece I'm working on that's on deadline."

"Really?"

"It's just for a blog."

"But it pays?"

She shrugged. "A little."

"Good for you," I said hoping my tone did not betray my jealousy.

Tessa wrote down her address and phone number on a napkin and handed it to me. The couple next to me watched us intently. They probably thought I was picking her up.

"Does Jaybird have a phone number?"

"Please." She laughed and shook her head. "The guy lives in the Stone Age."

I folded the napkin and placed it in my shirt breast pocket. "If you get any news on him, let me know, okay?"

I gave her my business card and walked out to the front of the restaurant. The cop car was gone. Somehow it made me feel at ease. Those two Maduros had me buzzing just enough that maybe I would fail a breathalyzer.

I got soaked running to my car. I started up on Ocean Boulevard. The rain was coming down hard. I drove leaning forward, squinting at the road. As I came to the stop on Higel Avenue, a car came up behind me, high beams burning the inside of my car like the sun. I turned on Higel and sped up just a little over the speed limit, trying to get a bit of distance from the asshole that stayed on my tail. Higel is a narrow two-lane road. Traffic was light. But the lights and the torrential rain were blinding.

I slowed down hoping the tailgater would pass.

He just stayed on my ass as we crossed the north bridge. Normally, I would take a left on South Osprey Avenue, but that's a two-lane road. I stayed on Siesta Drive to Tamiami Trail where I got the red light. The rain let up some, and with the streetlights and the illuminated signs from the bank and business, I could tell it was a cop car behind me. The traffic signal turned green, and I turned left on the Trail, heading north toward downtown. The cop car stuck to my rear.

I got into the middle lane. A few seconds later, blue and red flashed, lighting up the inside of my car and turning the rain to glitter.

I put my signal on, got into the right lane, and slowed down. Just as I was about to pull over, the Sarasota County Sheriff's deputy cruiser sped up on my left so we were side by side. Two seconds later, it took off—fast.

CHAPTER 11

IN THE MORNING, I went to find Joaquin del Pino to see what I could get out of him on Beach City Holdings, Inc. It was early. Court wouldn't start for at least another hour. I went straight to his office. There were already four people in the small reception area, one of them with a bandaged head like a cartoon character. Del Pino's secretary asked me to wait in the conference room. That was promising.

Joaquin del Pino and I went back a ways. He had been the key to my first case—if you could call it that. He was not an easy person to get information out of, but he had proved to be an ethical lawyer. Anyone with high standards and respect for procedure was not easy to crack. He was loyal to his clients. My hope was that since we now had a little history, he would be forthcoming with information and help me figure out about Liam Fleming's work. From what Bob Fleming had said, there had to be millions of dollars in property at stake. People kill for a lot less than that.

The conference room had a big long mahogany table and fourteen nice high-back chairs that made the room look tiny. I sat in a chair near the door. Not a minute later, del Pino stormed in. He was as short and as snappy as I remembered him. He wore pressed blue suit pants and a nice light-yellow Brooks Brothers shirt and a burgundy tie. Everything about him screamed lawyer—even his cologne.

"Dexter Vega," he said in a tone that let me know he was not particularly pleased to see me. "What is it now?"

I smiled. "It's nice to see you, too."

He pulled at his shirtsleeve and glanced at his silver watch. "I have five minutes. Use them wisely."

I stood. "Liam Fleming."

"Yes?"

"His company, Beach City Holdings. You managed the legal paperwork."

"That's correct."

"His body was found two Fridays ago floating in the Intracoastal around Osprey."

"I'm aware of Mr. Fleming's passing."

"The cops declared it an accident, but his father isn't so sure. So he hired me to check it out."

He raised his eyebrows and crossed his arms over his chest. "You're an investigator now?"

"I'm doing him a favor," I said. "But the thing is, I'm kind of beginning to agree with the old man."

"Get to the point."

"Beach City Holdings. What can you tell me about it?"

Del Pino didn't hesitate. He took in a quick breath and spilled a handful of beans. "About four years ago, Liam Fleming came to my office and hired me to draw up the paperwork for his corporation. In that time, he's purchased a number of real estate properties in Sarasota County. He brought me contracts to look over for him. That's it."

"What about his partner?"

"Terrence Oliver."

"Terrence Oliver," I mumbled to myself, thinking back to Keith telling me about Liam's partner. "You ever meet him?"

"Mr. Oliver? No. I never had the pleasure."

"You have his contact info?"

He smiled. "I'll have my assistant give you a copy of the corporate papers. They're public record."

"Geez," I said. "You are such a lawyer."

He didn't flinch. "Will that be all?"

"What did they do?"

"About what?"

"For money. What's the purpose of the business?"

"I just told you. They invested in properties."

"What kind of properties?"

"Houses, land."

"They flipped them?"

He shook his head. "Just bought. Mostly properties in distress. They're all rented as far as I know."

"Financed?"

"Cash. Every single one."

"How many?"

"I don't know. A dozen, maybe more."

I stared at him thinking, trying to figure out Liam's game.

"Anything else?" he said and again pulled at his shirtsleeve and glanced at his watch.

"Not for now."

He turned and walked out of the conference room. I heard him address his assistant as he made his way out of the office.

After about fifteen minutes, his assistant, a nice Latino lady with long dark hair and a medium-length skirt, came in with an envelope. "Mr. Vega," she said pleasantly. "The documents you requested from Mr. del Pino. Is there anything else I can help you with?"

I took the yellow folder from her and felt its weight. Light. "I'm good. Thank you very much."

The file on Beach City Holdings gave me very little information. The papers were just the articles of incorporation and yearly minutes, which said nothing other than offer proof of filing of minutes and payment to the State as required by Florida law. Liam Fleming and Terrence Oliver were listed as officers: president and vice president. No one else. The only address was del Pino's office and Liam's little cottage on Midnight Pass Road.

At least Bob Fleming wasn't lying about Liam's business. And it also explained the map with the red Sharpie marks in Liam's bedroom. Not much to go on except a name: Terrence Oliver.

When I left del Pino's office, I checked my car. I still had time in my parking space, so I crossed Main Street to the Sheriff's office to try and get a hold of Detective Fenton Kendel. The desk sergeant called him. I waited. Across the room a man was arguing with a woman, probably his wife. Something about their kid. Seemed he had been arrested the week before and had some fines to pay. A female deputy walked over and told them to keep it cool. The three of them walked outside.

I watched the desk sergeant pick up his phone after a couple of minutes. He gave a couple of yessirs, nodding his head like a good soldier, and hung up. "Vega," he called. "Detective Kendel's off today."

"Wasn't he off yesterday?"

He narrowed his eyes. "And he's off today."

I shrugged and walked out of the building. The female deputy was having a heated one-way conversation with the man and woman who had been arguing earlier. They were like children being scolded by their mother. I looked at the sky. Clear blue. It was going to be another scorcher. Last night's rain and the heat were turning the air into a steam bath. I broke into a sweat just walking to my car.

CHAPTER 12

I DROVE DOWN to Siesta Key. The island at midmorning had a unique quality of expectation. Last night's party had been cleaned up and the tables set for another long day and night of the same. Traffic was light. I passed a few joggers and a small group of bikers decked out in spandex and caps pedaling their speed bikes in a tight group. At the Village, things were somber. A short Latino-looking man was sweeping the front of the Old Salty Dog. An elderly couple were walking their pugs and peeking into the window of the Siesta T's souvenir shop. Except for Another Broken Egg and The Village Café, the other restaurants were closed.

Sun worshippers were taking advantage of the morning weather and slowly making their way to the beach in flip-flops, carrying their fold-out chairs and umbrellas. At the curve where Ocean Boulevard turned left onto Beach Road, I had to stop for half a dozen tourists on a Segway tour. To my right, just past the Terrace—an older, seven-story apartment building—I could see a group of people gathered at the end of Beach Road. They were holding signs: *Keep Beach Road Public.*

The car behind me honked. The Segways had passed. I started south on Beach Road, passed the old two-story beachfront condos to my right and a few vintage Siesta cottages and stucco two-story apartments with white shell and sand driveways that still retained the funky character I always loved about the key. It was a miracle developers hadn't taken over these places. It made me think of Beach City Holdings. According to Bob Fleming, Liam was buying up properties and holding on to them for when the time was right. Maybe Beach City Holdings was positioning itself to reshape the future of Siesta Key, build it up toward the sky just like downtown Sarasota had done in the past decade—turn this funky little island into Miami Beach.

This early in the morning, the public beach parking lot was half empty. Somewhere past the atrocious modern pavilion was the Gulf of Mexico with its aquamarine waters, gentle waves lapping against the powdery white sand that prompted journalists to give Siesta Beach the distinguished title of America's Best Beach, year after year.

I kept going south to Midnight Pass Road, past the entrance to the Sanderling and Turtle Beach, and pulled in to the driveway of Liam Fleming's cottage.

Everything was just as I had left it: blue VW Golf in the driveway, front door unlocked, magazines and papers strewn all over the place, empty pizza box, dishes in the sink. No one had touched anything. It was clear Jaybird had not been here.

I went into Liam's bedroom and looked at the map he had on the wall by his desk. I took a few photos of it with my phone. Then I walked out, got in my car, and drove north to the address on Calle Menorca that Tessa had written on the napkin the previous night.

* * *

A large green trash truck was backing up to the dumpster in the alley behind a two-story blue apartment building a block south of the Village. The place was typical 1950s Florida: concrete block, open on the front with stairs on both sides of the building, twelve units: six on the first floor, six on the second, doors at the front, screened porch at the back.

I drove around the block and found a parking space at the corner. Then I made my way back to the building and walked up the steps and knocked on apartment 8.

Tessa opened the door. She wore a Ramones t-shirt that was three sizes too big for her, and nothing else. Her hair was a sexy mess, like she'd just woken up after spending the night at her boyfriend's house.

She didn't smile. "I told you not too early."

"It's almost noon."

She squinted at the brightness of the day, then stepped aside to let me through.

Her place was nice, like an Ikea showroom: clean, modern, and accessorized with matching lamps, curtains, rugs, all in pretty pastel colors and paintings of the beach and shells and dolphins.

"Nice place," I said. "Martha Stewart help you decorate?"

"Shut up, smart-ass."

"Seriously," I said. "You can afford this on the *Sarasota Herald*'s salary?"

"I don't work for them anymore. I'm a bartender. That's where the money is."

"Too bad I'm not young and beautiful."

"I'm sorry," she said quickly. "Is that another joke?"

"A tired one."

"A misogynistic one."

I pointed to a chair. "Can I sit?"

"Sure. You want some coffee?"

"Thanks." I watched her go through the motions in the open kitchen across the room. I couldn't believe I didn't remember her from the newspaper. She was pretty, smart, and sharp with the tongue, qualities that would've stayed with me for a long time.

She set the coffeepot, ran her hand through her thick dark hair, and leaned on the counter. "Any news?"

"Of Liam's case?"

"Of Jaybird."

I shook my head. "There was no sign of him at the cottage. It didn't look like he'd been back."

"And what about the other?"

"I don't know. I might be wrong about that."

She pursed her lips, then turned and poured the coffee. "Milk and sugar?"

"Black, thanks."

She came around the counter with two cups. Someone in the apartment next door was making noise, moving furniture, heavy items scraping the terrazzo. The beeping of a trash truck backing up somewhere nearby started and stopped and started again.

"The thing is," I said, "I still can't tell if there was foul play."

"Listen to you," she said, getting comfortable on the seat across from me, her bare feet resting against the edge of the coffee table. Her toes were painted lavender, just like her fingernails. "You sound like a real PI. *Foul play.*"

"I'm not," I said. "I'm just not convinced. But it's all very murky. I was hoping you could help me."

"Sure, we can figure this out together."

I took a short sip of the coffee, hot and strong. I set the cup on the coffee table next to her feet. "The main thing right now is that the cops never found a kayak. So they're attributing that to a witness. A neighbor. But they didn't say that in the report."

"You think the cops deliberately left it out?"

"I doubt it. More likely it was an oversight. All in a day's work. We're talking the Sheriff's office."

"Amateurs," she said, rolling her eyes.

I smiled. "What I'm trying to figure out is—who was Liam Fleming?"

Tessa laughed. "You and everyone else."

"What do you mean?"

"I dated Liam for almost a year. The man's a mystery. He never really opened up to me, you know?"

"Yeah, well, maybe that's just a guy thing."

"No," she said and looked down at her coffee then tilted her head to the side. "It was more than that. Like he was secretive without being secretive."

"I don't follow."

She laughed. "You sound like my therapist."

"I'm certainly not the one to give you dating advice, but if it helps you to unload . . ."

She curled her legs under her and to the side. "There's nothing to unload," she said quietly and looked past me as she told me in a monotone how she met Liam at the volleyball courts in Siesta Beach two winters ago. They went to the same party at a nice house on North Beach Road. That was also where she met Jaybird. They hit it off and started dating right then. He lived in that little cottage on Midnight Pass Road and didn't seem to have a job, but every now and then he'd disappear for a whole day or two, or lock himself in his room and work. Other than that, he just hung out at the beach or went out on his kayak or stand-up paddleboard along the Intracoastal. He was into real estate. He was always checking out Zillow and the MLS site. But everyone in Sarasota was into real estate so she didn't think much of it. He didn't come across as a realtor. He was laid-back, funny. He had no problem making friends with anyone. And that was part of the disconnect.

"He had friends from different cliques," she said. "Like there was us, the Siesta Key bums: Jaybird and Cap'n Cody and that whole crew. But he was also friends with these wealthy businessmen and old people who'd been on the key forever."

"But that's a good thing, no?"

"Yeah, except he separated everyone. I was his girlfriend so I got to see some of it. But he'd never mix it up. He'd never take Cap'n Cody or Jaybird to a party at a friend's place in one of those downtown condos or up in Lakewood Ranch."

"So he didn't like to mix company."

"Exactly."

"Maybe he was embarrassed by them."

She shook her head. "He didn't bring his rich friends to the beach either."

"Maybe he was embarrassed by them."

She laughed. "Yeah, maybe."

"So what happened?"

"To us?"

I nodded.

"I don't know," she said. "What always happens, I guess. When I got laid off from the paper, I tried freelancing, so I was always on the go. I was desperate, he was like, not a problem in the world. Maybe I resented that he had money and could do whatever he wanted. I don't know."

"Most divorces are caused by financial strife," I said knowingly.

She looked at me and I could see she thought I was talking of myself. She said, "It wasn't that. I had to work. I wasn't there to party all the time. We argued about stupid stuff. But I think the main thing that bothered me was that he kept me at a distance. I was his Siesta Key girlfriend."

"You think he had a mainland girlfriend?"

"No." She laughed. "He wasn't like that. But I guess I felt I didn't have the whole of him. Liam's world was vast, and I was only part of a tiny section of it."

"So you broke it off."

She nodded.

"You stay friends?"

"Sure. Beach friends."

"Did he start dating anyone else?"

"Not that I know of. He might have. But he wasn't a playboy or anything. Or if he was, he didn't seem like one. He was laid-back about everything. He loved nature. He loved the beach and the waterways. He was a bird watcher. He always complained about the building boom in downtown Sarasota. Hated all the new buildings. And that new monstrosity right there on the corner of John Ringling Causeway and the Trail. The Westin. God, he hated that."

"And yet he was into real estate."

"See?" Tessa waved, flicking her fingers out, pointing at me in agreement. "That's what I'm talking about. He contradicted himself all the time. He was a developer who hated development."

"But he wasn't developing anything—not yet."

"I know. That's because his father was footing the bill. He had all the money he needed. And yet he lived like a bum. His house was always a mess. He never locked the door. He went around in ripped shorts and flip-flops. But then he'd be at a fund-raiser at the Ritz-Carlton or Michael's on East rubbing elbows with Sarasota's wealthy."

"Meanwhile, you had to work eighty hours a week," I said.

She frowned. "I didn't resent him. But I lost my job. And the newspaper world is dead. I mean, everything I had been working for all my life imploded: four years of college, two internships, a year at a small paper in Colorado, then the *Sarasota Herald*. You can't get a job at a newspaper anymore. And if you do, you can be damn sure you're not going to last."

"You're preaching to the choir, sister."

"Well," she said and leaned back in her chair. "That pissed me off more than anything. When I was with Liam, I was reinventing myself, I guess. If I resented anything about him, it was how he didn't have to try. But what was worse is that with all he had, he chose to live like a college kid, you know?"

"Maybe he liked that lifestyle."

"I don't know. Maybe." She took a sip of coffee, her big brown eyes looking at me over the cup. "I always felt he was putting up a front."

"A front for what?"

"I have no idea."

"Look," I said and leaned forward, resting my forearms on my knees. "Isn't that the whole point of being wealthy? That you can live any way you want."

"Like a bum?"

"Carefree."

"Not me," she said. "I'd have a nice place. And I'd travel."

"You have a nice place."

"It's not mine. And the rent's killing me."

I had to be careful with my words. It wasn't that I didn't trust Tessa. I didn't know her. And a vengeful girlfriend could be lethal. Crimes of passion are more common than crimes of greed.

"Here's the thing," I said, letting go of a little information to see where it might take me. "Liam had his own company and was using his father's money to buy properties on the key. And yet everyone I've talked to has told me he hated his father."

"Like who?"

"Jaybird and Keith. And you."

"Keith Peterson?"

I nodded.

She rolled her eyes.

"What's going on?" I said.

"It's complicated. Liam didn't hate his father. I don't think he was capable of hate. But he didn't like what he stood for."

"There has to be more to it than that," I said. "Tell me something I don't know."

We were quiet for a moment, our eyes staring at each other. My mind drifted, wondering what Tessa's life was like, who she saw, what she did. If she was dating someone now.

"Oh, Liam," she sighed. "What the hell were you up to?"

"You ever heard of Terrence Oliver?"

She shook her head. "No, why?"

"Right now," I said, "he's my main suspect."

"Why?"

"He's Liam's business partner. I figure he wanted to take over the company. Those properties have to be worth many millions."

"That's Liam in a nutshell."

"How do you mean?"

"An enigma," she said. "He hated corporate America. But he had his own corporation. Go figure."

"Beach City Holdings."

Tessa recoiled in her seat. "What the hell?"

"What?"

"That's the company I make my rent check out to."

CHAPTER 13

I DRANK ANOTHER cup of coffee while I waited for Tessa to get changed. She came out of the room in a flower pattern sarong and a white tank top that showed off her tan shoulders, and a pair of simple black flip-flops. She'd put her hair up in a bun and wore no makeup. We walked the back streets of the Village to Another Broken Egg and sat outside despite the midmorning heat. I had a Nellie's Delight, balsamic glazed chicken with smoked gouda on fancy bread. Tessa had a huge plate of Shrimp n' Grits. The waitresses knew her by name and every now and then someone passing by, walking their dog, or on their way to work somewhere in the Village would wave and say hello to her.

A block and a half away, at the end of Beach Boulevard, about half a dozen people still hung around holding signs that read, *Keep Beach Road Public.* Then a couple of teenagers came by handing out flyers asking people to sign the petition and attend a county commission meeting to voice their opinion against closing the small stretch of road. In big block letters, it read: *Tell Sarasota County Commissioner Troy Varnel he's not a dictator. You're against his land-grabbing policies and want to keep Beach Road public for everyone to enjoy!*

I had seen in the news that the county wanted to make a small stretch of Beach Road private. The road itself had been washed out for more than two decades. All that was left in its place was a bit of asphalt and sand. You could walk directly onto the beach from there. The County Commission, spearheaded by newly elected commissioner Troy Varnel, proposed closing the road. This would give the three homes on the block an extra ten to fifteen feet of property. It would also convert them into beachfront properties, probably doubling their value while closing off a wide swath of beach access to the rest of us.

None of it was new. And none of it was fair. Just a few years ago, after a number of petitions and protests against razing the Summerhouse Restaurant, a Siesta landmark designed by some famous architect, the county commissioners made a backhanded deal with the developer. Instead of destroying the building, the commissioners gave the developer a permit to build a nine-story condominium, going over the height limit for Siesta Key. The company kept the Summerhouse building for use as the condo's private community center.

"Look there." Tessa nodded across Avenida Messina. "It's Cap'n Cody."

The skinny, scruffy-looking man I'd seen the other day was walking toward Ocean Boulevard.

Tessa waved at him. "Cap'n Cody!"

Cap'n Cody stopped in his tracks and looked around. He stood in front of the Hub Baja Grill, dressed in faded jeans and a colorful Hawaiian shirt. His skin was tan and wrinkled from too much sun, his hair a mop of gray. He had a long gray goatee and a crooked smile that reminded me of Popeye. Another aging hippie, no ponytail. When he spotted Tessa, he nodded and crossed over to us, his flip-flops dragging over the asphalt.

"What's goin' on, little Tessa?" he said in a heavy southern accent and leaned over, gave her a kiss on the forehead the way a father might kiss his college-age daughter.

"Nothing," she said. "We're just trying to find out who killed Liam."

Cap'n Cody blinked. "Didn't they say he drowned?"

"Yeah," Tessa said and narrowed her eyes, whispered, "that's what they want us to believe."

"What who wants us to believe?" he said and shifted his gaze at me.

"The killers," she said.

Cap'n Cody looked at her and back at me, cracked a wide smile. "Ya'll pullin' my leg."

"Yes, we are," I said quickly. I couldn't believe Tessa's big mouth. I offered my hand. "Dexter Vega."

He shook it politely.

"Cap'n Cody's a musician," Tessa said. "Plays all over the key."

"Beach songs for the tourists," he said humbly.

"Come on." Tessa smacked his thigh with the back of her hand. "He's a real musician. He even recorded with the Allman Brothers and Mudcrutch."

"Tom Petty's early days," I said.

Cap'n Cody nodded. "That was a long time ago."

"You going to the protest?" Tessa asked.

Cap'n Cody looked up toward the part of Beach Road that was slated to close. "You think all that hullaballoo's gonna make any difference?"

"I don't know," Tessa said. "I sure hope so."

Cap'n Cody scratched the bottom of his gray beard, narrowed his blue eyes. "Politicians. They give it all away, don't they?"

"They say you can't stop progress," I said.

He focused on me. Didn't seem pleased by what I said. "I don't like it one bit. Been fightin' this crap all my life. I just 'bout had enough. Gettn' ready to throw in the towel."

"Come on," Tessa said. "Don't be such a grouchy old man. Sit with us. I'll buy you a cup of coffee."

Cap'n Cody smiled. "Thanks, darlin'. But I like being grumpy. It's my job. I'm an old man."

"You're not that old."

He laughed.

"Coffee?" I said.

"Nah." He shook his head and nodded to the side. "Gotta meet a friend for lunch. Maybe some other time."

Before he started off, I said, "You seen Jaybird around?"

"Nope. Can't say that I have. Everyone keeps asking for him. Little squirt oughta get a damn phone."

He walked off, making his way on the side of the road, crossing Avenida Messina and disappearing past The Cottage restaurant.

I looked at Tessa. "He's a character."

"There's one in every beach town."

"Did he really record with Tom Petty?"

She nodded. "I've seen the credit on the album. And he toured with them for a while. He also produced a couple of bands back in the eighties when he lived in Miami."

"You'd never know it from looking at him."

"It's funny," she said staring past me at the road. "Liam used to say he loved the beach because people were stripped of the accessories that defined who they were."

"How do you mean?"

"A man or a woman in a bathing suit is just that—a person. They're human."

"So you couldn't tell if they were rich or poor."

"Exactly."

"Or a killer."

She stared at me.

"Quick question," I said. "Why did you tell Cap'n Cody Liam was murdered?"

She shrugged, glanced at her plate. "I don't know. It just came out."

"Was he friends with Liam?"

"Yes, he was friends with Liam," she said angrily. "And he's a friend of mine. What are you trying to say?"

"Nothing. I just don't want it advertised that we're looking into it."

"What's the big deal?"

"First off, I'm not a licensed investigator. Second, I don't want people talking about it. If it gets to whoever did it, they can cover their tracks, take off. Who knows, maybe even come after us."

"Gimme a break, Dexter."

"We don't know anything, Tessa. Let's keep our work under the radar. Please."

"Fine."

I rolled my eyes and took out my wallet. I folded the flyer and shoved it between my cash. I signaled the waitress for the check.

Tessa ate quietly. Then she tossed her head to the side and apologized. "It's just, I kind of got excited about the case."

"It's not a case," I said.

"Then what is it?"

"We're just looking into things. See what we find out."

"Fine," Tessa said, her mouth half full of shrimp and grits. "So what's the plan, Sherlock?"

"I really would like to talk to the neighbor the cops talked to."

"But we don't know who it is."

"We?"

She squinted happily. "Yeah, we."

I didn't like the sound of that. But other than Jaybird, she seemed like the only person who could tell me about Liam. Besides, she seemed determined. And I actually enjoyed her company.

"Okay." I took a long breath. "First we'll go see if Jaybird's back at the cottage. Then we can knock on the neighbor's house."

"I love it," Tessa said. "Good, old-fashioned detective work."

CHAPTER 14

AS WE WALKED to my car, Tessa held her phone in front of her, her fingers clicking away like she was writing a novel. "I just checked in with the manager at The Dog. Jaybird was scheduled for a double today but didn't show up for the lunch shift."

"Let's hope he's at Liam's."

"He could be at the beach."

"Or at Walmart," I said sarcastically.

"Fat chance." Tessa laughed and got in the car. "Jaybird never leaves the island."

"Some life," I said and pulled out of my tight parking spot and headed south on Beach Road. "Guy doesn't have a car or a phone or a home."

"He's free."

"He's a hobo."

"Yeah, but think about it. He's not weighed down the way we are. He doesn't have to worry about slow internet service, software updates, rent, bills."

"And you believe in all that?"

She laughed. "You saw my place. I believe in comfort. I like things," she said and flicked her sandals off and put her feet on the dashboard. "But I won't deny that in principle, it would be nice."

"You mean in theory."

"Exactly."

"I like the part about no bills," I said.

Tessa shrugged. "I'm too ambitious. Gotta keep writing."

"You still believe, huh?"

"I have to."

"Yeah," I said sadly as if admitting defeat. "I guess I do, too."

"I do mostly fluffy pieces, travel and lifestyle and beauty articles. Not big investigative I'm-gonna-change-the-world kind of work."

"Well, I'm having a hell of a time finding *any* work that pays."

"Social media, my friend."

"What about it?"

"That's the key. People will give you work if you have a following."

"Like on Facebook?"

She laughed. "Yeah, Facebook, Twitter, Instagram. That's what they pay for: an audience."

"Sounds exhausting."

"If you can deliver the clicks, they'll deliver the cash."

"So, good writing is irrelevant."

"No. It matters. But so does the following."

"I don't know, maybe I'm old-school," I said. "I'll take paper over a screen any day."

"My God, you sound just like Jaybird."

We were passing the entrance to the Sanderling Club. I slowed down. A rented go-cart was moving slowly in front of us.

"It's really not that hard," she said. "I can teach you."

"Thanks. But I prefer to experience life face-to-face."

"Liam used to say the same thing," she said somberly. "He said the world was changing too fast. He said he was going to beat it at its own game."

"And what game is that?"

She took a deep breath and stared ahead at the road. The little go-cart turned off at the entrance to Turtle Beach. "Progress, I suppose."

"Liam Fleming, a fucking enigma."

She smacked my arm. "Don't say that. He's dead."

"You said it first."

"That's different."

"People usually fit a type," I said. "You can see the same patterns in them. Like the cliques in high school. Take the jocks. They'll always be jocks. They'll grow up, get jobs, maybe become some kind of asshole manager, put their kids in little league, and get into fights with other parents who were also once jocks. Then the cycle will repeat itself."

"Oh, my God. That is such stereotyping. There's no way people are that predictable."

"On the contrary," I said, "most people are. Jaybird might try to be free, but he's really just freeloading off of Liam. When that cottage goes, he's going to have to stay with someone else. But what's going to happen when he wants to have a family or travel? Or when he gets old and wants to retire?"

"Maybe he'll never want that. He'll be happy being a beach bum until he dies."

"I don't believe that. At one point everyone wants something tangible, something that's theirs. Like a legacy. It's the American way."

Tessa rolled her eyes. "You are such a square."

"Square?" I pulled into Liam's driveway. The VW Golf was still there, the surfboard still tied to the roof rack. "What are we in, the sixties?"

"I'm just saying. People don't fit into nice little patterns like that. And Jaybird is living his life the way he wants to live it. Give him a break."

"Okay," I said. "But I'm not a square."

Tessa came around to my side of the car. "Maybe not a square," she said and waved a finger at me. "But you sure seem to have your mind made up about people."

"Wait 'til you grow up."

"I am grown up!"

"I can see your future: living in one of those developments in East County," I said as we walked into the cottage. "A nice three-bedroom two-bath house with a small pool and a two-car garage. A husband, two point five kids. The works."

Everything inside the cottage was the same. Nothing had been disturbed. No sign of life whatsoever.

"What does that even mean, two point five kids?" She picked up a magazine from the top of the cable spool, flipped through it, and tossed it back. "What's the point five?"

"I don't know." I checked the kitchen counter, the fridge. "A baby or a dog."

"I'm a cat person," Tessa said and went into the bedroom. I followed. She handled the papers on the desk. "It's kind of sad," she said, her eyes scanning the floor, the dresser, the bed. "It's like it's frozen in time. I kind of imagine Liam walking in any minute and saying something like, 'Dude, shoulda been at Turtle, catch the sunset with me.'"

I followed her out. We stood at opposite sides of the living room. I pointed to the corner next to the stereo. "His drum's here."

"But no Jaybird."

An eerie silence came over us. Everything was too still, like a studio set, a place that wasn't real and had only been created for the purpose of make-believe. Like maybe there was no Liam Fleming and no Jaybird. It had been a play. And the play was over. Time to go home.

"Jaybird," I said to break the silence. "That guy. You'd think Jimmy Buffet wrote 'Margaritaville' about him."

Tessa blinked like she'd just come out of her own daydream. "Shall we go knock on the neighbor's door?"

* * *

The property had a long, paved driveway. The garden was neatly trimmed like at the golf course developments out east of I-75. The house was a huge two-story, peach-colored pseudo-Mediterranean with a grand entrance leading to a pair of large French doors with frosted windowpanes and a welcome mat on the floor. I rang the bell.

Someone yelled inside. Twice. Something about getting the door. A moment later the door opened, and a small woman, probably in her mid-fifties, looked out at us from large round plastic glasses.

"Yeah, what is it?"

I smiled. But Tessa beat me to the introductions. "We're friends of your neighbor, Liam Fleming."

"Don't know him," she said flatly. Her whole demeanor was defensive, the way she stood, how she pursed her lips, the pulsing vein on the side of her neck.

"He passed away a couple weeks ago," I said and nodded toward the water. "He drowned in the Intracoastal."

She poked her head forward. "Uh-huh?"

"The police said someone saw him on a kayak that night."

"And?"

"Did you see him?" Tessa said.

"Thursday night, two weeks ago," I said.

"You're not the police."

"No." Tessa laughed. "We're his friends."

The woman patted down her dress at the base of her stomach and touched her earring, a nice golden circle that weighed down her earlobe. "They had a lot of parties over there. Loud music and talking, going 'til all hours. Rather annoying if you ask me."

"Yeah." Tessa chuckled. "That sounds like Liam."

"Well, we don't take well to that. We like quiet. Between the parties and the motorboats and those water motorcycles . . . this place is driving me insane."

"Did your husband see him that morning?" I said.

She drew a breath and turned to the inside of the house. "Charlie!" she yelled in a shrill voice. "You see the neighbor ridin' a kayak last Thursday night?"

"Two weeks ago," I corrected her.

A voice inside the house yelled back, "What's that?"

The woman raised her voice so it echoed across the large open living room. "I asked if you seen the neighbor last Thursday?"

"What neighbor?"

"Jesus Christ," the woman muttered, then she yelled again, her pitch cracking from the effort. "The one from next door. The kid. Did you see him on his canoe last Thursday?"

"I didn't see anything," the man yelled back. "I dunno what you're talking about."

The woman turned to us with a sad grin.

"You didn't tell the police that you saw him that morning?" I said.

She studied Tessa for a moment, then addressed me. "I just told you. We didn't see anything. We don't know the neighbor. We don't know any of the neighbors here. We keep to ourselves. That's how we like it. Peace and quiet."

"And you didn't talk to the police," I said again.

She frowned and spoke real slow and mean. "We. Did. Not. Talk. To. The. Police."

Tessa smiled and reached for the woman's shoulder, but the woman's eyes grew wide, and she pulled her shoulder away. Tessa froze, her hand hanging between the two of them.

"Anything else?" the woman said.

I shook my head. "Thanks for your time."

We walked back toward Liam's house in silence. Just as we reached the driveway, Tessa laughed. "She wasn't very nice, was she?"

"Proof that money can't buy you happiness," I said.

"There you go again," she said. "You sound just like Jaybird."

"Well, maybe he's on to something, after all."

We entered Liam's cottage. I went to the kitchen and looked in the fridge. I guess it was an impulse. I wanted a beer, but it wasn't my house. And I had work to do.

Tessa sat on the sofa where Jaybird had slept earlier and picked up one of the real estate brochures. "What now?"

"I don't know," I said. "There're too many angles. I have to talk with Detective Kendel, get the name and address of this witness of his. But I also want to go home and look up the properties of Beach City Holdings, see if I can find anything on Terrence Oliver."

"We can go to my place." Tessa tossed the magazine aside and stood. "You can use my computer. I don't have to be at work 'til five."

We walked out of the house, leaving the door unlocked. I drove north on Midnight Pass. Just as we came upon the entrance to the Sanderling Club, a white Maserati GT pulled out ahead of us.

"Well, hello," I said.

"What?"

"That car," I said. "It belongs to the Flemings."

"You suspect his folks?"

"I suspect everyone."

CHAPTER 15

WE FOLLOWED THE Maserati off the key over the Stickney Point bridge then north on Tamiami Trail.

"What if they're just going to Publix?" Tessa said.

"Then we'll go to Publix." We stopped at the traffic light on Bee Ridge Road, three cars behind the Maserati. "And we can get a six-pack of beer and some snacks."

"Fun job," she said.

"But if they're not going to Publix, that's another story."

The light turned green. The Maserati weaved easily through the light traffic all the way down the Trail, around Sarasota Bay, and got into the turning lane for John Ringling Causeway that led to Lido and Longboat Key. We were six cars behind. I could see a sliver of the curved white rear panel. I followed the little Italian sports car as it revved up, taking a left onto the causeway and then a quick right up the ramp to the Ritz-Carlton Hotel.

Tessa smiled. "Beats the Publix."

The Maserati pulled up at the entrance. Three valets ran up to it.

I stayed back on the crest of the drive about twenty yards away.

A valet opened the door of the Maserati and offered his hand to the driver. Brandy Fleming stepped out of the car wearing a sexy purple minidress with no sleeves and a low V that showed off her tan back. She wore her hair down. At the end of her curvy legs she had on a pair of shiny black stilettos. She looked hot the way an expensive escort looks hot.

Tessa leaned forward. "Who's that?"

No one came out of the passenger side. Brandy paused at the back of the car. She raised the trunk and pulled a cream-colored Louis Vuitton bag from it.

"Liam's stepmom," I said.

Brandy smiled at the young valet who offered to carry her small bag. Instead of giving it to him, she slung it over her shoulder, tossed her hair to the side like a pro, and marched into the Ritz like she owned it.

"Damn," Tessa said. "She's a fine piece of ass."

I looked at Tessa. "Really—"

"Well, she is, isn't she?"

"Yeah. And she knows it."

"So, what do you think?"

"I don't know, late lunch with the bridge club?" I pulled the Subaru slowly to the entrance. "Go inside and see where she goes."

Tessa gave me a conspiring grin. She hopped out of the car and skipped quickly into the Ritz. The valet came to the car, pulled the door open for me.

I stepped out. "I'm just picking up a package from the desk. Can you keep it close?"

"Certainly, sir."

Sir. I liked that. I figured people like Mr. and Mrs. Fleming were used to that kind of treatment. The only people who called me *sir* were the valet parkers at the Ritz and the grocery clerks at the Publix.

When I walked into the foyer, the finely groomed bell captain started toward me with a friendly smile. I raised my chin toward Tessa. "I'm with her."

I walked straight past him to where Tessa was standing, staring up at the numbers atop the elevator doors.

"What's up?"

Tessa pointed to the numbers as they illuminated one after another. It stopped on the ninth floor. "There. She went to the ninth floor."

"Really?"

She turned to face me. "The lady," she said sarcastically, "walked into the lobby, paused at the front desk where she was given a key and a smile. Then she walked with confident strides to the elevators and went up to the ninth floor. Any questions?"

"Yeah," I said. "Why?"

"Really?" she said and smacked me on the chest. "Are you that dense, Dexter?"

"Come on," I said. "Let's go get a drink and wait this out."

She looked at her watch. "I have to be at work in a couple hours."

The bar didn't offer a good vantage point to spy on the elevators and the entrance to the hotel, but if Brandy Fleming was meeting someone for a little afternoon delight, it would probably take a while for her to come out. I leaned on the polished counter and was pleasantly surprised to see a tap for Copek's Siesta IPA.

Tessa ordered a rum and Coke.

"You seem like a . . . I don't know, a chocolatini type," I said.

"I am, but not in the middle of the afternoon, dressed like this."

"You're so . . . Margaritaville," I said and quickly scanned the bar—plush chairs, mahogany tables, dark amber lights—empty except for two men in business suits sitting at opposite sides of a table near the windows that faced the back.

The bartender came with the drinks. I paid and raised my glass. Tessa touched it with hers. "Here's to us," I said. "May we be successful in our search for truth."

She smiled, turned the little blue straw in her glass, then fell serious. "And may Liam find peace."

That shut me up fast. I hadn't known Liam. I saw him as a project, a puzzle I needed to solve. Tessa reminded me he'd been a person, someone with feelings. A nice guy. And now we shared a friend.

Damn.

I had to shut down the neurosis. This was neither the time nor place to evaluate myself and my relationship with Liam and Jaybird. And Tessa.

I turned in my seat, took a long drink of beer. Tessa pointed to the side of the bar with her little blue straw at a large red sofa between the elevators and the wide staircase that led to the backyard of the hotel. "Let's sit over there."

I followed her to the divan. From that place, we could see the side of the elevators and the three main doors to the front entrance. I knew Brandy Fleming could go out another way, but she would have to get her car. There was a decent chance she would exit this way. Besides, she had no idea we had followed her here.

"So, tell me." Tessa leaned back and crossed her legs, her flip-flop dangling from between her toes. "How did you get into this line of work?"

"It's a long story."

She glanced at her wrist. "I've got, oh, I don't know, an hour or two."

"Coincidence," I said honestly. "It's not as if I do this all the time. After I got laid off, I met some guy, a creep who roped me into a complicated case that almost got me in a heap of trouble." I pointed at my ear. "Even got myself a little battle scar."

She leaned forward and examined the side of my face. "Yeah, I noticed that last night."

"Too polite to stare?"

She shook her head. "Just didn't get a chance. What happened?"

"Guy put a cigar out in my ear."

"Ouch"

"You're not kidding."

"Why?"

"To get me out of Mexico City."

"That's crazy."

"Anyway, I guess I got a bit of a reputation after I solved that case. The editor of *Sarasota City Magazine* recommended me to Bob Fleming."

"Does it pay well?"

I shrugged, leaned forward, forearms on my thighs, glass in both hands. "Better than journalism, that's for sure." But I had mixed feelings about all of it: the life, the job, the money. It felt dirty, yet I kept telling myself I was helping someone. "And I guess I'm pretty good at it."

"At tailing women?"

"Funny," I said. "Helping people."

"I remember you from the paper. You were like, the superstar. Everyone talked about how you wrote some phenomenal article that nailed a bunch of bad cops."

I smiled at my beer. "Those days are long gone."

"Yeah, but it must've been great for you. Everyone in the newsroom was in awe."

"It's all in the past."

"I had such a crush on you."

"Oh, come on."

"It's true." She smiled and brought her glass to her lips. "Well, sort of. You were going through a divorce, I think."

I laughed. "Journalists, we thrive on gossip, huh?"

"Ain't that the truth."

I stared ahead at the elevators wondering why we were here. I didn't imagine that whatever Brandy Fleming was doing here had anything to do with Liam's murder. What I really needed to do was check out the property listings for Beach City Holdings, try to find Terrence Oliver. And nail down Detective Kendel for the name and address of the witness. I glanced at the clock on my phone. We hadn't been here an hour.

"Getting impatient?" Tessa said.

"No," I said, "but there are a million other things I'd rather be doing."

"Oh, like what?"

I sat up and took a sip of beer. "I don't know, like getting drunk."

I stared ahead at the deserted lobby, hoping Brandy wasn't planning on ordering room service and spending the night. Then I glanced at the bar, at the two men in suits. One of them was in his forties, portly, round cheeks and chin, bald head. The other was younger, maybe early thirties, blond, good looking in a Young Republican kind of way. He looked vaguely familiar. But I couldn't place him.

"You keep changing the subject," Tessa said.

I looked at her. "No, I'm not."

"So, how did it work out?"

"How did what work out?"

"The divorce."

I was no longer angry about my divorce. I didn't blame anyone but myself. I just hated how bitter things can turn when two people are supposed to love each other. And then, of course, there was Zoe. Having her so far away—not just in a physical state but in a mental way—turned my stomach sour.

"I mean, if you wanna talk about it."

I studied the pattern the foam made at the top my glass, like a thin round island in an amber sea. I held up the glass. "You're going to have to pump a lot more alcohol in me to get that story."

She looked past me at the bar. "I don't know. At these prices?" Then she frowned. "Is Fleming taking care of your expenses?"

"Yeah, but that's not how it works. If you want to get me drunk, you have to pay for it."

She turned away and stared at the front of the building. My eyes traced the outline of her profile, the angular line of her jaw and cheekbone. She seemed like someone who was very much in control of her life—and having a good time. I imagined she got hit on by drunk frat boys all the time. She had to be quick with the comebacks. Take nobody's shit.

"Why don't you tell me about you and Liam," I said.

She tilted her head to the side, her pretty brown eyes on me. "I already told you."

"I mean tell me more. What was the relationship like? Were you in love?"

She laughed and held up her rum and Coke. It was almost empty. "You're going to have to buy a hell of a lot more of these to get that kind of juice out of me."

"Well." I stood. "I'm ready for another."

I went to the bar and ordered another round. When I came back, I glanced at the time on my phone. "I don't know how much longer we should stay."

"She could be here all night," Tessa said. "If it were me, and I was rich, and I was meeting my lover, I'd stay a while. I'd order room service, champagne, the whole shebang."

I raised an eyebrow at her.

"Maybe we should get a room," she said. "You know, for surveillance."

I grinned. "I thought you had to go to work. Besides . . ." I gestured toward the lobby with my beer. "Don't you find this a little too much?"

"What, the hotel?"

"The opulence. It's so over the top: the chandeliers, the uniforms, the smiles, all the yessirs and yes ma'ams. It's so not me."

"Oh!" Tessa laughed. "You're one of those."

"One of what?"

"You hate the rich."

"No," I said sharply. "I hate show-offs. And I hate waste."

"Wow. I don't believe it. Dexter Vega, you're jealous."

"What the hell are you talking about?"

"You're jealous of the people who can afford a place like this."

"That's ridiculous."

"Yes, you are. You don't like people who are better off than you."

"You don't know what you're talking about."

"You're going to tell me you wouldn't like to bring your lover to a place like this and be pampered? Have a couples massage, drink champagne, have a decadent meal at Jack Dusty's?"

"Sorry. Not my thing."

"God!" She laughed and took a drink of her rum and Coke. "That explains everything."

"Explains what?"

"That chip on your shoulder. You've got a vendetta against the one-percent."

"Gimme a break, Tessa."

"You're more like Jaybird than you know."

I laughed. Jaybird. I was sure that skinny hawk-nosed rasta had the answer to the puzzle. Almost one hundred percent. "We need to find him."

"I'll tell you one thing," Tessa said, "if he doesn't show up at work tonight, he's going to need to find another job."

"I'm serious," I said. "He has to know more than what he's told me. When I talked to him at the drum circle, he was pretty out of it—"

"The witness!"

"Goddamn it," I cried and stood, looked around the bar. "He must've been the one who spoke to Detective Kendel. But . . ."

"But what?"

"When I spoke with him, he didn't say he'd been there or seen Liam going out in the kayak."

Tessa covered her mouth with her hand. "And?"

"That son of a bitch."

"No. Let's not jump to conclusions. Maybe he was high. Maybe it just escaped him. I mean he's a little strange but—"

"A little?"

Tessa forced a cough and nodded toward the front of the hotel. "Heads up."

Brandy Fleming had just strutted out of the elevator, her stiletto heels clacking on the tile all the way to the front desk.

"Keep an eye on her." I set our drinks on the closest table and pointed to the end of the bar. "I'm going that way."

I walked quickly around one of the large columns and stood by the side, hidden from view. Brandy Fleming was still wearing her sexy purple minidress. But she looked a little different, hair slightly disheveled. Maybe it was my imagination, me thinking of what had gone on in a fancy suite on the ninth floor. She set her bag on the counter. She seemed to be paying for the room—cash. Tessa stood in front of the elevators, looking up at the numbers and turning away, pacing back and forth, stealing glances at the front desk.

After she paid, Brandy walked out. The valet ran off to get her car. She glanced at her watch, tossed her hair to the side, struck a pose: one foot forward, one to the side, showing off those fine, tan, muscular legs. She took quick inventory of the area around her, left then right. Like maybe she was trying to see if there was anyone who might recognize her. A couple of minutes later, the white Maserati drove up with a low rumble. The valet hopped out and stood by the door with a goofy smile on his face. She tipped him, leaned into the car, then walked to the rear and put her bag in the trunk. She ran her hand over her mane of black hair then got in the car and drove off toward the Tamiami Trail exit.

Tessa walked out the door. I followed, coming out of the building two doors down. Tessa joined me. We walked back to the main entrance to where the valet was standing, still looking to where the Maserati had disappeared down the driveway. "You got my keys, friend?"

He pointed at me. "Red Subaru, right?"

I nodded.

He walked slowly back to the valet station, pulled my keys off a hook, handed them to me, and pointed in the opposite direction of where the Maserati had gone. My old red car sat like a joke at the end of the circular drive.

I gave him a five-spot and didn't wait to see if he was happy with the tip. There was no left turn out of the Tamiami Trail exit. She had to be going south.

"We're gonna follow her?" Tessa asked when we reached the Subaru.

"I don't know. Let me think."

"So why were we waiting here for two hours?"

"It was a lead, okay? I didn't know where it was going to go. It happens."

"So Liam's stepmom having an affair means nothing."

"We don't know for sure if she's having an affair."

"Seriously?"

"She's probably driving home," I said. "Sometimes you find something, sometimes you don't."

"Well that went nowhere quickly."

I looked toward downtown where a large crane was moving slowly over the row of mega condos in the bay front. "We have to find Jaybird."

Tessa glanced at her phone. "I have to be at work in half an hour."

Just as I was about to get in my car, an older cream-colored Toyota Land Cruiser climbed up the driveway to the entrance of the hotel. On the door was the sign: *Sun n' Surf Adventure Kayak Rental.*

"Keith. Fucking. Peterson."

"What?"

"Brandy Fleming's having an affair with Keith Peterson."

Tessa looked back at the entrance. Keith got in his SUV, tipped the valet, and the Toyota started down the driveway toward Tamiami Trail, right blinker flashing.

"I have to go to work."

I pulled out a twenty and handed it to Tessa. "Take an Uber."

"What?"

"I have to follow Keith, then I'll come by the Salty Dog."

"Are you serious?"

I stepped on the gas just as a black Mustang convertible came up the drive to my right. I slammed on the brakes. Our bumpers stopped inches from each other. An older man got out of the Mustang. I backed up the Subaru, shoved it into first, and sped around the motherfucker and down the driveway. When I turned on the Trail, I got the red light. I was stuck in the shadow of the new Westin, searching past the intersection where the road curved along the bay. No sign of Keith's Toyota.

CHAPTER 16

WHEN I GOT the green light, I weaved through the traffic along the curve of Sarasota Bay. The sailboats bobbed gently on the windless day. To my left, the wall of condos separated me from downtown. But there was no way. By the time I came to where Tamiami Trail and Washington Boulevard came together, it was clear I'd lost Keith before we even got started.

I went a little farther and took a right on Hillview Street just after the hospital and pulled over at a spot in front of the Pacific Rim restaurant.

What the hell was I doing?

I was chasing too many tails and it was leading nowhere. I had to prioritize. I took a deep breath, went through each problem one at a time: Brandy Fleming's affair was not what I was supposed to be investigating, but the fact that it was with Keith Peterson counted for something. Maybe there was something there. Maybe not. But I could always catch up with Keith at Turtle Beach. I didn't have to chase him.

Finding Jaybird was now priority number one. He was the one closest to Liam. He was probably Detective Kendel's witness. He saw Liam going out in the kayak. So, Jaybird either saw Liam the night he died, or he was lying, which pushed him to the top of my list of suspects.

And then there was Terrence Oliver. I imagined he had the most to gain from Liam's death as the new sole owner of Beach City Holdings and all the properties. Or maybe they just had a falling out, a business deal went bad, a difference of opinion on buying or selling a property. Or just plain greed. I'd read too many crime stories where business partners double-crossed each other for control of the company—or for a few dollars more.

Or maybe my imagination was taking me on a long ride to nowhere.

* * *

I drove home and browsed the property records on the County Appraisers website for Liam Fleming and Terrence Oliver. Nothing. Neither of the two men owned a damn thing in Sarasota County— at least under their own names. But when I looked up the records under Beach City Holdings, I hit pay dirt. The company owned a decent amount of acreage in east Sarasota County where farms and ranches were being turned into subdivisions. The company also owned some very nice property on Siesta Key: Liam's cottage, a few lots south of there, near Midnight Pass, a beachfront lot south of Turtle Beach—a place that would probably be washed away in the next hurricane—two houses at the end of Beach Road just north of Siesta Village, as well as the apartment building where Tessa lived. All together there had to be at least fifty million in real estate— probably more.

I pushed my chair back and stared out the window at the empty lot where Dieter & Waxler were getting ready to build The Majestic. Their real estate man, Alex J. Trainor, was poised to make a real nice chunk of change. I was never very good at math, but nine floors with at least four units per floor at say, a million plus per unit.

Yeah. Real estate was gold in this town. That was a hell of a lot of motivation right there. Terrence Oliver just moved a notch above Jaybird on my suspect list.

I tried getting ahold of Detective Kendel again, but got more of the same: unavailable.

I called Brian Farinas, my old friend and handy-dandy-lawyer.

"No," he said flat out before I'd even asked.

"But—"

"You only call when you need something. And I can't right now, Dex, I'm working."

"Please."

Silence.

"It's important, Brian. I swear."

He sighed.

"Detective Fenton Kendel."

"What about him?"

"He's giving me the runaround."

"And?"

He was lead investigator in a case I'm looking into and—"

"Active case?"

"No. They ruled the drowning accidental. The victim's father asked me to look into it for him, make sure it was on the up and up."

"And you think it's not . . ."

"Feels like it. The report states the victim was in a kayak, but there was no kayak found. The responding Sheriff's Deputy said Kendel got the info from a witness, but it's not in the police report."

"You think they're lying."

"I don't know. The report is incomplete. I'd like to talk to the witness."

"And you want me to do what exactly?"

"You're a criminal lawyer. You spend a lot of time at the courthouse. Maybe you can find Kendel and ask him about it."

"Jesus, as if I don't have enough to do already."

"Come on, Brian, help me out here."

"You really think it was murder?"

"It's weird about the report. Why would Kendel leave out a major piece of information like that?"

"The kayak?"

"And the witness. And fucking Kendel won't call me back."

"Maybe he knows he messed up. You do have a reputation."

"Give me a break, Brian. Just ask around, see if you stumble into something that can help me. Maybe call someone at the Sheriff's office."

"What's in it for me?"

"The usual."

"No. I'm tired of the pub. How about the Beer Garden?"

"Seriously? It's like a million degrees out."

"You want your information?"

"How about Copek's brewery."

"No way. Sitting on plastic chairs in a warehouse next to a bunch of kegs is not my idea of a good time."

"He's got a tasting room," I said.

"Bullshit."

"He just built it. Even has a chickee hut."

"Seriously?"

"He's having an event tomorrow."

"And it's on you."

"Absolutely."

He seemed to hesitate. Then he said, "Okay, what's the victim's name?"

My next call was to Rachel Mann.

"What do you need, Dex?"

I sighed. "I was just calling to say hi."

"Funny. Out with it. I'm on deadline." She was all business.

"Okay, then. A drowning two Fridays ago. Liam Fleming. You know who wrote about it?"

"Maybe Kirkpatrick. He's our crime guy."

"Can you do me a huge favor and send me whatever you all have on it?"

"Sure, 'cause I have nothing better to do with my time."

"Please, Rachel."

"You ever heard of Google?"

"Just do me this one favor. I'll never ask for anything else. Ever."

She sighed, held the line for a moment. "I won't be able to get to it 'til tomorrow."

"That's fine."

"Cock & Bull tomorrow?"

"What about Copek's thing?"

"After Copek's. The Funky Donkeys are playing. I need you to come with."

"And I guess I'm buying the drinks."

"Why, certainly."

"You and that chick are getting serious again?"

"That *chick's* name is Dana. And yes, we kind of got it on the other night. But we agreed to see other people, so we're not like girl-friend and girlfriend, you know. We're—"

"Free spirits? Swingers?" I had nursed a few of Rachel's broken hearts in the past. And, in most of them, Dana had played a major role.

"Whatever, Dexter. It's all just labels."

We hung up. I went to the fridge, pulled out a cold Siesta IPA, and took a long thirsty gulp. It was perfect for a hot afternoon like this. Just looking out the window made me sweat.

I poured a little food for Mimi and turned the stereo on. I let the tubes warm up while I selected a record. I was in the mood for something old school: Pink Floyd, *Wish You Were Here,* the British Harvest label. I set the needle down, sat on the couch, and tried to chill.

The music was medicine. I almost fell asleep listening to side one. But while I'd been lying there something kept poking at my brain: the properties Beach City Holdings owned did not make sense to me. Both the acreage and the lots in Siesta Key were like a patchwork, a chessboard. It didn't look as if they could be put together for a development, or a condo building. Maybe that's what Liam was waiting for. He wanted to fill in the gaps.

I pulled out an old road atlas from the bottom of a bookshelf and studied the length of Siesta Key—top to bottom, north to south. Midnight Pass Road ended at Pointe, a condo development. No land after that, just the Intracoastal. But at the end of Blind Pass Road, just past Turtle Beach, there were a few lots. Then there was a long swath of land. This was Midnight Pass, the opening the Corps of Engineers closed back in the eighties. It was undeveloped until the north end of Casey Key—where development started all over again.

I pulled out my phone and looked at the photograph I took of the map in Liam Fleming's bedroom wall. The red Sharpie marks coincided with the properties I had seen on the County Property Appraisers website: three lots south of Turtle Beach. One on Midnight Pass Road just before the gates of the condo development. And of course, Liam's cottage.

Maybe the county would one day approve building on that land. When Fleming said his son had a long-term plan, he wasn't kidding.

In addition to owning the apartment building where Tessa lived, Beach City Holdings also owned two of the three houses on the north end of Beach Road, that little stretch of road that was causing a heap of trouble thanks to County Commissioner Troy Varnel.

But if the county got its way, Beach City Holdings' two properties there were poised to gain ten to fifteen feet of land and become beachfront houses.

A great investment.

I got up and turned the record over and looked at the cover, the man burning, shaking hands with the businessman. Pink Floyd at their zenith. I set the record back down and cranked the volume up on "Shine on You Crazy Diamond."

My mind kept drifting back to Brandy Fleming and Keith Peterson. What if Liam found out about their affair and was threatening to tell his father? It sure didn't feel like Brandy wanted me snooping around Liam's case. She either thought I was a con or she thought I'd find out about her affair, that Liam had found out, that he was going to tell his father, that Brandy panicked, that she had Keith kill Liam.

I sat up. I believed it and didn't believe it—or didn't want to. Either way, it was a serious possibility. I typed up a list into my Fleming document:

Jaybird (motive: uncertain, probably told cops he saw Liam leave on kayak then lied to me)

Terrence Oliver (motive: greed, control of Beach City Holdings)

Brandy and Keith (motive: fear of having their affair revealed by Liam)

I procrastinated a moment, thinking of something that had been gnawing at my gut. I didn't want to see it like that, but I had to be honest with myself. Trust my intuition. I couldn't allow myself to be fooled by talk and friendship. It was certainly a possibility. Finally, I added the last name to the list:

Tessa (motive: jealousy, crime of passion)

CHAPTER 17

IN THE EARLY evening, about an hour before sunset, I called the Salty Dog but neither Tessa nor Jaybird were in. Too early for the dinner shift. I drove down to Siesta Beach to see if I could find Jaybird at the drum circle. Heavy clouds hovered low over all of Sarasota—storms to the east, south, and west.

When I got out of the car, lightning flashed out in the ocean followed by the crack of thunder. People were coming off the beach in a hurry, carrying their chairs, folded umbrellas, towels flapping in the strong wind.

Just as I got to the beach, a hippie with his drum passed me by on his way to the parking lot.

"Hey!" I went after him. "What happened to the drum circle?"

He waved at the sky. "Canceled 'cause the shitty weather."

"Is Jaybird back there?"

He shook his head. "No one's there."

Lightning struck near the water's edge. Thunder followed with a tremendous roar. The hippie disappeared into the parking lot. Cars were pulling out of spaces. People were laughing as they rushed to their vehicles, threw their beach gear and toys in the back. The sky was dark gray. The wind picked up. It was getting ready to pour.

I made my way back to my car just as the rain started. It came down in sheets. I started the car, turned the AC on low, and waited for the storm to pass. Summer. We never caught a break.

Hot, humid, rainy, and infested with mosquitoes. But as fierce as the storms were, they passed quickly. About fifteen minutes after it started, the storm moved north. The rain lightened up.

I drove down Midnight Pass to Liam's cottage. I parked in the driveway next to the VW Golf and walked into the house. Everything was exactly as it had been the last time I was here. Jaybird's drum was in the same place, the same beers in the fridge. The red kayak leaning against the wall outside the lanai.

I went out to the front and checked the mailbox. I grabbed the bundle of mail and walked back in the cottage, sat down on the couch, and went through the envelopes.

It was more of the same: a water bill from the county, real estate advertisings, a copy of *Surfer Magazine*, two general coupon flyers, and the Publix weekly savings.

I tossed it all on the coffee table next to the purple bong and leaned back on the rattan couch that stank of mildew and cheese. I considered drinking one of the beers in the fridge. I went back out on the patio and looked around. It was getting dark and the mosquitoes and no-see-ums were out in force. I made my way to the end of the narrow dock and came back and around the side of the house and got in my car.

Too many bugs to enjoy the evening.

I called the Old Salty Dog again and asked for Jaybird. The person on the phone sounded distracted, said he wasn't there. Hung up quickly. I didn't get a chance to ask for Tessa.

I started the engine and turned up the AC and waited, thinking, trying to figure out what to do next, where to go. Finally, I backed out and started north on Midnight Pass. The Old Salty Dog. I figured I'd sit in the bar, have a beer and talk to Tessa.

I knew what was happening. My conscience was waving an angry finger at me telling me not to. She was as much a suspect as Jaybird and Keith Peterson. But I couldn't help it. I was falling for her.

I enjoyed her company. She was funny and smart. And pretty. I passed the public beach. It had stopped raining, but the storm had left puddles and palm fronds and debris on the road. Just as I was coming up on the Village, my cell phone rang.

Rachel Mann.

"Hey, you know what's weird?" she said.

"A lot of things," I said.

"True. But you know how you asked me for the clippings on that drowning?"

"Yeah, you got them for me?"

"We did nothing. It was just a few sentences lifted directly from the Sheriff's report."

"Really?"

"We have no staff."

"What do they pay Kirkpatrick for?"

"Fuck if I know."

"What a way to run a business," I said.

"But listen. I just heard on my scanner that they found a floater down by Blackburn Point Road."

"What?"

"A body floating in the Intracoastal. I'm headed there now."

* * *

I got off the key, drove south on the Trail, and turned right on Blackburn Point Road, toward Casey Key. As I came to the bridge, I could see the flashing blue and red. First responders were staged at the park on my left just before the bridge. Two Sheriff's cruisers blocked the entrance to the parking lot.

I pulled over on the right side of the road where there was a marina, and made my way back and across the street to the park. No cordon had been set up, but the park was crowded with cops, divers, and an ambulance.

In that part of the Intracoastal the water made a small bay that separated the park in two. The first responders were on the large section that was more of a paved parking lot with a wide boat ramp. That's where I was headed.

Running parallel to the road, a walkway led to a smaller unpaved little park. I could see Rachel on that side. She was standing between a row of Australian pines at the water's edge, taking photos. Two sailboats and a large cabin cruiser were moored a few feet out.

One of the deputies on the scene saw me when I was halfway to the walkway.

"Hell no," he said in a deep, commanding voice. "Can't be here. This is an active crime scene."

"I'm with her." I pointed at Rachel.

He looked me up and down. "You press?"

"That's right."

"Let me see some ID?"

I pulled out my wallet. I had no press ID. "I forgot it," I said. "I heard the call and ran out on dinner with the folks."

"Right," he said and pointed to the other side of the road. "Find someplace else to go and let us do our job."

"Who's in charge of the investigation?"

The deputy nodded toward a group near the water's edge by the boat ramp. And there, in the middle of the crowd of uniformed men and women, was a heavyset old man with a squat hat and a handlebar mustache. Detective Fenton Kendel of the Sarasota County Sheriff's Office.

The deputy spread his arms and then pointed to the road. "Now back it up, buddy."

"Can I talk to Detective Kendel real quick? I want—"

"I said, back it up. I'm not gonna say it again."

I backed away, keeping my eyes on Kendel, just in case he looked my way.

He didn't.

I stood under a streetlight, crossed my arms over my chest, and watched Sarasota's finest do their work. They had already raised the body and bagged it. It was lying on the small dock next to the boat ramp where Kendel and a handful of officers were standing, shooting the breeze with a man and two kids, maybe early teens.

I could see why Rachel went to the other side of the park. She had a clear shot across the water. When the officers put the body in a gurney and rolled it away to one of the ambulances, Rachel set down her camera and started back across the walkway to our side of the park.

I waved to her. "Rachel!"

She turned. So did one of the EMTs and two deputies standing near the ambulance. It was a big group of officers for a drowned person. But then again, maybe it was a slow night.

Rachel came over. "What's up, Dex?"

"I just got here."

She bowed her head and browsed through some of the images on the back of her camera. "Looks like a couple of kids were fishing and caught a body."

"From here?"

"Yeah, I guess they were casting out from the end of the dock." She nodded in the direction where the investigators stood. "They ended up pulling the body up. They called the cops."

"Anything on the victim?"

She set her camera down and glanced at me. "Listen to you, you sound like a real live investigator. You working for the police now?"

"Don't fuck around," I said. "Do they have anything?"

She shook her head. "Looks like a homeless guy. No ID."

"What did he look like?"

"He was already bagged when I got here."

"Do they have any idea how long he was under?"

"Maybe two days. But the medical examiner'll make the call."

I looked past her at the group of cops on the dock, talking. Then refocused on Rachel. "Can you ask Kendel to come talk to me?"

"I have a deadline, man."

"Please."

She shook her head and walked toward the dock. She stopped by the crime scene van and talked to her friend, Dana, her on-and-off girlfriend. She placed her hand on her arm for a moment and then walked on to where the officers were huddled. She interrupted whatever was going on, took out her notepad. She pointed at one of the deputies with her pen, nodded. Wrote down a few notes. Then she pointed at me. Kendel and two other officers glanced my way. Kendel shook his head and turned back to the officers. Rachel walked back to the crime scene van and showed some of the photos she had taken to Dana. Then she came to where I was standing, waiting.

"And?"

She shrugged, shoved her notepad in her back pocket. "Nothing."

"What the fuck?"

"I told him and he looked over and then went back to whatever he was yapping about to his admirers."

"Jesus fuck."

"Okay, I gotta go file. What're you doing later?"

"I don't know, sleep."

"You owe me a drink."

"I know. Tomorrow."

"I'm filing this and then going to the Shamrock on Ringling in case you change your mind."

I nodded toward the crime scene van. "She going, too?"

"You jealous?"

I smiled. "Maybe."

She smacked my arm and walked past me to her car.

"Dexter Vega." Detective Fenton Kendel was walking toward me. He was a big man, wore a baggy short-sleeve shirt, jeans, and a regulation Glock strapped to his wide waist right next to a shiny Sheriff's gold star badge. He was older, gray with a bushy handlebar mustache, small wire-rim glasses, and his trademark black leather pork pie hat that had seen better days.

"Detective Kendel," I said. "I've been trying to reach you all week."

"I am aware of that," he said. His voice was raspy with a touch of angry southern. "Is that why you're here?"

"Rachel Mann gave me the heads-up."

He took out a square of nicotine gum, unwrapped it with his thick fingers, and tossed it in his mouth. "What can I do you for?"

"Whatta you got here?"

"Drowning. Male, mid-thirties, five-five, hundred fifty pounds."

"No ID?"

He shook his head just slightly, chewed his gum like it tasted good. "One of the deputies says he's a bum—hangs around Siesta Beach. Goes by Jaybird."

CHAPTER 18

I DROVE STRAIGHT to the Old Salty Dog and parked myself at the bar. Tessa glared at me, then ignored me. I didn't fret. Besides, my mind was reeling—stunned. In shock.

Kendel had said they were looking into the drowning as a murder. It appeared Jaybird's body had been tethered to a cinderblock. Someone had drowned him.

After a few minutes, Tessa came over to the end of the bar where I was sitting. She looked pissed. "What can I get you, sir?" Her voice was sharp, lips pursed, and the *sir* came out of her like she wanted to spit.

"Two beers, pints. Make it that Big Top IPA you have on tap."

"Two?"

I nodded.

She shook her head, picked out two glasses, and poured. She came back and set the beers in front of me. "You're an asshole, Dexter."

I grabbed a beer and downed half the pint in three long gulps. Then I looked at her, my eyes quivering. "Jaybird's dead."

"What?"

"Yeah . . ." The words came out of me slowly, like bits of shattered glass. "Someone . . . killed him."

Her eyes locked on mine. Her lower lip trembled. Then she stepped back, slowly brought a shaking hand to her mouth, covered it just as it opened. I thought she was going to cry, scream. But she just stood there in the middle of the bar, one hand over her mouth, dark brown eyes welling up, staring at me as if they were collecting all the information through telepathy.

"Why?" Her voice was barely audible.

"I don't know."

"How?"

I hesitated. I didn't know how much to tell her. At least at the moment, in this place, it was too ugly to get into. I stared at my half-empty glass, the white thin foam clinging to the rim, forming the hole I was falling into.

"Someone tied him to a cinderblock and tossed him in the middle of the Intracoastal."

She gasped. The lines in her face were sharp as she winced, eyes shut tight. Then she turned away.

I closed my eyes. And in that small parcel of darkness, I saw Jaybird. I opened them. Took another drink of beer.

"I don't believe it," she said sharply. "Where did it happen?"

"Blackburn Point Road. By the little park there."

"Jesus."

In the background, Bob Marley was singing one of his uplifting tunes, something totally incongruous. One of the customers at the other end of the bar yelled at the ball game on the TV.

A waiter walked up to the corner of the bar by the steps and glanced in our direction. He must have sensed something was wrong, probably from Tessa's expression or body language. He turned his eyes on the other customers at the bar, then down at his tray where he had his order written on a pad.

Finally, Tessa whispered, "But why?"

I was as lost as she was. A part of me wanted to laugh at the ludicrous hours we'd spent looking for him. I thought of when I went out on the kayak to explore what Liam might have done that fateful night. And when I came back, Jaybird was gone from the couch. That was the last time I'd seen him, tired, stoned Jaybird asleep on the couch, cockroaches crawling out of his blond dreadlocks.

What if I'd stayed in the house?

"Order up," the waiter finally said. Tessa and I jumped, turned to look at the man leaning forward on the counter, smiling at us. Tessa hadn't shed a tear. She turned her eyes to me. I could tell she was working hard to hold it in. It made me imagine the moment when she got the news of Liam's passing. We'd never talked about that—how she learned he was dead. It must have been tough. Did she break then?

She moved away, went to the end of the bar, forced a smile for the waiter, and took a long time reading the order. She poured two pints of Guinness, her movements completely mechanical as if she was running on autopilot. She set drinks on the round tray in front of the server, went back to the cooler and fished out three Coronas, used a large opener to pop the tops, set them on the tray, fished out three lime wedges from the condiments tray at the end of the bar, set them on three-pint glasses, which she set on the tray with the other drinks. She smiled again, but this time it didn't come off right. Her lips twisted and her eyes narrowed. Then she came back to me, grabbed one of my beers, and drank.

I did the same.

I set my empty down. Tessa held hers up and forced a grin. "Here's to Jaybird."

I watched her drink, her throat moving up and down. She offered me the glass. I took a long sip.

The customers at the end of the bar were staring at us. It was a rare sight to see a bartender drinking on the job.

Then Tessa laughed one of those fake chuckles to prevent her from crying. "Joey," she said and wiped her lips with the back of her hand. "Joey, the manager. He was just bitching about Jaybird, how he was going to fire his ass."

I had no words. The only two people to drown in the Intracoastal in at least a decade were Liam and Jaybird. No one could tell me it was a coincidence.

When I spoke with Detective Kendel earlier, I asked him about Liam's case. He didn't seem pleased. Asked me if I was a licensed investigator.

"The case is closed," I told him. "I'm just going over it for his father. It seems there was a witness—"

"Where'd you hear that?" he barked.

"Deputy Norton said you spoke to a witness."

"The fuck does he know?" he said, his fat face chewing hard on the nicotine gum, his little beady eyes staring at me—almost daring me to cross him. Me, I didn't have an issue with Kendel. He was old school and respectable as far as I knew. And I'd known him for years. His behavior at the moment was surprising.

I said, "He was there."

"Kid's a goddamn rookie," Kendel said.

"Was he your witness?" I asked nodding toward the ambulance.

"Who, Norton?"

"No. Jaybird."

"Hell no."

"Well then, who was?"

His eyes were cold, his expression hard. The mercury vapor lights of the park and the street cut nasty shadows across his old tired face. For a moment, I was a little afraid of him. But then his little round eyes softened. It was difficult to tell if he smiled because his mustache shielded his mouth.

He nodded to the side of the park. "Let's walk."

I stepped beside him, and we made our way slowly to the little bridge that led to the other section of the park where Rachel had been taking her photos. Then he stopped and turned to face the water, leaned forward, forearms resting on the wooden rail.

"There was no witness," he said quietly.

"Then how did you know he was out on a kayak?"

"I didn't."

"But the report said—"

"Fuck the report," he said and turned his head to look at me. "This is between us. Off the record."

"Go on."

He ran his hand over his mouth, his thumb and index fingers pressing down the sides of his long mustache. "I got four months left," he said. "Retirin' in December. Thirty-two years in the Sheriff's office, twenty-one of those as a detective. That kid we fished out a couple weeks ago checked out as an accident, plain and simple. There was nothin' to indicate any different. I called it how I saw it."

"So, what, you just invented the kayak?"

"What difference does it make if he was on a kayak or if he just'd gone out and gotten drunk and fell off a pier or one of them stand-up boards?"

"Maybe someone pushed him off," I said and nodded to where the first responders were wrapping up their work. "Just like this guy."

"Not the same."

"You surprise me, Kendel. You're a good detective. Why do this?"

He leaned back and stretched his left arm out, rubbed his shoulder with his right hand. "Son, I'm looking over the fence. Four months from now my day's gonna be filled with golf and fishing."

"So you shoved Liam Fleming's case in the accident pile."

"It *was* an accident," he said and tapped his chest with his thumb. "I know for a fact."

The smug motherfucker. I nodded at the place where the ambulance was backing up, flashers off. "What about Jaybird. Is he an accident?"

Kendel smiled. "You can't win them all, can you?"

"It gets worse," I said. "The guy you found two weeks ago was living in the same house as Jaybird. They were roommates."

He eyed me suspiciously. "How do you know that?"

"Because I spoke with him a couple days go. I was at the cottage on Midnight Pass Road when he disappeared. Wake the fuck up, Kendel. Liam Fleming and Jaybird were murdered."

CHAPTER 19

TESSA SERVED ME another pint and gave me a short, empathetic smile. Then she walked off to take care of the handful of customers at the bar. They looked like regulars, older, scruffy fishermen with gray hair, unshaven, sun-faded t-shirts. She went about the transactions in a robotic way, pouring the rum, filling a glass with Coke, twisting open a Bud Lite and handing it to one of the men.

"What is it?" she said when she finally came back to where I sat.

"Nothing."

She took a short sip of my beer and narrowed her eyes. "I can see the wheels turning in your head, Dexter. What's going on?"

"I don't understand," I said. "Why would someone want to kill Jaybird?"

"Why would anyone want to kill anyone?"

I held her stare for as long as I could. But there was too much hurt in her eyes and too many lies in mine. I wasn't telling her everything I knew—what Detective Kendel had confessed.

The deaths of two people close to her took its toll. I could see her struggling to hold it together. A part of me wanted to walk across the counter like a ghost and put my arms around her and hold her tight, tell her it was okay to cry. And yet another part of me was not as sympathetic. Instead, I withheld information because two people close to her had been murdered. I knew nothing about Tessa. She could be anyone. Yes. She could be—a killer.

"Thing is . . ." I said, thinking carefully of what I wanted to say. "At first I thought Liam was killed for money. Maybe his partner wanted to take over the company. People are greedy like that. But why Jaybird?"

"It doesn't make any sense."

"My other thesis was totally different," I said. What had been a job, a gig, a quick buck, had turned into a nightmare. I couldn't imagine Jaybird being drowned that way. And I couldn't—or didn't—want to imagine Tessa or any of the people I'd met in Siesta Key being involved in such a horrible crime.

"Was?"

I took a deep breath. "When we saw Brandy Fleming and Keith at the Ritz, I got it in my head that maybe it had been Keith."

"But they were all friends. Liam and Jaybird and Keith."

"I get it. But maybe Liam knew about their affair and was going to tell his father."

"That's possible."

"Was," I said. "When they found Jaybird in the Intracoastal, it killed that idea."

Someone at the other end of the bar called for Tessa. She glanced over her shoulder. "Be right over," she said and turned back to me. "So we scratch both those theories."

She went over to the other end of the bar to check on her customers. I took a long drink of beer. The buzz was helping my nerves cool off. I'd expected a quick, easy job. But it was just beginning. I focused on two possibilities: Jaybird had witnessed Liam's murder. Or at least knew who did it. So that person had to keep Jaybird quiet. And that could be anyone: Keith, Terrence . . . or even Tessa.

When Tessa came back, I told her another possibility. As far as I could tell, it was the only answer to the case: "Drugs."

"Seriously?"

"Maybe they were both in cahoots with a dealer. Owed money. Or double-crossed someone."

"Listen to you: double-cross. What is this, a seventies TV cop show? All those two ever did was smoke dope and drink beer. And Liam not so much. No hard stuff."

"Honestly?"

She raised her right hand. "I swear."

"Never."

"Okay, sometimes when we worked closing, we'd go out, hang out at the Beach House or the Daiquiri Deck, or we'd meet up with the guys from the Oyster Bar and go to my place or Liam's and party. There was always booze and pot. And occasionally a little coke. But that's it."

"And that's not enough?"

"No. Absolutely not. And it wasn't a big part of Liam's life."

"I don't know. Coke's heavy stuff."

"And?" She drew back. "I don't snort. And neither did Jaybird. Not that I ever saw."

"What about Liam?"

"He was pretty straight. He had his shit together. But then again, he had money and a real business. This," she said and waved a hand from left to right, "is our livelihood. The day shift bartender's got two kids and a husband on disability. And the waitress, Amanda, is putting her kid through college. There's a couple of guys at the Daiquiri Deck who also go to school. As far as I know, most everyone is holding two jobs to make ends meet."

"Sarasota's an expensive place."

"You're not kidding."

"Where'd the dope come from?"

"I don't know about the coke. Like I said, someone would just pull out a gram or two. It wasn't a regular thing."

"What about pills, heroin?"

"God no!"

"And the weed?"

"What about it?"

"Where did it come from?"

Her eyes turned to the steps that led out of the bar into the dining room. "Felipe."

"Who's Felipe?"

"The dishwasher. He hooks everyone up. I mean, I never bought any, but I know he deals. Jaybird bought from him."

"And Liam?"

"Not while I was dating him."

"Really?"

"Really, Dexter. You're chasing the wrong lead. Besides, people don't kill for a couple of joints."

"If only," I said because I knew better. People killed for a lot less than a buck. And more often than not, drugs or alcohol were part of the equation. But I understood where she was coming from. And I didn't believe it myself. Liam and Jaybird and Tessa and Cap'n Cody and Keith and the hippie girl at the drum circle—none of them looked like criminals. They didn't seem capable of it.

Tessa's brown eyes seemed to grow bigger, tender, friendly. After a moment, she turned away and went to check on her customers. When she returned to me, her eyes were moist, red.

"Is Felipe working tonight?" I said.

She nodded.

"Does he know about Jaybird?"

"How would he?"

She shoved off and went to attend to a waitress who called out her order. A moment later, the blender was screaming, crushing ice as Tessa prepared more of those fancy tropical fruity drinks: a Pony

Ride Margarita, an Awesome Rum Haven CoCo LoCo, a Fido's Pain Killer.

I drank my beer and watched her move, her slim body leaning to the side to grab a beer from the cooler, her movements alert, sharp, professional. Slowly, a voice inside my head convinced me that she was okay. I scratched her off my suspect list.

When she finally came back, she pointed to my beer. "You okay there?"

I raised my glass. "Fine. But I need you to do me a favor."

She gave me a tired nod.

"Can you hook me up with Felipe?"

"You wanna buy pot?"

"I want him to think that. I just want to talk with him."

"He didn't do it, Dex."

"You know that for sure?"

For a moment she seemed suspended, as if she couldn't decide whether to tell me to fuck off or hug me. "He's a good guy."

"Don't worry. And don't tell him about Jaybird."

She sighed, took a quick look around the bar. "Go around the back and hang out by the dumpsters. I'll have him meet you there."

I stretched my legs and dug for my wallet. She placed her hand on my arm. "It's on me."

* * *

The back of the Old Salty Dog stank like burnt grease and trash— typical restaurant shit. There were half a dozen cars parked right up to the building and a small path to the green industrial dump- ster. The back door of the kitchen was held open by a cinderblock. White light spilled out into the alley in a perfect rectangle. About thirty yards away, near the street, was another light. Behind that, the glow of the gas station gave the night a seedy ambiance. Didn't quite feel like beautiful Siesta Key.

I stood near the door but just outside the rectangle of light so I wouldn't stand out. The heat and humidity seemed worse back here. There was no breeze. Not too far to the east, a flash of lightning caught my eye. It was going to rain again—hard.

About five minutes after I got there, a short middle-aged Latino man with dark brown skin, wearing a plastic apron and a hairnet, came slowly out of the Old Salty Dog.

"Felipe?"

"You Tessa's friend?" he said in a thick Spanish accent.

"That's me."

"So wha's going on?"

I came closer. He had deep brown eyes that made him look sad, and an old scar between his chin and his lower lip. I extended my hand. He shook it.

"I'm also a friend of Jaybird's," I said.

He nodded.

"I wanted to pay whatever money he owes you."

He looked to the side, shook his head. "Jaybird don't owe me nothing."

"I thought maybe he did. You know . . . for the stuff."

"For the weed? No, man. He's good. He don't buy that much. And he always pay. No problem."

"That's good to hear," I said. "You know him pretty well?"

He crossed his arms over his chest. "We work together, yes."

"So." I nodded and kicked at the ground. "Something happened."

"Wha' happen?"

"To Jaybird."

"He okay?"

"He's dead."

Felipe glanced away at the darkness for a minute, kicked at the ground. "You for real?"

"I'm sorry."

He pulled his hairnet off, held it with both hands against the top of his stomach, looked at me. "What happened?"

"Someone killed him."

"What? Jaybird? *Pero* . . . Why?"

"I don't know," I said. "I'm trying to find out. I thought maybe he owed you money and—"

"And you think I kill him?"

"I thought because of the drugs—"

"I don't kill nobody, *carbrón*. Never. I just sell a little weed to my friends. Don't hurt nobody."

"I know," I said. "I just had to make sure."

"You a cop?"

I shook my head. "I'm a friend."

"Yeah." He gestured with a wave of his hand, as if he were tossing something out. "A friend. *Chinga tu madre.*" Then he turned and started back to the door of the Old Salty Dog.

"Hey, hold on."

He stopped and turned. In the light that spilled from the open door of the restaurant, I saw a glint in his eyes.

"Look," I said. "I'm sorry, but I had to check. Okay? I had to make sure."

He spat to the side, put his hairnet back on.

"Let me ask you . . . Did he buy drugs from anyone else?"

He shook his head.

"He ever buy coke or pills, any hard stuff?"

"No, man. Jaybird just smoke weed. To relax, he say. He was . . . *como se dice?* Easygoing. Always like no problem."

"Who do you get your shit from?"

His eyes narrowed and his jaw tightened. "You don't want nothin' with them."

"Is there any chance they could've hurt Jaybird?"

"They don't know Jaybird, man. Shit. They want nothing to do with this. They sell a little weed to me. I sell to my friends. No one mess with Jaybird."

"Well, someone messed with him pretty bad."

He shook his head. "Jaybird never leave the island. He always say he live free. Never messed with anyone es'scept that guy from the county that wanna close the beach."

"What guy?"

"With the county government. He wanna close Beach Road."

"What, Troy Varnel?"

He nodded. "I think that guy."

"When you say he messed with him, how do mean? What did he do?"

"Nothing. He just complain like everyone."

"But he didn't do anything to the commissioner?"

"He start the petition to keep the road open."

"But that's it."

"And complain." Felipe smiled. "He complain all the time. Everyone complain about the beach all the time."

"All right," I said. "But that's all he did."

"And Tessa, too. They love the beach."

The moment I felt I had something, it flew away. Varnel's proposal to close Beach Road—a proposal that still had to be approved and passed by the commission and the board of development and possibly the courts.

"So, the petition and complain," I said. "That's all he did, right?"

"Yes." Felipe nodded. "That's all. *Pinche* Jaybird. He talk a lot and he bang on his drum." He turned and started back to the Old Salty Dog.

"Felipe . . ."

He stopped and stood in the rectangle of light outside the kitchen door.

"I'm sorry."

He bowed slightly and then disappeared into the restaurant. I slapped a mosquito on my neck. Then I made my way around to the front of the restaurant and went back to the bar.

CHAPTER 20

THE YOUNG MAN behind the bar came over and gave me a fake smile. "What can I get you, pal?"

I nodded to the taps. "A glass of that Big Top." I looked up and down the bar, populated by the same customers, tourists, a few scruffy old fishermen. No sign of Tessa.

The young bartender came back and set my beer on the counter. "Wanna see a food menu?"

"I'm good," I said. "Where's Tessa?"

"She went home. Wasn't feeling too good." He pointed at my beer. "You wanna start a tab?"

* * *

I left the Old Salty Dog without finishing my beer, walked quickly through the Village in a blur of neon lights and pastel colors and the smell of suntan lotion and booze. The Siesta Key Oyster Bar was packed. Someone—I imagined Cap'n Cody—was playing the guitar. The Daiquiri Deck had pulled down plastic shields along its outside deck to cool their guests with AC. Tourists strolled up and down the sidewalk, flip-flops, t-shirts, glowing red faces, kids chasing lizards. The Beach Club was jamming. A light breeze picked up just enough to warn of a coming storm.

I could feel my emotions getting the best of me. I felt like crap about Jaybird. Maybe it was because I'd thought he was the key to

Liam's murder, or maybe it was because he came across as such an innocent man—someone who was ignorant of the world around him. But there was also Tessa. Maybe I was reading too much into her body language, the way she touched my arm, how she tossed her hair to the side, laughed at my stupid comments, how she looked at me—her beautiful brown eyes cutting into a part of me I usually kept guarded. Maybe my feelings were getting in the way of my objectivity and that was why I wandered to the blue apartment building, walking around it twice before going up the stairs and knocking on apartment number 8.

Tessa opened the door and looked through me, her eyes red and distant. She had an odd expression, one of either absolute relaxation or absolute exhaustion. Or, she was stoned.

"You okay?"

She nodded and moved aside to let me in. I walked past her. She turned and kept her eyes on me. In the soft light of the apartment, it was clear she'd been crying.

I went to her. She raised her hands to hold me at the same time that her lower lip trembled and her mouth twisted letting out the first of many sobs.

I held her. She leaned her head against my chest, arms around my neck, tight, cheek pressed against me. And she let it all out: the fear and the anger and the sadness of everything that had happened in the last two and a half weeks. She cried like a child alone in a room with her pain. It tugged at my own feelings more than I cared to admit even to myself. So much so that I clenched my jaw as tight as I could and swallowed the tight ball that was rising in my throat.

We stayed like that in the middle of the living room of the pretty apartment, the sound of her weeping like a soft memory from my childhood, for what felt like a lifetime. I caressed her hair, took in her smell of shampoo and sweat. And for a moment I actually closed my eyes and felt so close to her it would take a crowbar to pry us apart.

But just as I fell into it, she pulled away. She wiped her tears with the sides of her hands and forced a chuckle. "I'm so sorry."

I wanted to hold her, take care of her. Protect her. Her eyes moved through me as if there was something past my skin.

She backed away a step. Two. Then she turned and walked into the kitchen and grabbed a paper napkin from the counter and used it to wipe her cheeks, blow her nose.

"I'm sorry," she said. "It's just . . . it just hit me, you know? I was standing behind the bar after you left and remembered how Jaybird used to walk out of the kitchen with his goofy smile and that hawk nose of his, giving me a wink to let me know he and Felipe were going out back to smoke a joint. And then . . . and then I . . . I imagined him fighting to get out of the water, struggling."

"I understand," I said.

She sobbed, blew her nose again. "Christ," she cried looking up at the ceiling. "I hate this."

She tossed the napkin in the trash and pulled out another and held it up to her face, dabbing the corners of her eyes.

I walked farther into the living room. "I don't know what's going on," I said. "But people don't go through all the trouble of tying someone up to a cinderblock and tossing them in the water because of a dime bag of weed or a couple grams of coke. There has to be a strong motive."

Tessa came out from around the kitchen counter and sat on the couch. I followed her and took the place next to her, my head low on my shoulders as I tried to process the scene, what Felipe had said.

Tessa leaned forward, her forearms resting on her knees. She looked ahead at the sliding glass doors that led out to the narrow balcony, and beyond it the low glow of the lights from the Village.

"He was a good guy," she said. "Jaybird was Siesta Key—old-school Siesta Key. He was always at the beach or hanging out around the Village. Everyone knew him. He was a big part of the drum circle and he helped organize volleyball tournaments, even though he never played. He was just a nice guy. He organized protests against the developer that wanted to tear down the Summerhouse."

"You can't stop progress."

"But you can manage it," she said wisely. "Jaybird used to say that all the time. It wasn't about stopping development or progress. It was about integrity winning over greed."

"Tell that to the developers," I said, thinking of Dieter & Waxler and the nine-story building they were erecting next door to my little cracker house.

"Jaybird started the petition drive to keep Beach Road public." She sat up and straightened her back and pointed to the corner of the living room. "It's one of the coolest parts of Siesta and the county wants to give it away to the homeowners."

To Beach City Holdings, which meant Terrence Oliver. Liam Fleming's partner now owned two properties on Beach Road. His company could tear them down, build a beachfront condo. I tried a little math: seven stories, two units per floor at three or four million per unit. It sure gave one Terrence Oliver a hell of a lot of motive to kill Liam. Maybe Jaybird knew—maybe he was a witness. Maybe he was going to go to the cops. Maybe Terrence wanted to silence him.

"How did Jaybird find out about Liam?" I said.

"That he drowned?"

"Yeah. How did that go about?"

"I told him," she said quietly. "I saw it in the news that afternoon before work. At first, I thought it was a mistake. I couldn't believe it."

"And you went to work and told Jaybird?"

She nodded.

I hadn't noticed my right hand was clenched in a fist. Tessa placed her hand on it and forced her fingers into it, eased her fingers between mine.

"Take it easy," she said soothingly.

"I can't. It bugs the hell out of me." I took in a long deep breath and leaned back on the sofa. Tessa looked at me with sad, apologetic eyes.

I was barking up all the wrong trees. Maybe I was trying to rush, trying too hard to solve something that had to play itself out. I had to find Terrence Oliver. He had the clearest motive as far as I could tell.

At least Detective Kendel couldn't brush Jaybird's murder under the rug—call it an accident. It was an active case. There was certainly going to be an autopsy. And maybe Kendel would get off his fat ass despite his impending retirement and do a little work. Something might turn up.

I pulled my hand away and stood. She looked up at me with red, wanting eyes. "What is it?"

I glanced at the clock on my phone. It was just after midnight. "I should get going."

"Stay." She stood, took my hand in both of hers. "Please."

I studied her face, so pretty, so sad. Then my eyes drifted down to the couch. "I really need to get a good night's sleep."

"You don't have to sleep on the couch," she said and pulled me toward her.

"No." As much as a part of me wanted to stay, in that room, in that bed, with her—I couldn't. I had to stay objective, keep my mind clear. "I don't think that's a good idea right now."

"What?"

Tessa probably didn't get rejected very often, but I couldn't stay. I had way too much in my head. I had been burned once pretty damn bad after being blinded by lust. I didn't want to make the same mistake twice. I don't think I could deal with that kind of betrayal again. As much as I didn't want to accept it, Tessa was still one of my suspects.

"It's been a crazy couple of days. I'll call you in the morning. Promise."

She let go of my hand like it was diseased, glared at me. "You're serious."

I backed away toward the door. "You're hurting right now."

"Yeah, I am," she said angrily. "And I really don't want to be alone."

"I'm sorry." I opened the door. "You'll probably thank me in the morning."

She hung her hands on the sides of her hips. "Don't count on it, buster."

I walked out of the apartment and down the stairs in a hurry. I was feeling queasy about the whole thing. I was afraid I'd turn back and dive into the kind of mess that would send me back on a bender, reeling and lamenting my pathetic life. I had a job to do. I had to keep my head above water.

In the dark night, the flashy lights of the back streets of the Village seemed to turn into an artificial movie set. A light rain fell. It wouldn't last. There were no *light* rains in Florida summers. It either poured or it didn't.

The soft rhythmic thud of a bass from the music in one of the bars on Ocean Boulevard accompanied me all the way to my car. I got in and closed the door just as the rain turned into a torrent, coming down in heavy gray sheets. Across the street, behind the Old Salty Dog where the back door was slightly ajar, I could see Felipe sitting on the cinderblock by the door, smoking a cigarette—or a joint. The man looked sad, alone.

And Tessa. She also seemed morose, lonely. Here, in the heart of Siesta, behind the veil of sun, it was a different world. The creatures that frolicked in the sand now found themselves in dark holes of their own making. Even Tessa's want for me seemed to be more than just an invitation for sex, or company. It was fear. I suffered from the same malady, of the dark places that inhabit us when we're alone. Except I didn't hide it. I flaunted it. Being alone at night was like cutting Xs and Os into my own heart with a razor.

I started home and drove slowly along the narrow road out of the key, the rain crashing against my windshield, pounding hard on the roof.

I kept thinking of Jaybird being fished out of the water. According to Keith and Tessa, everyone in Siesta Key knew Jaybird. He had a lot of friends. Maybe someone saw something. If Detective Kendel did his job right, someone might come forward, offer him a clue.

I turned left on Higel Avenue. A truck appeared behind me, raced up to the rear of my Subaru and stuck there, tailgating me.

I checked my speedometer. Thirty. I brought it up to thirty-five. The truck rode my ass, high beams turned on, lighting up my car like a parade. I adjusted my rearview mirror. Squinted at the road. The rain and the brights of the truck made it difficult to see. The bridge to the mainland was coming up. From there I would be back in civilization. I gave the Subaru a little throttle, forty-five—ten over the speed limit.

The truck stayed on me.

Fuck it. I let off the accelerator and inched into the bike lane on my right. Let the bastard pass.

He didn't.

As we approached the bridge, the truck merged to the opposite lane, sped up, and came level on my left—red late-nineties pickup, jacked up, large tires, tinted windows.

It closed in on my lane.

I merged farther into the bike lane, right wheels spinning gravel on the shoulder. No place to pull over. I stepped on the gas. Climbed up to forty. A car was coming toward us in the opposite lane, just off the bridge.

I sped up.

The truck did the same—stayed parallel to me.

I stepped on the brakes, inched to the right, shaved the hedge with my passenger-side rearview mirror.

The oncoming car flashed its lights, merged to the right, honked its horn. The three of us passed on the two-lane road, inches from each other.

I stepped on the gas. The truck stayed on my side, its big diesel engine roaring like a pissed-off redneck. The entrance to the little park before the bridge was to my right—then the bridge. I was hitting forty. Fifty. Rain splashed on the windshield. The truck swerved, hit the side of my car. The rearview mirror flew off in pieces—metal on metal.

The Subaru hydroplaned. The all-wheel drive stabilized. Then the truck hit my side again, pushed me hard. I flew off the road, slammed on the breaks and turned the wheel. The car skidded over the wet crushed shell, smashed head-on against the trunk of a Palmetto palm. I flew forward. The seat belt stopped me. The air bags failed to deploy.

It took me a minute to get my bearings. I glanced up at the bridge. The red pickup was speeding away. Couldn't get a license.

I stepped out into the rain. The left side of the car, from the front bumper to the rear quarter panel, was dented like wrinkled paper. Pieces of the rearview hung by wires. The right headlight was gone. All the plastic trim at the front busted—dent on the bumper.

The tree had saved me. Ten more yards and I would've gone into the Intracoastal.

CHAPTER 21

WHEN I WOKE up the next morning, I felt as if it had all been a bad dream: Jaybird, Tessa, my car. I sat up in bed and looked across my bedroom at a painting of a blue pig, a big expressionist piece I'd bought from an artist I'd met a few years back when I had money. I must've had a deep sleep, because as I stared at the brushstrokes on the painting for a long time, it felt like it was a decade earlier, before the mortgage crisis, before we all hit rock bottom, before my divorce.

Then my eye caught Mimi strutting her stuff across the dresser. She hopped down on the chair where I'd tossed my wet clothes last night. It all came back: starting up my car, backing away from the Palmetto palm, driving home slowly, my hands trembling, my eyes squinting at the rain, pulling up to my house, going inside, pouring a shot of tequila, taking a shower, drinking another shot.

Now it was almost noon and the summer sun was sneaking into the house in slivers between the horizontal blinds. As the fog in my head cleared, my anger rose. That damn truck—rednecks trying to run me off the road like in some fucking B movie. Not a coincidence. I was sure of that.

I shuffled into the kitchen and poured myself a tall glass of ice water. Mimi hopped on the counter and stretched. She stared at me for a moment then jumped down to the floor and rubbed against my ankles.

I peeled off a couple of slices of ham, folded them into a slice of Havarti, and made my way to my desk and turned on my laptop. I found the story on Jaybird in the *Sarasota Herald*. It wasn't an article, just Rachel's photograph: first responders at the boat ramp standing around a body covered in a white sheet. The information was just the basic police report: unidentified male, pulled out of the Intracoastal. Dead.

I knew that.

What I didn't know was who the hell put him there.

I pushed my chair out and stretched my legs. I picked up my phone. I had one message. Tessa. From this morning. She apologized for her behavior. Said she'd been very emotional.

Well, maybe. But I'd been a bit of an ass myself. I owed her an apology as well—a big one. In person.

At the moment, instead of checking in with her and having a nice chat about how everything was okay, I called Detective Kendel.

Big surprise. He wasn't in. But the sergeant said he was down in Siesta. I grinned to myself. Old Fenton Kendel was following my lead. Glad I could be of help.

Next up I called Officer John Blake, my inside man. He was Sarasota PD and had access to the computers. Helped me out whenever I was in a bind.

"I'm kind of busy right now," he said when I got him on his cell.

"I'll be quick," I said. "Promise."

"Go on."

"I need whatever you can dig up on a couple of people," I said. "Keith Peterson—"

"Address?"

"I don't have one."

Blake sighed. "Sarasota?"

"I think so. Yeah."

"What's the other one?"

"Liam Fleming," I said and gave him the address on Midnight Pass Road.

"Got it."

"—and Blake," I said, hesitating.

"What?"

"Another one," I said quickly. "Tessa Davidson. Calle Menorca, Siesta Key."

Blake said he'd get back to me later in the day. I took a quick shower and walked out of the house. Then I saw the damage to my car. It was worse than I'd thought.

Last night in the dark, I couldn't see the metal crushed like an accordion, the obliterated right headlight and signal light, fog lamp. The plastic bumper cover was hanging by a clip.

I had no collision insurance. Repairing this mess was going to be on my dime. Jesus Fucking Christ.

I kicked the bumper a few times just to make sure it was going to hold. Then I drove to Siesta Key. I had intended to stop by Tessa's place and take care of that piece of business, but I kept going. I passed the Village and the public beach and went straight down Midnight Pass Road to Liam's place.

The cops were all over it. There was a crime scene van, three police cruisers, and an unmarked car. I had to park on the shoulder, the back half of my car sticking onto the street.

"Hey." The deputy by one of the cruisers pointed a thick finger at me. "You can't park there."

I looked back at my car but kept walking.

"I said you can't leave your car there." The officer stepped away from the cruiser and started toward me.

"Who's in charge here, Kendel?"

The cop looked me up and down. "Yeah." Then he cracked a tiny smile and crossed his arms over his chest. He was standing just to the side in front of the cordon of yellow tape that marked off the driveway—Liam's property.

I reached for the yellow tape. "Hey," he barked. "You can't cross the line."

"I have information for Detective Kendel."

"What about?"

"About the murder he's investigating." I pointed to the house. "This murder."

He stared at me. His eyebrows slightly furrowed, sweat beads building over his brow and upper lip. It was shit duty to stand in the sun and guard. But it wasn't my fault he drew the short straw.

I turned around and started back to my car. "No problem," I said. "Just have him call me whenever he's ready for my confession."

"Hey!" he yelled in that nasty cop voice, like a little league coach whose team is down in the ninth. "Hold on."

I came back. He raised the yellow tapeline for me. "He's out back. Go around the side of the house. And don't touch anything."

Inside they were dusting for prints, going through everything. I was pretty sure they'd find my prints all over the place. But I wasn't worried about that. Not yet.

Detective Kendel stood in the patio looking in the direction of the neighbor's house, his pork pie hat pushed back on his head, both blue-gloved hands over his brow, shielding his eyes from the harsh noon sun, mustache like the tusks of a walrus. He wore a pink and cream Tommy Bahama shirt and gray pants. When I came around the side, his eyes shifted toward me. He didn't lower his hands.

"Dexter Vega," he said. "Nice of you to swing by and lend a hand."

"How you doing, Kendel?"

"Busy."

"Yeah," I said looking around at the deputies searching the patio. "I guess there's no excusing this one as an accident, is there?"

"If you got somethin', spill it."

"Tell me what you got," I said.

"It ain't much. We're waitin' on the autopsy report. Victim was tied by the left ankle to a cinderblock. Cause of death was most likely drowning, but we're waiting on toxicology and the coroner to make it official. We still don't have an ID. No suspects, no motive—yet."

At least they were digging into it. Good. I said, "What about Liam Fleming?"

"What about him?"

"He drowned in the Intracoastal a couple weeks ago. Same MO."

"Not the same at all," Kendel said with a grin.

"If you know everything, you solve the damn case," I said and turned to go.

"Vega!"

I stopped.

"What are you not tellin' me?" he said.

"I'm telling you to look into Liam Fleming's death," I said. "Treat it like a murder investigation."

"You're a broken record, my friend."

I nodded and took a couple of steps back. "Don't you think it's weird that the two men who lived in this house were both drowned in the same place?"

"Wasn't the same place."

I raised my hands and took another step back. "Fine," I said. Why did cops have to act like they're the smartest people in the goddamn room? No one else can have a theory or be right about anything. It's a wonder they ever solve a case.

I said, "Keep in mind that Fleming was a strong swimmer, competitive in college. And take a look at how many drownings you have in the calm waters of the Intracoastal in the last few years. Then talk to me about coincidences."

Kendel seemed to finally register what I was saying. He wanted his retirement, but he was going to have to work for it, figure this last one out.

"Tell me somethin'," he said. "How well d'you know the deceased?"

"That's another thing," I said. "Jaybird told me he'd been interviewed by the cops. Told them everything he knew about Liam. But you said you didn't interview a witness."

"When did he tell you that?"

"A couple days ago. Right before he disappeared."

"What gives, Vega?"

I moved closer to him and whispered, "If you hadn't swept Liam Fleming's murder under the rug, maybe Jaybird would be alive."

"Ah, spare me the—"

"No. Something's going on here," I said, my tone like a goddamn knife. "Two people are dead. And all you can think about is fishing and golf. Get off your ass and do your damn job."

That didn't go so well. The last bit touched a nerve. Kendel grabbed my arm, squeezed tight like a vice, and frowned. "Don't you ever talk to me like that again. You got that?"

I stared right back at him. I wasn't going to take shit from a tired old cop.

"I'm gonna look into this real close," he said between clenched teeth. "When the medical examiner's report comes in, we'll know a hell of a lot more. Then I'll go down my list of suspects. And you, my friend, will be at the top of that goddamn list."

"Now that's what I'm talking about," I said and tore my arm away from his grip and walked away.

CHAPTER 22

I MARCHED AROUND the side of the house, ducked under the yellow tape, and glanced across the street at Turtle Beach. Keith Peterson. The mangroves of the lagoon blocked my view of the parking lot. For a brief moment, I considered walking across the street and around the park to the beach. But it was too damn hot.

I found Keith's cream Toyota Land Cruiser sitting in a patch of shade by the lagoon on the parking section reserved for trucks with trailers. It had the windows open, a long paddleboard tied to the roof. No trailer.

I parked on the beach side on Blind Pass Road and crossed the street, over the wooden barrier that separated the parking lots, to the boat ramp. He wasn't there. I went back to my car and took my shoes and socks off and walked to the beach.

The sand at Turtle Beach was grayish-brown and so hot it burned the soles of my feet. I walked quickly to the water's edge, let the ocean cool me down. It wasn't crowded. Maybe two dozen people. And most everyone had set themselves up on the stretch directly across the parking lot. Toward the north, the beach looked deserted all the way up to where it ended at the Sanderling Club. To the south, a few people were gathered in small pockets. Then it was deserted except for the two last low-rise condo buildings and a few houses. Then Midnight Pass began. A few people fished from the shore in front of the last buildings. One of the groups had three men. Two of them stood together holding fishing rods, a blue cooler at their feet.

The third man was Keith.

I walked on the wet sand. As I came closer, the two men glanced at me, then at Keith, who had a can of Bud Lite in his hand. Then they looked back at the sea, paying attention to their rods. One of the men reeled in, checked his bait, and cast. He stole a quick glance at me before turning back to the water.

Keith stepped away from the water, separating himself from the two fishermen. He took a long drink of beer.

"What's up?" I said.

The two men nodded, looked at me over their shoulders and back at the water. They looked scruffy, unshaven, older—maybe late fifties. Both men wore slacks, short-sleeve shirts. They reminded me of the fishermen at the Old Salty Dog, except these two looked like they were better fed, paunchy. One of them had a nice gold chain around his thick neck.

"Catch anything?" I said.

"Nothin' worth keeping," one of the men said without turning to me.

Keith tossed his golden hair to the side, pointed at me with his can. "What's goin' on, brah?"

"Just checking out the beach," I said, sounding obvious and stupid. "Saw a bunch of cops over at Liam's place."

The two fishermen and Keith glanced back toward the parking lot. Liam's cottage was on the other side of it, on the other side of the lagoon and the road. "Yeah," Keith said. "I saw. Guess they're looking into the drowning."

"I guess." I didn't know if he was referring to Liam or Jaybird. I left it open—for now.

The two men ignored us, stared at the sea. About thirty yards out on the ocean, a small flock of seagulls floated, squawked, and dove into the water, fishing.

"You ever find Liam's kayak?" Keith said.

I shook my head. "I'm told it could've drifted all the way to Venice."

"Totally possible." He took a long sip of beer, then pointed at the cooler. "You wanna cold one?"

"I'm good."

One of the fishermen took a few steps forward, feet in the water. I nodded toward Midnight Pass. "Can I talk to you for a minute?"

Keith glanced at the fishermen then turned and started walking south. I took a few quick steps to catch up. We walked side by side. I kept to the wet sand, an inch or two of water.

"I can't find Jaybird," I said. I imagined that, despite the cops crawling over Liam's cottage like ants, Keith had no idea Jaybird had been killed. The brief in the paper didn't name him. For now, he was just a John Doe.

"Did you try the Salty Dog last night?"

"Yeah. And he wasn't at the drum circle, either."

"That's weird," he said and let out a nasal chuckle. "Unless he shacked up with some babe."

"Maybe."

"Jaybird's his own person, you know. Free as a bird."

"I like him. He has . . . character."

Keith laughed. "That he does. But not everyone takes to him."

"Can't imagine him having any enemies."

He stopped, shook his head. "Enemies? Dude . . ."

I laughed and let it pass. "I mean, people who don't like him."

"Everyone's got some of those, brah."

"People who dislike them?"

He shrugged and started walking again. "But people are people, man. Like in winter. Sometimes we get some mighty righteous waves down at Blind Pass. But you get some surfers down there from Englewood and shit—think the beach belongs to them."

"I don't surf."

"Well, there ain't no need for anyone to be nasty, brah. The ocean is vast."

"I always thought surfers were a friendly bunch."

He laughed. "Most are. But not when it comes to waves. People can be total assholes—even surfers, yeah?"

"There are assholes everywhere, I guess."

He pointed at me with his beer can. "That's the thing, brah. That's the thing."

"So," I finally said, getting into what I really wanted to talk about. "I was at the Ritz-Carlton yesterday."

"Yeah?" He leaned down and picked up a Styrofoam cup and a candy bar wrapper and shoved them in his shorts pocket. "Why do people have to litter?"

"Keith, about the Ritz?"

"Yeah, fancy digs, that place, no?"

"You know it?"

"Yeah." He laughed that nasal laugh, like he was mocking the place. "Though I don't really hang out there. Not my style."

"You didn't see me?"

"What?"

"Yesterday. I saw you there. I tried to catch up with you."

"I was working."

"You work there?"

"No way." He laughed again, took a sip of his beer, kept walking, his arms swinging freely. "I work for myself, brah. Rent boards and kayaks, yeah?"

"Right."

He said nothing more. I waited. He took another sip of his beer, tilting the can all the way, draining it. Finally, I said, "So what were you doing there?"

"Meeting clients."

"Seriously?"

He nodded. "People see my ad, call me up. We meet and make a plan. I rent them boards, lead a group, whatever."

"I see."

He stopped walking. Turned around. The two fishermen were small figures like toys in the sand.

"I work." His words had a sharp edge to them, his head forward as he poked his chest with the empty can. "I have a family. An ex-wife, two kids. I love my kids, man. I support them in every way. It ain't easy, and sometimes you feel like just bailing. But not this cowboy. I'd do anything for them."

"And the Ritz?"

"Shit. So sometimes I sneak into the hotels to meet the clients. We're not supposed to solicit guests. Not here at the beach and not at the Ritz fucking Carlton. So they call my cell, we make an appointment. I meet them at the ramp or Lido. But tourists that don't know the area sometimes ask me to come to their hotel or to meet them at Starbucks. Gotta be discreet, though."

"Look, Keith—"

"I was meeting a group of tourists, alright?"

"Hey. I was just asking."

He stared at me a moment, then started walking back to Turtle Beach. "What's the fucking problem, brah?"

"I saw Mrs. Fleming there."

"So what the fuck, brah?"

"I thought maybe . . ."

"You think me and her . . ." He laughed . . ."that we were doing the nasty? Man, your imagination's working overtime, brah."

"I'm sorry. It just struck me as odd."

He looked to the side, focused on my eyes. "I got a call from a tourist. Two families from some place in Michigan heard about the mangrove tunnels in Lido and wanted to go out on kayaks. But they wanted to talk to me first, look at the map. It's just business. But it's against the policy of the Ritz."

For that brief instant, during that defensive monologue, it seemed his surfer drawl had disappeared. "Where did you meet them?"

"At the hotel, brah. I just told you."

"What part?"

"At the bar, man. We sat at one of the tables in the back and made a plan. That's all." He stopped walking. "Why am I even explaining this shit to you, brah?"

"Look," I said, "I'm just trying to find out about Liam. And now it seems Jaybird's disappeared."

He stared at me, his blue eyes piercing through me as if he were looking for something hidden in the back of my brain. "Well that Jaybird ain't the type that hangs out at the Ritz, brah."

I raised my hand, held it up between the two of us. "Don't get me wrong, Keith."

Then his face froze. "You think Jaybird . . . Oh, brah, really? You think he did Liam in?"

"I don't know," I lied. "But I can't find him."

"Dude."

We started walking again. "I don't know what to make of it," I said.

"Why don't you just let the cops do their job?"

"I am."

"Jaybird's a strange little dude. Maybe he had like a double personality or something."

"Maybe."

We were coming closer to the two fishermen. Behind them the crowd at Turtle Beach had thinned out. A single engine Cessna flew over Siesta Beach to the north pulling a banner behind it.

"Those two guys you're hanging with," I said. "They surf?"

"No way, brah." He laughed and tossed his head to the side, moved his hair out of his eyes. "They just fish. And not very well."

"Good friends?"

"Just beach people, brah. We hang out." He raised his empty beer can. "Gave me a cold one. Can't say they're not cool."

"The brotherhood of the beach," I said.

"No shit." He touched my arm with the can and nodded. "The brotherhood of the beach. That's who we are, brah."

CHAPTER 23

I LEFT KEITH and the fishermen at Turtle Beach and got in my car, cranked the AC, and waited for it to cool off. When I pulled out of the parking lot, I turned right on Midnight Pass Road just to check out the action at Liam's house. There was still activity, but just one crime scene van, a cruiser, and the unmarked Grand Marquis.

I went a little farther down and made a tight U-turn at Ophelia's on the Bay and drove back north, passing the house again.

My instinct kept screaming that Keith was guilty. But my brain kept getting in the way. Brandy Fleming wasn't Liam's real mother. And from the sounds of it, Liam didn't spend any time with his father—or Brandy. So why would he care, tell his old man about Brandy's affair?

And then there was Jaybird. How did his murder play into that scenario?

It was just after three in the afternoon. I drove to Tessa's apartment. There was no answer at the door. I walked the few blocks to the Old Salty Dog. Things were quiet. Just a few tables. It was that time of day when restaurants seem to catch their breaths after the lunch rush. A change of shifts: a slow winding down from the first and a slow prepping for dinner of the second. In this town, with all the old people, dinnertime started at about five p.m. with early bird specials beginning at four.

A waiter was moving from table to table, checking ketchup bottles and salt and pepper shakers, wiping down tabletops with a rag, tucking in chairs. The woman who'd been working as a hostess last night was parked at the wait station near the kitchen, rolling silverware into paper napkins. The bartender, a lean white guy with a hipster haircut gelled to the side, was folded over the counter, carefully slicing limes into neat wedges.

I sat on a stool. I was the only one there. When I inquired, the hipster bartender said Tessa had the night shift. Came in at five. I asked for a pint of the JDub's and a plate of fish and chips.

After I ate, Felipe came out of the kitchen wearing a long white apron, his hair in a black net. He sat beside me, looked straight ahead at the bottles of booze on the shelves. "So, you find anything about Jaybird?"

I shook my head. "But the cops are all over it."

"Good. I hope they catch the motherfucker."

"Me, too."

He sniffled and looked to both sides, left and right. We were alone except for the bartender who was at the far end of the bar, his back to us, stocking his condiment rack with olives, maraschino cherries, cocktail onions, sliced pineapple triangles, and strawberries.

"Jaybird was a simple guy," Felipe said quietly. "But what I don't understand is why he get so pissed off about Beach Road."

I pushed my plate away and looked at him. "The county wanted to take away his beach."

Felipe shook his head. "I know is about the beach. But is also about the houses. He was very angry when some rich guy buy a house on Beach Road."

"I'm not following."

"One night last summer, we were out back taking a break, smoking a little *mota*, no? And Jaybird very angry. I say, '*que pasa,*' and he say, 'Some piece of shit rich fuck wanna buy up Beach Road.'"

Liam and Terrence Oliver. Beach City Holdings.

"I say to him take it easy," Felipe went on. "There is plenty of beach for all, no?"

"Maybe," I said. "But I get him. Developers are taking away the beach, the views. One day there'll be nothing left for the rest of us."

The average residents were losing the battle. Our representatives were selling out to the developers. Always. When the building boom exploded in downtown Sarasota a couple decades ago, they passed a noise ordinance to appease the condo owners. A friend explained it to me a while back. Behind the ordinance were a couple real estate guys who were having a hard time moving units. The noise ordinance took care of that. No loud music after eleven p.m. meant no more clubs and bars. No more live music. The people that brought downtown back from the dead were kicked out by the developers, the real estate agents—and city council.

Now there was this little stretch of road that was not even a road. Our county commissioners were making a gift to the homeowners across the beach. Liam and Terrence Oliver and whoever owned the third house were poised to receive a stretch of oceanfront property. Everyone else lost.

I didn't get it. Who in the hell was buying all of these multimillion-dollar one-bedroom condominiums?

Felipe shrugged. "A couple of months later the county decide to close the road. That's when Jaybird start the petition to stop them. Make a big fight for them."

Weird. Maybe Jaybird didn't know he was protesting against Liam. Two friends at opposite ends of a battle. Liam knew about Jaybird. But Jaybird didn't know about Liam and Beach City Holdings. Unless of course, he did.

No. I couldn't see Jaybird killing Liam. And then who killed Jaybird?

Felipe pushed himself off the stool and gave me a pat on the back. "I go back to work," he said and disappeared down the steps back to the kitchen.

The bartender pointed at my empty glass. "Another?"

I shook my head. "Just the check."

But I really wanted to stay because I wanted to hang with Tessa. I wanted to sit at the bar of the Old Salty Dog and talk with her, try to figure out if Jaybird knew Liam owned Beach City Holdings—if he knew he was protesting against his best friend's investment.

That's when Rachel Mann called.

"What's up?"

"Copek's happy hour thing," she said. "You're going, right?"

"Shit." I'd completely forgotten about the event. And it had been my idea: Charley's guests would write slogans for the beer, and whoever had the best slogan got a free case of Siesta IPA. The little contest would free me up from writing slogans for him. Besides, I had promised Brian Farinas a few drinks.

I'd had my head buried in the sand—literally. Three days in Siesta trying to figure out this mess: Liam and Jaybird. And Tessa. Now the other part of my life was catching up with me.

"Swing by and pick me up," Rachel said.

"What's wrong with your car?"

"Nothing, but I'm drinking. And we're going to the Cock & Bull later to check out Dana's band, right?"

"I don't know." I was thinking of Tessa, the case.

"Come on, Dex. Be cool."

"It's not that." I glanced at my watch; it was still early. "I was going to catch the sunset at the beach."

Rachel laughed. "Since when?"

"It's just—"

"Got a romantic date?"

"No. I—" But she was right. I wasn't going to catch the sunset. And it wasn't a date. It was Tessa. I just wanted to sit with her, enjoy her company. It had nothing to do with Liam and Jaybird.

"All right," I said, trying to man up to my responsibilities. "I'll be at your place in an hour."

Before heading out of the key, I drove by Tessa's place. She wasn't in—or didn't want to open the door. Then I drove up to Beach Road. I parked a block away where the road ended and became that tiny stretch of sand and asphalt.

I made my way up to the end where it ended and back, looked at the three houses. There wasn't much to them. Small, old-school cottages from the forties or fifties: one story, concrete block, small windows. In another neighborhood, they would be worth a hundred grand, maybe less. Once, a long time ago, that was Siesta Key.

But I guess that was everywhere.

You can't stop progress. You can't paralyze the future. And it wasn't as if everything was perfect back in the day, in the fifties or the sixties—or even a few years ago. It's strange how we cling to a past, to the way things were. Nostalgia is a peculiar bird.

I sat on a rock on the beach side of the washed-out road. The sun burned down on me without mercy. Clouds far to the north and east. Maybe today we'd be spared the summer afternoon storm.

Maybe not.

At least there was a pleasant breeze. A group of tourists on pastel-colored beach cruiser bikes came riding to the end of the road and stopped. Their faces glowing red. One of them pointed to the water. They got off their bikes and pushed them onto the beach to where there used to be an old concrete pier. Yeah, a long time ago. Now it was just rocks. On one side, a gang of teenagers hung out smoking and drinking and having a good time.

This was what Jaybird was fighting for. This was what he wanted to keep.

I walked to the other side of the road where the property to one of the houses began with a small low fence about three feet high. I counted the steps across the road: ten steps, about twelve feet. There was a sign in the yard of one of the houses: *Private Property Keep Off.*

I imagined a fence or a wall separating the properties from the beach and the place where the road started again toward the Village. Even if they allowed a path for beach access, a wall or signs telling people to stay off would limit the openness of this part of the beach. Past the road on the beachfront were a few low condos ending with the Terrace, that big seven-story monster on the corner where Ocean Boulevard ended and met Beach Road.

Problem was, some realtors promised homebuyers they owned the beach in front of their house, but it's not that simple. Florida's coastline is public. In some parts, like Point of Rocks and North Lido, when the storms come and erode the sand, the beach becomes narrow, sometimes right up to the property lines. In order to pass, people are forced to walk over the backyards, pissing off the homeowners. All the county commissioners and the State can do is spend millions of tax dollars to re-nourish the beach by pumping sand back from the sea. Tax dollars mean public property: public beach.

No. You can't beat nature at its own game.

CHAPTER 24

RACHEL'S LITTLE GARAGE apartment off Osprey Avenue was nice and cool. She'd had her AC running on high all day, so when I walked in, I got a whoosh of freezing dry air. Her couch was covered in camera gear.

"What's going on?" I said.

"For tonight," she said. "I have to take pictures at Copek's and the Funky Donkeys at the Cock & Bull."

"For work?"

"Copek is work. The band is a favor. For Dana."

"So you guys getting back together?"

She grinned. "Kind of."

"Why, you dirty girl, Rach."

She smacked me on the arm and leaned over the big lens she had on her lap, moving a small cotton rag over the front element before placing it in a tan Domke bag. "A girl's gotta live, baby."

"You're a slut."

"I am. I admit it. I am. And I fucking love it."

I took a seat on a chair in the little dinette that separated the tiny living room from the tiny kitchen. On the other side was Rachel's work desk with two large computer monitors.

"So," I said. "What're you doing for Copek?"

"He needs some close-ups of his beer and some party shots, you know, drunks having a good time."

"Is he paying you?"

She grabbed a flash from the couch, checked the batteries. "Why?"

"How much?"

"I didn't say he was paying me." She shoved the flash into the bag.

"But he is."

She looked away.

"That son of a bitch," I said. "He's paying you but he's not paying me."

"I don't work for free, Dex. You know that. And Copek knows that."

"Neither do I."

"You made a trade. I told you not to do that. You start doing that shit, you set a precedent. Fucks you over every time. People talk. You know how this town is. No one will ever pay you again. Always a fucking trade." She poked her chest with her thumb. "I don't do that."

"I can't believe Copek did me like that."

"You did it to yourself. You chose beer over cash."

"Yeah, but he said he couldn't afford to pay me."

"Whatever," she said and pointed at me with one of her lenses. "But you're part of the problem."

"What the hell, Rach?"

She set the lens in the bag and picked up one of her cameras, checked the memory card, checked the settings, and placed it in her bag.

"Dex, I've been doing this for too long. You just started freelancing. You make your choices and they stick with you. If the words you write are worth money, if you want to make a living at this, you need to charge everyone. You can't live on beer alone."

"I beg to differ."

When Rachel talked shop, she turned into a badass—hardcore. Which was probably why she survived in this town as a freelance photographer.

"But you know," she said, "you seem to be doing okay as an investigator."

"It's either my good luck or my bad luck," I said. "I can't decide which."

"Maybe you should get licensed. Advertise. Get more work."

"You're serious."

"Why not?"

"I don't know—it's dangerous."

She stood and went over to the kitchen counter, stuffed her pockets with cash, keys, her wallet. "There's a lot of rich people in Sarasota," she said. "You could make a killing."

Maybe Rachel had a point. Perhaps it was something worth looking into. I'd been paid well by my first client, although I felt like a dirty rat afterwards. But this gig with Fleming felt right. I was helping solve a crime. If it weren't for me, Liam Fleming's death would always be remembered as an accident. Bob Fleming wouldn't have the closure he sought. Besides, the gig paid well. And the old man never tried to negotiate or do a trade.

I stood and waved my finger at her. "Maybe you're on to something, Rach."

She smiled and grabbed her camera bag, and we walked out of the cool apartment into the hot afternoon, the sun just over the trees to the west.

We made our way down the stairs. "Holy crap," Rachel cried and walked around the car. "What the hell happened?"

"Some asshole ran me off the road."

She ran her fingers over the crushed sheet metal. Then she pointed to the broken headlight. "You better get that fixed, or you're going to get a big fat ticket."

"With what money?" I said. "I work for beer, remember?"

* * *

The chickee hut at Charley's brewery was still not finished. Not that it mattered. It was steaming hot out, and his little palm-thatched patio was going to look onto the parking lot. When it was finished, we could all sit out there and drink beer while staring at the damn cars.

For now, Charley had taken matters into his own hands and converted part of his warehouse into a small tasting room. It was cold and plain with no windows. It had a small bar with three beers on tap and six tall wooden pub-style tables and stools. Copek had added a few nautical decorations, a fake schooner wheel, a pair of brass lamps, a vintage longboard, and a small fishing net. None of it did much to hide the fact that we were sitting in a warehouse in a strip mall in Sarasota.

"What's up, guys?" The young hipster working the bar greeted us with just a bit too much enthusiasm.

"Cold beer," Rachel said and set her camera bag on the floor by the bar. "It's hot as shit out there."

I ordered an IPA.

"The same," Rachel said. "And a glass of water."

The bartender smiled. "Two Siesta IPAs comin' right up."

I gave Rachel a look. "I wonder how much he's getting paid."

She smacked my arm with the back of her hand. "Cut the shit. Try and have a good time. This was your idea. Remember?"

The bartender set two goblets on the counter. "This IPA's brewed with fresh organic Citra hops from Washington State and a touch of locally grown grapefruit and lemon and—"

"We know," I interrupted and held my glass under my nose. The brew smelled crisp like a spring morning. It had a slightly opaque yellowish hue and a nice half-inch head of foam. "Charley Copek and us," I said, "we go way back."

"Awesome. So, you know all about Blind Pass Brewing. We're coming out with an amazing Chocolate Porter in the fall." He pointed at my beer. "But that right there's what's gonna put us on the map. By the way," he said and pointed to a bowl with small strips of paper and half-size pencils, "we're having a slogan contest. If you come up with the best slogan for the brewery, you get a free case of beer."

I ignored the contest and took my first sip of beer—a blast of flavor. Actually, the second one was, too: fresh hoppiness and citrus jolting my taste buds. After that, the brew settled nicely into a mild flow. It was comfortable, not too much of one thing. I guess it's what they refer to as complex. I drank down half the glass, just to get in the mood, ready to sail.

We sat at a table. Rachel didn't waste any time. She pulled out her camera, set a flash on the hot shoe, and went over to the only other customers, two older men and a woman sitting at one of the tables.

She started joking with them, taking a few photos of them drinking and laughing. A couple of minutes later, she was climbing the stools, getting high up to get different angles.

Another group came in, hung out at the bar, tasting Copek's three brews. Rachel was on them like a damn paparazzi at the Oscars, getting right into their faces, posing them, ordering them to look this way and that, hovering over their beers, her flash going off like lightning in a summer storm.

I was about to walk up to the bar and order another IPA when Charley Copek's big barrel frame came marching into the tasting room. His little blue eyes moved quickly from left to right. He marched over to the bar, checked the bowl with slogans: only a handful of entries. But it was still early. He greeted his customers, made small talk, paused to check the taps, then adjusted the fake schooner wheel hanging on the plain white wall—as if anyone would notice it was crooked.

Finally, he came to my table and gave me a pat on the back. "So what do you think?" he said and scratched the side of his bushy red beard.

"Nice to see you, too," I said.

He leaned closer, placed his hand on my forearm, and whispered, "I'm freaking out, Dex. I don't know . . . what if it doesn't work out?"

"What're you talking about?"

"My investor," he said. "What if he changes his mind?"

"You never mentioned that you had an investor."

He shrugged and looked around the room. "Technically, I don't. Not yet. But this dude was pretty stoked about pumping a little cash into the brewery."

"A little?"

He winced, then gave me a short grin. "He talked of going national with Blind Pass Brewing."

"That's great," I said, thinking of the money I wasn't getting paid for writing copy for the website.

"Yeah," he mumbled. "If he shows up."

"You think he's on the up and up?"

Charley shrugged. "I'll be honest with you, Dexter. I'm scared shitless. I'm just getting started. I don't even know what I'm doing here. Flying by the seat of my pants, you know?"

"Relax, man."

"Easy for you to say. I have my life tied to this place. Everything."

"So, what's the problem?"

He shook his head, ran his hand over his bald head. "I can't sleep at night. I worry about everything. I have nightmares that we put parched yeast in the vat and—"

"Come on, Copek. You've been brewing this shit in your garage for years. As far as I can remember, you never had a problem."

He straightened his back and seemed to ponder this while watching Rachel making her way around the bar, leaning to the side, snapping shots. Charley turned to me and smiled. "Those were the days, eh?"

Back then I used to go over to his house and we'd put on an old Stones album or some early Rod Stewart and chill on lawn chairs in the driveway, drinking whatever magic brew he'd come up with that month.

For a moment, Charley seemed lost in his nostalgia. Then he glanced at his phone, pressed a few buttons, and whispered to himself, "Come on, Terrence, where the fuck are you?"

It came to my ears like an echo. I said, "Terrence?"

Copek nodded. "My phantom investor."

"Bullshit."

"You know him?"

"What's his last name?"

"Oliver. Terrence Oliver."

"Bullshit."

"What?"

"I'm looking for him."

Charley grinned. "Good luck with that. Guy's impossible to get a hold of. I've gabbed more with his lawyer than with him."

I almost didn't want to ask because I was sure I knew the answer. "What's his lawyer's name?"

"Joaquin del Pino. The guy from TV. You know, Justice for All."

"I can't fucking believe it. He's coming here?"

"At least he said he would. But I'm beginning to think those two are just talk."

"Which two?"

"Terrence and del Pino."

Just then my phone beeped. I glanced at the screen. A text from Brian Farinas: *can't make it tonight,* followed by a sad-faced emoji.

Charley stared at my half-empty beer, then at me. He smiled and walked over to greet a group of customers that had just walked in.

By eight thirty p.m., Terrence Oliver had not shown up. Most of the customers had moved on. Copek collected the bowl with the slogans.

Rachel shoved her camera gear in her bag and gave me a slap on the back. "So what's the plan, Kemosabe?"

"Kemosabe?"

"Yeah, Kemosabe. I got it from one of the old guys at the bar. Sounds cool, no? I think I'm going to adopt it."

"It's kind of racist," I said.

"Really?" she said and rolled her eyes. "And you're so damn PC."

I ignored her and turned to Copek. "No news of Terrence Oliver?"

He shook his head and glanced at his watch. "I gotta lock up the place and pick up the wife at work."

"Crap." I set my empty glass on the table. "You don't happen to have his number, do you?"

"Yeah." Copek pulled out his phone and pressed a few buttons. "I'll text it to you right now."

CHAPTER 25

AFTER RACHEL AND I had a quick bite at the Thai sushi place in Gulf Gate, I tried Terrence Oliver's number. Twice. No answer. Each time I got the automated voice mail from AT&T. I left messages, said it was urgent. Then we went to up to the Cock & Bull on Cattlemen Road—a beer joint from the days before craft brews even existed. The place was in an old barn. Inside it was all wood with a long counter made with slabs of center-cut wood laid out like big oval tiles. There were half a dozen full-size refrigerators behind the bar with hundreds of different beers and an offering of at least twenty taps. Beer lover's heaven.

The Cock & Bull was one of the few places left in town that had live bands that played original music. Most of the time they featured acoustic sets. But tonight, The Funky Donkeys were opening for the Belching Penguins.

To the left of the long bar was a foosball table and darts, to the right was the stage and a few tables and chairs. Jimi Hendrix was playing low over the speakers. The place was mostly empty except for a handful of beer aficionados enjoying rare brews at the bar and a few old punks hanging around the back door that led out to the deck. The stage was in the corner opposite the bar. The band was setting up, rolling in their amps and speakers, putting together the drum set, hooking up their mixer, guitar pedals.

Rachel set her cameras down and went to the bar and ordered drinks. Got me a Goose Island IPA. I didn't complain. She had a Saint Arnold's Pub Crawl Pale Ale.

She took a long sip and licked her lips, all the while watching Dana setting up for the gig. She looked nothing like the crime scene investigator I'd seen at Jaybird's murder scene. The khakis, pressed police polo shirt, and blue latex gloves were gone. Now she was all Goth: black fingernails, black straight hair, thick black eyeliner, black lips—the works. She knelt beside the drum set and pulled a dark purple Rickenbacker from a case, focused on tuning the instrument.

The band had two guitarists. The other was also the singer. He had a bald head and a face covered in piercings. The drummer was older, clean cut, and wore khakis and a blue and white checkered shirt. Looked like he belonged on a golf course with Fenton Kendel.

When the band finished setting up, Dana set her axe on a stand and came to where we sat. She ignored me and scowled at Rachel. "Whassup, bitch?"

Then she marched off to the bar.

Rachel watched her go. Then she turned to me with a wide smile. "She's so fucking hot."

She was, in a Dracula kind of way. I was here for Rachel, but I also had my own secret mission: I was hoping to have a little time to ask Dana if she'd found anything peculiar in Jaybird's drowning.

After Dana got her beer, she walked up to the stage, took a long drink, and looked over the sparse audience. The singer was flattening out a sheet of paper with their song list. He kneeled, placed it in front of him, and held it down with the guitar effect pedals. He quickly crossed himself, stood and slung the strap of his Fender Strat over his shoulder, touched a couple of stings, turned a tuner knob.

Finally, he glanced at Dana and the drummer and the bass player who looked like he could be fourteen. Then he walked up to the microphone and said, "Thanks for coming. We're the Funky Donkeys."

He turned, nodded to the drummer who banged his sticks: one, two, three, four. The singer jumped in the air and came down with a stroke of his guitar and the band dropped in with an explosion sound: vintage Cult shoved in with the Red Hot Chili Peppers, thanks to the intensity of the kid jamming on the bass. The guitars sounded like breaking glass. Dana carried the melody, saved the band.

Rachel pulled out her camera and changed lenses. "Aren't they great?"

I nodded. She smiled, checked the settings on the camera and went to work, moving on and off the low stage like she belonged there.

They played five songs, one of them a monotonous ballad with the singer screaming over the weeping lead guitar. It was pretty annoying. Afterward, the singer announced they were taking a short break. Halleluiah.

Rachel came back to the table, sat, and scrolled through the images on the back of her camera.

Dana set her Rickenbacker on the stand and stepped off the stage. She was walking past us when Rachel pushed out a chair with her foot, blocking her path.

Dana's eyes narrowed. She turned the chair around and straddled it, her legs spread, her armpits resting on the backrest.

Rachel glowed like a teen meeting her idol. "You guys rock, babe."

"Oh, yeah?"

Rachel nodded toward me. "You know Dexter?"

Dana glanced at me with tired eyes. "I seen you around." Then she turned to Rachel. "He work at the paper with you?"

"Used to."

Rachel and Dana. The two of them dated for a few months, then broke up and then slept together one drunken night, then broke up. I guess now they were working it out again. To be young, beautiful, and gay.

Dana nodded at the camera. "How do they look?"

"Awesome."

"You stayn' for the whole set?"

"Hell yeah."

Dana grinned. She reached over the table, took Rachel's Saint Arnold's, and tossed it back. Then slammed the bottle on the table. "Excellent."

"Hey," I said, "aren't you investigating that drowning in the Intracoastal?"

"And?"

"I was wondering if there was anything that could tie it to that other drowning a couple of weeks ago."

"Yeah," she said. "They both drowned."

"I'm serious."

She glanced at Rachel, then at me. "The one we fished out last night was tied to a cinderblock with a surfing leash."

"What's that?"

"One of those plastic straps surfers use on their surfboards so the boards don't go far when they wipe out."

"I didn't know that."

"Learn something new every day," Rachel said, annoyed.

Dana glanced at her and stood.

"What about the other one?" I said.

"Nothing. He was just a floater."

She marched off to the bar to get a drink. Rachel frowned at me. "What the fuck, Dex. You messing up my game."

"What game?"

"With Dana. We're trying to patch things up, and you come up with that murder shit."

"Really?"

"She's off work, man. Lay off."

"Jesus, Rachel. Check her out. She's all about death. She's probably happy to talk about dead people."

"It's her job. Do you want to be thinking about work when you're chilling?"

"I'm always thinking about work."

She rolled her eyes. "Right. I forgot who I was talking to."

"Take it easy. I'm going to finish this beer, and I'll be out of your hair."

A couple of minutes later, Dana came back, a beer bottle in each hand. She leaned over our table and pointed at me with one of the beers, a Ballast Point Manta Ray. "You know what, that other floater had a red mark on his right ankle."

"What was it?"

"I didn't think anything of it at the time. Just an old mark or something. Maybe from surfing. The guy had blond hair, a deep tan and shit. Made sense."

"Maybe that's what it was," Rachel said.

"Maybe," Dana said. "It was on his right ankle. If the guy surfed with his left foot forward, sure. But if it was the other way around, that's another story." She took a sip of one of the beers and pointed at Rachel. "We're doing one more set. You gonna take more pictures or what?"

Rachel leaned over her camera, fiddled with the controls. Changed memory cards. Dana marched off to the stage, set one of her beers on the ground next to a speaker.

I stood and felt for my keys, glanced at Rachel. "I'm outta here."

* * *

On my way out, I noticed a rack of free publications by the door. Real Estate. The cover had four photos of four very expensive looking houses. But what caught my eye was the name at the bottom: Alex J. Trainor, Realtor.

I picked up the magazine. Looked at the thumbnail portrait. Alex Trainor was the one selling the condos next door to my house. But there was something else. He was the same man I'd seen at the bar of the Ritz-Carlton the other day.

I tossed the magazine back on the rack and walked out, passed a group of skinheads smoking near the door. Behind them three Harley-Davidsons. At the end of the building was my dented Subaru. I got in and started the engine. Dana had given me something to go on. I figured Keith or Tessa might know Liam's surfing stance.

* * *

I pulled out of the parking lot and headed south on Cattlemen Road, then turned right on Bahia Vista. My mind kept drifting back to the real estate guy: Alex J. Trainor. Why did real estate agents insist on putting their picture on their ads? They loved that shit. During the real estate boom, almost every bus stop had a picture of some real estate agent—as if someone who was riding our intermittent public transportation could throw down a load of cash for a new home. Was it ego? Or was there some marketing manual that told them to do that? I mean, shit. I wouldn't buy a house from half the realtors in this town just from their looks. Criminals in suits.

Just as I was passing Beneva, in the heart of the Pinecraft neighborhood, the blue-and-red police lights flashed behind me.

I immediately did an inventory of my drinks: three beers at Copek's then dinner, two at the Cock & Bull—all in the span of four and a half hours. If I blew into the breathalyzer, I'd be fine. I was stone sober.

I slowed down, set my blinker, pulled over onto a parking lot on the opposite side of Bahia Vista from Yoder's Restaurant. I turned the engine off and put my hands on the steering wheel.

The police car's PA blared: "Step out of the car, hands where I can see them."

I didn't move.

The spotlight on the driver's side of the police cruiser beamed on me. The cop repeated his command.

I didn't like it. I'd been told by an officer to always turn the engine off, put my hands on the wheel, and wait for the officer to walk over. But one time, Brian Farinas told me never to argue and do exactly what the cops said.

Either way, I was fucked.

I lived with the memory of my father: the patrolman ordering him to step out of the car. When he did, he pumped him full of lead: two in the chest, one in the abdomen, one in the arm while he knelt with his hands up in the air. They said he died instantly. I saw it all from the back seat. Eight years old. My dad knelt, then turned to look at me. The fear in his eyes etched into my heart. Then boom-boom. He fell back, one leg folded awkwardly under him, and one arm extended out, the other half-over his chest. Blood on the pavement.

The cop repeated his command. "Out of the car. Now. Hands where I can see them."

I took a deep breath, pushed the door open, stepped out with my hands at my sides, but slightly separated from my body so they could see I was clean.

The officer adjusted the spotlight on me, blinding me. I narrowed my eyes, brought a hand up to shield my eyes.

The officer yelled, "Don't move."

I yelled back, "I'm not."

The officer in the passenger side stepped out and started slowly forward, holding his long flashlight over his shoulder—the other hand at his side, too close to his gun for my comfort. "You been drinking, sir?"

"I had two beers in two hours," I said. I couldn't see him. The driver also stepped out, moved forward, same manner, but no flashlight. "I'm sober," I said. "I'll be glad to take the Breathalyzer."

When the driver stepped in front of the spotlight, I saw they were Sheriff's deputies. Then he stepped to the side and the light blinded me again. "What was that?"

"I said I was sober."

"You were doing forty in a thirty-mile speed zone."

Maybe it was true. I wasn't paying attention. We were in the middle of an Amish neighborhood. They rode bikes.

"I'm sorry," I said. "I didn't notice there was a change."

They came closer. Then I saw the deputy's name tag: *Norton.*

"You know you're driving with a broken headlight?" the other deputy said as he came around my car.

"Yeah. It just happened last night. I haven't had—"

"Let's see your driver's license, registration, and insurance, please."

"For a broken light?" I cried.

"License, registration, and insurance," Norton repeated.

I ducked into my car and got the registration from the glove box. Then I came forward and handed my documents to Deputy Norton.

The other deputy said, "Do we have your permission to search your car, sir?"

"What?"

Norton about-faced and went back to the cruiser. Checked my docs. The other one pointed at my car. "Sir?"

I stepped to the side. "Sure. Whatever."

I watched him search the car. Then come out. He ran his hand over part of the dent near the door. Looked at me. "Did you report this?"

"What?" I was getting a little pissed off. "That some douchebag ran me off the road last night? No. What for?"

Deputy Norton stepped out of the cruiser, walked slowly toward me and the other deputy. Behind the cruiser, next to the sidewalk, I could make out the shape of three Amish men, heavyset, older, bushy beards and hats, sitting on their tricycles, staring at the show.

"Will you turn around, please?" Deputy Norton ordered.

I clenched my jaw, did what he asked.

"Hands on the roof," he said.

I did as he said. A second later I felt the handcuff going around my right wrist. Then he pulled my arm behind my back and started with the Miranda rights.

CHAPTER 26

MOTHERFUCKERS WOULDN'T TELL me why they arrested me. I sat in the back of the cruiser asking, again and again. But the two deputies were like stones. It was just me and the occasional crack of the police radio. I took a deep breath, straightened myself in the seat, and stretched my legs. I noticed Norton take a quick glance at me through the rearview.

I had to keep calm and not make a scene. I'd learned from the past, from Brian Farinas: say nothing. I figured there was probably video. The footage would prove I did nothing wrong. I'd offered to take the Breathalyzer. I kept my head down, my mouth shut, did exactly as I was told. I was as docile as an ex-con who knew he was guilty.

They took me straight to county and handed me off to a female deputy who fast-tracked me through booking. The charge was fleeing the scene of an accident.

They sent me to the drunk tank with three homeless men that stank of piss. I didn't protest. I knew they had the wrong guy. And in the back of my head, I even hoped it had been the assholes in the red pickup who had reported me. Brian would rip them a new one in court.

* * *

At one in the afternoon, I was marched with a handful of other losers out of the cell and into a room at the jail for first appearance via closed-circuit video to the courthouse. The judge on the monitor screen couldn't be bothered. Ran us all through like a factory on deadline. Brian Farinas was there. He told the judge there had been a misunderstanding. Deputies had jumped the gun. It wasn't the same accident that had been reported off Fruitville Road and Honore. He asked that the case be dismissed. But the judge wouldn't have it. At least he released me without bond. And why not? I had no record and—according to Brian—was an outstanding and valuable member of the community.

* * *

"Don't say anything until we're in the car," Brian said when I walked out of jail and met him in the lobby of the Sheriff's office. He placed his hand on my shoulder, drew me close, and whispered in my ear. "You don't want to piss anyone off. Not now, okay?"

He stank of yesterday's booze. I looked sideways at him, said nothing, just as he asked.

"I have a splitting headache," he said as we made our way out of the County Building and down a couple of blocks to the parking lot, up the steps to the third floor where his Range Rover was parked.

He started the car and cranked the AC. He stared ahead.

I waited, taking in the cool air.

Finally, Brian took a deep breath and spoke real soft. "Okay. Tell me what happened?"

I told him about being run off the road in Siesta and being at the Cock & Bull with Rachel. "They're trying to nail me for the wrong accident. I was never near Fruitville and Honore."

"No problem." He continued to stare ahead. "If you're telling me the truth, then the paint won't match. Besides, you have Rachel to corroborate your story and—"

"What the fuck, man? This shouldn't even go to trial."

"Please let me do my job," he said quietly. "Now, why didn't you report the accident on Siesta?"

"Because I didn't get a license plate. What was I going to tell the cops?"

"You tell them what happened. Keeps things clean and legal."

"Right."

He turned to face me. He looked like crap, red eyes, dark bags under them, sagging like old paper. "Is there anything you're not telling me?"

I grinned. I could tell he wasn't in the mood for jokes, which was rare for him. I said, "Why don't we go to my place. I'll cook us up a little breakfast. You look like you could use it."

He smiled and put the car in reverse. "So could you."

We backed out and made our way out of the parking lot and out onto Ringling Boulevard toward Washington. We stopped at a crosswalk where a large group of men and women in suits walked in front of us, from the County Building to the courthouse.

"Look," I said and smiled at Brian. "A herd of lawyers. I've never seen one in the wild before."

He didn't find it funny. "That's your county government at work."

I watched them walking slowly in a tight group as if they were scared to break off the group—like elementary school children on a field trip.

"What's their deal?" I said.

"They wanted to see how the Sheriff's office operates because they're requesting more money."

"For riot gear, no doubt."

Brian glanced at me. "For a guy who just got out of jail, you sure sound peppy."

"Did you just say *peppy?*"

Brian looked away, didn't smile. I watched the commissioners and their assistants, folders and papers under their arms. One of them looked familiar: oval face, slightly bald. Looked like the kind of guy who managed a tire shop.

"We elected these guys?"

Brian shook his head. The crosswalk cleared, and he stepped on the gas. It had been a long time since I'd seen Brian in such a mood. No fun, no talk. Just business. I figured he must've had a hell of a night.

When we got to my house, I picked up my copy of the *Sarasota Herald* from the front porch and tossed it on the coffee table, then I went straight for the fridge and popped open a couple of Siesta IPAs and handed one to Brian.

He finally cracked a little smile. "You can tell, huh?"

"You look like shit."

"I met a woman."

"Well, good for you. That's why you bailed on me?"

He nodded.

I raised my beer. "Is it love?"

"It is for me," he said with an honest smile. "I think. Or at least lust."

"She a lawyer?"

"Works at the county clerk's office."

"Nice. Government job. Great benefits."

We sat on the couch, both of us looking like we'd had a terrible night and were ready to just tune out and crash. The beer helped. I sat on the floor and flipped through my records, see what music to put on.

"So," Brian said, "you gonna tell me what's going on, or what?"

I picked out *Frampton Comes Alive*, side four. I wanted to hear "Do You Feel Like We Do." I set it on the old Thorens and let the Scott do its magic.

I stood, grabbed my beer, and leaned against the counter that separated the kitchen from the living room. "I just told you. Some asshole tried to run me off the road the night before last."

"No," he said. "The job. What's up?"

"I was hired to look into the death of Liam Fleming, a kid, twenty-seven years old. Drowned on the Intracoastal a couple of weeks ago."

"What, you're Sherlock Holmes now?"

"I need the money."

"So what's the deal?"

I didn't have an answer, but I knew I was getting close. "It's weird," I said and moved into the kitchen, started on breakfast: scrambled eggs and hot dogs and Sriracha sauce. The frying pan sizzled with hot oil as I broke five eggs into it. "The cops are calling it an accident. Turns out Fenton Kendel is retiring and chose to take the easy way out. Then two nights ago the guy's roommate was also found drowned in the Intracoastal—only his is definitely a homicide. Someone tied him up to a cinderblock and dropped him in the deep end."

"How do you find these cases?" He stood and came over to the counter and looked over my shoulder. "Smells good."

"Nothing like a hot greasy breakfast to cure the blues."

He nodded and held up his beer. "And this."

I touched his beer can with mine. "Indeed."

I got us two more beers and we sat down to breakfast in the dining room. Mimi appeared out of nowhere and joined us at the table. I shoved her off. She sat on the floor and complained, begged, then moved around our feet, rubbing against our ankles, meowing incessantly.

"Tell me about your arrest," Brian said, his body folded over his plate and shoveling food into his mouth.

"Not much to tell. They followed procedure. Except one of the deputies is the same one who was the responding officer when they found Liam Fleming in the Intracoastal."

"You think he's involved?"

"I don't know. Coincidence?"

"Could be," Brian said. "They'll probably drop the charges on you. But if it happens again, report the accident. Even if you don't have the license plate. It creates a record. Gets you off the hook."

"What are the chances of two hit-and-runs in the same twenty-four-hour period?"

"Better safe than sorry," he said.

* * *

After Brian left, I sat back on the couch to take a nap. I grabbed the newspaper from the coffee table and browsed the pages, mostly news from the AP wire. Then I saw Rachel's photo from the night of Jaybird's murder off Blackburn Point Park. There was a small brief. The body had been identified: Terrence Oliver.

CHAPTER 27

I TOOK A quick shower and ran out of the house. But the driveway was empty. My car was in Pinecraft, or the pound. I went back inside, called Rachel.

"I can't," Rachel said.

"Come on," I pleaded, "just drop me off at Yoder's."

"First of all, I'm up here by the airport—"

"So?"

"In bed."

"I can wait."

"With Dana."

"Oh."

"And I have a shoot in a couple hours up in Bradenton."

"Well . . . have a nice time."

Rachel giggled. "I already did."

I had an Uber pick me up a few blocks from my house in the parking lot of the Women's Exchange on the corner of Orange Avenue and Oak Street. I found my car where I left it in Pinecraft. No ticket.

I drove straight to Siesta Village.

I parked in a neat little spot on the side of the blue apartments and ran up the stairs to number 8. No answer. I ran back down, already breaking into a sweat.

Across the street, people were making their way to the corner and disappearing down to where Beach Road turned into the short, narrow dead end along the Gulf. I could hear chants, drumming.

I crossed Ocean Boulevard at the Siesta Key Oyster Bar and turned right to the little section of Beach Road where at least two dozen people, hippies and surfers, most of them familiar to me from the drum circle, had gathered. They held signs, chanted, and danced. A couple of men tapped their drums.

I recognized Cap'n Cody standing on the sidewalk with his arms crossed, staring at the show. Behind him were the two houses that belonged to Beach City Holdings.

The hippie girl who had first pointed out Jaybird to me a few days ago at the drum circle climbed up on a rock. The crowd cheered. She raised her hands and motioned for everyone to be quiet.

"Guys," she said, "guys . . ." The drumming died down. "Friends. We all know why we're here, yeah? We need to work together to stop the closing of this little stretch of road. Everyone who's here needs to be at the county commissioner's meeting on Tuesday, yeah?"

The crowd cheered.

"I will take our petition with all the signatures. If we all crowd in there and each one of us speaks their piece, say whatever, talk about keeping this road open, and the access to the beach public, we will beat them."

Someone yelled: "Preach it, Willow!"

"That's right," Willow said. "We all count. We vote. And we'll be there at the meeting and make our collective voices heard, yeah?"

The crowd clapped and cheered, and the drummers tapped on their tribal instruments. Willow, the hippie girl, raised her hands. "*Namaste*, my friends!"

She jumped off the rock and was hugged by another hippie girl and a young man who looked like a surfer. Standing outside the perimeter of the crowd, a few older people paused to watch, looking a little bewildered, beach chairs and umbrellas in hand.

A man in a yellow swimsuit and long black hair climbed up on the rock. He extended his arms out over the crowd like Jesus and said, "People. Just a reminder. Next Sunday at sunset we're having a celebration of life for Jaybird. The event will take place at the drum circle. We'll be spreading his ashes and remembering him as someone who truly lived a full and generous life. Jaybird was a friend to all of us. And he was the best friend Siesta Beach ever had. We'll never forget him."

Someone yelled, "All right, Jaybird!"

People cheered.

"Everyone's invited!" he cried and hopped off the rock.

I turned to cross the street to ask Cap'n Cody if he'd seen Tessa, but he was already walking away toward the Village with his head bowed. I didn't catch up to him before he turned and went into the Siesta Key Oyster Bar.

I crossed Ocean Boulevard and followed Calle Menorca to the place where I'd parked my car. A part of me wanted to call Detective Kendel, bring him into the loop: two business partners murdered. But I still had no proof that Liam had been murdered—and no motive. I had to find out who was poised to benefit from Beach City Holdings now that the two partners had been killed. I put my Keith and Brandy Fleming theory—that Keith was trying to keep Liam quiet about the affair—on the back burner, and shifted my focus to Jaybird and Liam: killed because of a business deal gone sour. Either someone got greedy, or they pissed off the wrong person, owed money—something.

When I got to the alley next to the blue apartments, my car was gone. In its place was a blue Hyundai Accent. I looked around, made sure I was in the right place. Then I saw the sign half hidden by the big round leaves of a sea grape tree: *Tow Away Zone. Residents Only.*

Welcome to Siesta-Fucking-Key.

I went around the side, ran up the stairs to apartment number 8, and knocked. No answer.

A chill ran up my spine. What if Tessa . . .

No. I shook my head and erased the image of her being pulled out of the Intracoastal by Detective Kendel and his crew.

The Old Salty Dog.

I ran down the stairs and raced across the street.

"Dexter!"

It was Tessa. She was crossing the parking lot of Morton's Siesta Market, bags with groceries in both hands.

My heart stopped. Then started again at a comfortable beat.

"I'm sorry," I said and took some bags.

"What do you mean?" she said.

"About the other night."

"It's cool," she said. We came up to her building, walked up the steps. "I was feeling pretty bad. I wasn't myself."

"I know," I said, "but I acted like a total asshole."

"No. You were right. You were a gentleman."

"It would've been awkward," I said and watched her struggle to get her keys from her purse and open the door. "The last thing I want to do is hurt you."

She laughed. "Don't flatter yourself, Dexter. I wasn't trying to go to bed with you. I just didn't want to be alone. And it was late. I thought you could just crash. I was offering you half my bed."

I followed her inside. I could see in her eyes that she was serious. I bit my lip.

"I'm not as weak as that," she said, and we set the bags on the kitchen counter. "Trust me. I've been in worse places with worse people."

"I misunderstood. I apologize."

She opened the fridge and started putting away the groceries. "No apology needed. So long as we understand each other."

She closed the fridge. I sniffed the air. The apartment smelled of smoke. "Leftover pizza," she said and went to the sliding glass doors. "I was reheating it in the broiler and burnt it."

I followed her. From the balcony, I could see the next building and the alley below. A car was having trouble parallel parking. Past the building across the alley, all that was visible was another building and the blue of the sky. No beach. That was the argument for Beach Road. People wanted to keep it public because it was the only place where someone could drive and see the beach from their car. It was all that was left from the old days.

"Did you hear?" I said.

"What?"

"Jaybird was Terrence Oliver."

"Liam's partner?"

"The one and only," I said.

"But Jaybird was a bum. He cooked at the kitchen of the Old Salty Dog and smoked pot and didn't have a care in the goddamn world."

"I don't understand it either. But those are the facts."

She shook her head. "I don't believe it."

"This means whoever killed Liam probably killed Terrence—Jaybird. And I think it's pretty obvious it has to do with Beach City Holdings."

"Do the cops know this?"

"I don't know," I said. "Was Liam right-handed?" I said.

"What?"

"Was he right-handed or left-handed?"

"Left-handed."

I ran my hand through my hair and glanced out the window trying to think of a surfer's stance. "Which foot came forward?"

"What are you talking about?" Tessa came to my side and curled a strand of hair behind her ear.

"When he surfed. Did he stand with his right foot forward?" I imitated a surfer's stance to demonstrate.

Tessa shook her head and glanced out the window as if all our answers were floating between the buildings. "I don't know," she said. "Liam didn't really surf."

"What? There's a surfboard on the roof of his car."

"Jaybird surfed. Keith surfed. Almost everyone did. Liam was just learning. But it wasn't his thing. He was a nature lover. He would rather be out on his kayak, or paddleboard."

"I don't believe it."

"What's the matter?"

"It means he was murdered the same way as Terrence Oliver."

"How do you know that?"

I took a couple of steps back and eased myself onto the couch. I was so tired. My head was buzzing from exhaustion, stress, jail.

Tessa came around the other side of the coffee table and sat next to me, leaned forward. She smelled of citrus and sugar, brought back memories of my ex, of when we first met. Of the good old days.

I massaged my temples where a tension headache was slowly building. Tessa stared at me. Outside, two people were arguing, something about a parking space. Siesta Beach, the Village. I imagined the noise here at night, especially during spring break when all the kids came down and the population exploded around the Village. One big eternal party. The island was theirs now. Most of the houses and apartments on the key were owned by corporations. They were making a killing on seasonal rentals: a one-bedroom apartment like Tessa's could go for more than twenty-five hundred a week during peak season.

"I broke up with Liam because I found out about his company," Tessa said in a monotone.

I turned, looked at her dark, sad eyes.

"We all used to hang out, right?"

I nodded.

"Liam was mister outdoors, right?"

"Yeah, so I hear."

"I loved him for that. I mean, here was this guy who cared deeply about nature, enjoyed it. He loved Siesta and the people we hung out with. He loved the vibe. And he gave Jaybird a place to live."

"Terrence Oliver."

She sniffled but if there were tears, she did a great job of holding them back. "That's the thing. I hated his secrets. Most of us knew his father was wealthy. He was cool about it. He never flaunted it or acted superior to anyone."

"Earlier you said he was very laid-back."

"And he was. He lived a simple life, like he wanted to be one with nature. Did you know he used to go out on his paddleboard early in the morning and meditate?"

I shook my head. I knew nothing—nothing about Liam or Jaybird or Terrence.

"One day I walked in on him. He was on his computer studying the County Appraisers website. He wouldn't tell me what he was doing. So I pressed him on it. I wouldn't let it go.

"That's when he told you about Beach City Holdings?"

"Well . . ." Tessa hesitated. She drew in a deep breath, her chest rising and falling when she exhaled. "I didn't know about the company. He didn't say anything about that. Certainly not the name."

"What did he say?"

She shrugged and then the first tear found its exit. She wiped it with the back of her hand and went on. "He told me he was handling these multimillion-dollar properties for a company."

"What's wrong with that?"

She wrung her hands and tossed her head to the side. "You don't see it?"

"He was a businessman—"

"Exactly. He was *the* enemy. He preached one thing but did the total opposite."

"So you didn't like that he was working for a developer."

"It was more than that. He was using us to find properties before they went up for sale."

"But that's smart business," I said. "A little sneaky, but—"

"He was a cheat, Dexter. He had no integrity."

"Please," I said. "It's not as if any of the drum circle hippies owned any land."

"No, we didn't," she said defensively. "But the people we came in contact with did. He used us as his eyes and ears. Me at the bar of the Old Salty Dog, Lonnie at the Daiquiri Deck, Jaybird at the beach and the volleyball courts. Keith in Turtle Beach. We all hear things. Just a few weeks ago, Troy Varnel, that county commissioner who's trying to close Beach Road, was at the Siesta Key Oyster Bar talking with a couple of developers about some empty lot on the Intracoastal."

"He wants to develop it?"

"The developers probably do. They must've been asking for his help. That lot is like a secret kayak launch for some of us. Instead of going all the way down to Turtle Beach, we can go there. It's just south of the Stickney Point bridge."

"And that's the kind of thing you'd tell Liam."

She nodded. "But he was one of them."

"So you broke up with him."

"Well," she said and curled a loose strand of hair around the back of her ear. "It was really because of Lisa Schmidt."

"Who's that?"

"A teenager who hung out with us in the winter. Her grandparents owned the house where she stayed at the very end of Midnight Pass. Anyway, we were all hanging out on the patio at Liam's place, beer in a cooler, a joint going around. Cap'n Cody was strumming his guitar. It was real nice, right? So Lisa says in passing how her neighbors were in the middle of a messy divorce. Suddenly Liam's ears perked up. Man, was he interested."

"Okay," I said. "So he was a fake."

"Don't defend him," Tessa cried. "You should've seen him fawning over Lisa. Nudging his way to meet her grandparents and the neighbors. He was such a weasel."

"Did he get the property?"

"What do you think?"

I knew the answer was in the affirmative. But none of it helped build a case. There was no motive. Unless Lisa Schmidt's neighbors...

"He was a hypocrite," Tessa cried. "All this love for Siesta and nature, the kayaking and the paddleboarding. His love for the beach. It was a front to scope out properties on the cheap."

"If he didn't snatch them up, someone else would."

"I couldn't trust him anymore," she said sadly, her eyes looking down at the terrazzo.

"But you stayed friends."

"We did," she said with a shrug. "He was a nice guy. I just couldn't date him anymore."

"He also has a lot of acreage near Myakka and in East County."

"And what are developers doing out there?"

We both knew the answer to that. That part of the county was being developed at an incredible pace. A few years back, when Rachel and I worked for the newspaper, we did a story on the ranchers who were selling—or losing—their properties to developers because they were being priced out by rising property values and taxes. That small pocket of rural Florida was now a small city.

I didn't like it any more than Tessa. And yes, it made me angry—at Liam and Terrence for being part of it. But I also had to admit it had been pretty genius of him to live like a beach bum to find the bargains in the key.

"Look," I said and took Tessa's hand. "I appreciate you telling me all this about Liam. But people don't kill people over a plot of land—"

"Are you kidding me?" Tessa cried and leaned back on the chair. "People wage wars for a bit of land."

She was absolutely right. My problem was that I didn't see a connection. I sighed and looked out the sliding glass doors. "I suppose he must have crossed the wrong person."

"Yeah, but who?"

CHAPTER 28

TESSA'S QUESTION ECHOED in my head: Who?

Except I was thinking of a different who. Now that both Liam and Terrence Oliver were dead, what was to happen to Beach City Holdings? Who was to benefit? Was there a will?

I stood, took out my phone, and dialed Joaquin del Pino.

"He's gone home for the day," his secretary said impatiently.

I looked at my watch. It was just after four p.m. I said, "Kind of a short day for him, isn't it?"

"His court case adjourned early," she said, sounding a little testy. "Would you like to leave a message?"

I told her to have del Pino call me as soon as he arrived in the morning. It was urgent.

When I ended the call, I took out my wallet and looked for the business card for Thomas Pearlman, Esquire.

Couldn't find it.

I glanced at Tessa. "Can I borrow your car?"

"Why? What happened to yours?"

"It got towed," I said. "I need to rush downtown and see Bob Fleming's lawyer."

She jumped up. "I'm coming with!"

"No," I said quickly. "I need you to do something else."

"Spy on someone?"

I frowned. "Look up Beach City Holdings' properties on the computer."

"You already did that," she said.

"I know. But I wasn't sure what I was looking for."

"And now you do?"

"Not exactly." I went to the kitchen counter. "I need you to look at each property and write down the date of purchase, the purchase price, and the name of the previous owner."

"Why do I get the boring part?"

"I'm serious, Tessa. It's important. It's possible there was a recent transaction that turned bad, didn't sit right with a family member."

She huffed, but still handed over the keys to her Fiat. "Please be careful."

"I swear, if Bob Fleming hadn't hired me to look into the murder, I would be putting him at the top of my suspect list."

"You have a suspect list?"

I hesitated, looked away quickly because she was still on it. "It's my job, right?"

"Care to share?"

"Not yet," I lied. "It keeps changing."

"Dexter . . ."

"I'll be back in a couple hours," I said with a grin and ran out the door before she could drill me for more info.

* * *

Just as I pulled Tessa's teal Fiat 500 out to Ocean Boulevard, I stopped at the crosswalk. A couple of tourists carrying big folding lawn chairs and two kids on skateboards passed in front of me, followed by a man in a casual khaki suit whom I recognized right away as Alex J. Trainor, real estate agent. I watched him make his way up the steps of the deck of the Siesta Key Oyster Bar and take a seat at a table with a group of older men in Hawaiian shirts. The son of a bitch wasn't just selling condos downtown—he was moving real estate on the key. The car behind me honked and startled me out of my dream.

I didn't want to cause alarm or disrupt the Fleming household. I was banking on Pearlman knowing if Bob Fleming had an arrangement with Beach City Holdings in case of dissolution, bankruptcy, purchase, public offering—or death of the officers, for that matter.

And I didn't really suspect Fleming, but he was a businessman—and from the looks of it, a shrewd one. I didn't believe he would give Liam millions of dollars for a company without having any guarantees in case Liam decided to break with his partner—or die. I mean, helping your estranged son is one thing, but feeding money into a company where you have no stake, financial or otherwise personal, made zero sense.

I parked on Palm Avenue and went up to the sixth floor of the Orange Blossom building. Vivian McCutcheon, the friendly secretary, was there, again dressed in a blue skirt suit, looking very well groomed, sitting erect as if she was expecting me. There was no one else in the dark, paneled room.

"Is Mr. Pearlman in?"

She frowned and made a slight tilt of her head. "And you are?"

"I'm Dexter Vega, the investigator Bob Fleming hired to look into his son's death."

"Ah, of course. I'm sorry." She smiled, stood quickly, and strutted around the desk. "May I tell him what specifically you'd like to see him about?"

"About Liam's Fleming's death."

"I understand. But could you be more specific?"

"More specific than what?"

"What about Liam's death is it you'd like to inquire about?"

I took a deep breath, ran my hand over my hair. "I want to talk to him about Beach City Holdings. Specifically."

"Good. Thank you. I'll see if Mr. Pearlman can see you."

Vivian turned on the spot and click-clacked her heels across the office to the other side of the large wooden door.

A moment later she came back and held the door slightly open for me. "Mr. Pearlman will see you."

I walked in. She closed the door behind me.

Pearlman's office was not big, but it looked it. No shelves or books or art or anything that might give it a personal or professional feel. It was just a large mahogany desk with a few papers, a computer, a telephone, and the pungent smell of cigar smoke that seemed to hover over the man sitting behind the desk.

"Mr. Pearlman?"

"That's me," he said without getting up or extending his hand. His eyes did all that without effort. Then he grabbed the cigar that was resting on an ashtray, brought it to his mouth, and sucked in a long drag. He replaced the cigar on the ashtray, and a soft cloud of blue smoke escaped his mouth as he spoke. "What is it you need to know, Mr. Vega?"

Pearlman looked like a southern lawyer in a bad Hollywood movie: a nice pressed shirt, gold cufflinks, a red bow tie, a pair of thin gold-rim glasses hanging on his nose. He had a nice head of salt-and-pepper hair. The clean shave, the perfect hair, clothes, manicure, it all screamed money—and plenty of it.

There was no place for me to sit. Obviously, Pearlman did not receive visitors in his office. I figured if he had to talk with Mr. Fleming, he would go to the house on Sanderling, or meet him at some fancy restaurant over drinks.

"I've been looking into the death of Liam Fle—"

"To the point, Mr. Vega."

"Beach City Holdings," I said quickly. "What's Mr. Fleming's stake in the company?"

"Bob's been very generous with Liam. He's funded the company."

"That's not what I asked," I said—getting back to the point.

Pearlman raised an eyebrow. "As far as I know, he doesn't own any of it."

"And you would know because you're his lawyer."

"You assume correctly. Mr. Fleming believed in Liam's real estate business. He is a true believer in long-term investment. It was how he managed his hedge fund, and he was proud of Liam for taking such a long-term view with his own plans. Mr. Fleming doesn't believe in what you'd call a quick buck."

"What was Liam's long-term plan?"

"To develop and sell the properties, I assume. I wasn't privy to the details."

"So you don't know if there is a provision in the corporation in case of the death of its officers."

"I do not."

"So you could say that with the death of Liam's partner, Bob Fleming's lost his investment."

"I believe Liam's lawyer could answer that better than me."

"Joaquin del Pino."

"I can assure you that Liam's passing is worse for Mr. Fleming than the loss of any investment."

"I thought those two didn't get along."

He smiled sadly. "Father and son."

I nodded.

He tugged at his sleeve and glanced at his little wristwatch, then stretched his hand and picked up his cigar and held it up in the air. As far as lawyers went, I could tell he was as loyal to his client as a dog to his owner. I wondered if he would go to jail for Mr. Fleming.

"Did you like Liam?" I asked.

His eyes opened just a little wider, giving away his poker face. "Why, I didn't know him."

"You never met him?"

"I'm afraid not."

"But you knew of him. And you wrote some pretty big checks for him."

"I did."

"And you probably heard stories or complaints from Mr. Fleming."

"What are you getting at?"

"You must have had some kind of an opinion of him."

"That's not my job."

"But you're human. You must've felt something."

That stopped him. I could almost hear the wheels in his head turning. He set his cigar back on the ashtray and brought his hands together on the desk. "Between you and me, Mr. Vega, I thought Liam was taking advantage of his father."

"Because of the money?"

"Not so much the money. Mr. Fleming has plenty of it. I think it was more his love . . . and I believe perhaps guilt."

"So you think Liam was playing him?"

He grinned. "I've known Bob a very long time. He is an extremely smart and strong-willed individual. But he's older. He's changed."

"Softened?"

"I think he wanted to make up for not having been there for Liam and his mother."

"But money can't buy you love, huh?"

He pursed his lips and narrowed his eyes. "Mr. Fleming seemed happy to be helping his son, even if it didn't bring them closer together. I would say he saw a day in the future when they would reconcile."

"A long-term investment," I said drily.

His mouth twitched like he was going to grin, but changed his mind. "Is there anything else, Mr. Vega?"

"As a matter of fact, there is," I said. "The current Mrs. Fleming..."

"What about her?"

"What's her deal?"

"Deal?"

"Who is she? Who was she before she became Mrs. Fleming?"

He glanced at his cigar on the ashtray, a thin stream of blue smoke rising. Then he looked back at me. "Brandy Weston, of New Haven, Connecticut. Her father was an obstetrician. He passed away when she was fourteen. Her mother fancied herself an artist, painted landscapes, which she sold locally at a gallery in New Haven and took on commissions, portraits mostly. Brandy took after her. Became an artist herself."

"Any real money in the family?"

"Comfortable," he said. "But not rich. No."

"Brothers and sisters?"

"None."

"How did the two meet?"

"At the club."

"Which club?"

"The Founders Club."

"She was a member?" The Founders was probably the most exclusive golf club in the county. Like something trying to rival Trump's Mar-a-Lago.

"Brandy was having an art exhibit at the clubhouse."

"I see."

"What are you getting at, Mr. Vega?"

"I didn't want to go to Mr. Fleming with this. But right now, as things stand, I'm pretty sure Liam was murdered."

"So Bob was right."

"It's looking that way."

"And you suspect Mrs. Fleming is involved?"

"Did she sign a prenup?"

"A prenuptial agreement. Yes. Absolutely."

"If she divorces Mr. Fleming, she'll lose everything?"

"Not everything. But she will certainly lose a lot. Mr. Fleming agreed to set her up . . . rather comfortably."

"Right. But she'd lose the cushy lifestyle?"

Pearlman tilted his head and studied me with his beady blues. Then he picked up the cigar and took a long draw, two loud puffs like he was kissing the stogie, then set it down again. "There is something you haven't told me," he said when he replaced the cigar on the ashtray.

I crossed my arms over my chest and took a deep breath of cigar smoke. "I'm pretty sure Mrs. Fleming's having an affair."

The side of Pearlman's lip turned up in the slightest hint of a smile. "It wouldn't be the first time," he said.

"You're kidding me."

"Bob's been married to Brandy Fleming for five years. She's had affairs before. Both men were discreetly paid off and the affairs ended. Bob tolerates it only so much. But he understands. Mrs. Fleming is still young and beautiful. And he—"

"And he's an old drunk."

"Mr. Vega—"

"Like you said, let's get to the point. Fleming's quite the drinker. So they have this arrangement, or at least he accepts that this will happen. I'm not judging. But it means my theory that Mrs. Fleming and her lover were found out by Liam doesn't hold any water."

"I beg your pardon?"

"I had a suspicion. I thought Liam had found out about Mrs. Fleming having an affair and was going to tell his father. I imagined Mrs. Fleming plotted to have Liam killed in order to keep him quiet."

"I see," he said without batting an eye at my preposterous theory. "Mrs. Fleming knows Bob would not divorce her for having an affair so long as she's discreet."

"And since she's done it before and hasn't been sent packing by Fleming, she wouldn't be worried about Liam telling on her."

"Excuse me?"

"Just thinking out loud," I said.

He stared at me. "Have I answered all your questions?"

"Yeah," I said quietly. He didn't offer a hand or a nod. "I'm good."

I took a short step back, turned around, and walked out that big, heavy door. Vivian McCutcheon was at her desk, sitting erect in her blue suit just like a pretty robot.

CHAPTER 29

WHEN I CAME out of the building, the sun was beginning to turn toward the horizon, stretching shadows along Main Street so that the pattern of the cafés and cars parked at an angle made a psychedelic blanket of man-made objects. At the end of Main Street was Sarasota Bay. Despite all the development and the big condos, Sarasota was still a beautiful town.

My meeting with Pearlman had thrown me off. He was one cold character. But I guess he was the kind of guy you wanted on your team if things ever got tough. Fleming's bulldog. I couldn't blame him for being how he was.

And the marriage contracts and prenups. I didn't know what to make of that except that being a millionaire must be a shitty way to live. Even love was a commercial transaction.

I made my way across Main Street and then across Palm Avenue straight to the bar at Two Señoritas. I'd been craving a tequila for days now, and the conversation with Pearlman had melted away whatever resolve I'd had to curb my intake of hard liquor until I was done with the case. Liam's and Jaybird's murders had me stumped. I had nothing. I didn't know where to go next. No leads. No suspects. No motives.

I took a stool at the deep end of the bar and ordered a shot of Siete Leguas and three limes. When the Mexican bartender set the drink in front of me, he smiled and nodded at the clear liquid in the glass. "Good stuff, eh? *Salud.*"

I nodded and took in the smell, the mild smoky and bitter agave bouquet. I took a short sip. It went down and spread inside me like a soft firecracker. Lifted me to the heavens like an angel. I sighed, leaned back, tried to think, clear my head of the noise—just think. Motive, motive, motive.

Just as I ordered another tequila, I heard a familiar voice. "Mind if I sit here?"

Vivian McCutcheon. She was still in her blue lawyer costume and medium heels, but she had let her hair down. And I was pretty sure she had applied a layer of fresh lipstick around her pleasant smile.

"Absolutely not," I said and pulled out the stool for her to sit. "Please."

She set her purse on the counter and sat, and in a single swift motion, signaled the waiter for two of whatever I was having.

"Long day at the office?" I said.

"Long week," she said. "It might not seem like much when you come in, but we're constantly working on one thing or another. And Mr. Pearlman, a gentleman most of the time, can be quite curt when things get complicated."

"And all that just for old man Fleming?"

"One client," she said and nodded at the bartender who was setting down the drinks, one shot for her and another for me, and a little plate with more lime wedges and a little hill of coarse salt at the center.

She touched the rim of the shot glass with the tip of her fingers, studied it. "Yes," she said and held up her glass, "but Mr. Fleming does have a company and a foundation and a trust, all of which need constant attention."

I touched her glass with mine, making a dead clink. Then she said, "Well, here goes."

"No, no," I said and put my drink down.

She frowned.

I placed my hand over hers holding the glass of tequila. Guided it back down on the counter. "Don't drink it like that. This is good stuff. You're not supposed to drink it in a shot."

"But that's how everyone drinks it."

I smiled. "Not everyone. Just take a sip. Enjoy."

"And the lime and salt?"

"You can follow with a bit of that if you like. Try and take in the flavor. It's an ancient Aztec drink. Respect it."

She gave me a look like I was nuts. Then she took a short sip of the Siete Leguas and smiled. She set it down, took a lime, and touched her lips with the lime.

"Good?"

She nodded and took another short sip and set the drink down. She licked the tip of her pinky, picked up a dab of salt by pressing it on the plate with her finger, and then placed it in her mouth—a very sexy move.

"So," she said and tossed her head to the side. "My understanding of all this is that Liam might've been murdered."

"It looks that way," I said. I had to keep things short, vague. I didn't know Vivian. And I didn't know her intentions. Why was she even here?

She lowered her head. "It's a shame."

"Yup."

"He was a great guy."

"A great guy with a few too many secrets." I leaned forward and looked into her big brown eyes. "How well did you know him?"

"We dated in college," she said. "But that was a while ago."

"Really, UF?"

She nodded. "I was pre-law, but after graduation I came to the realization that I couldn't afford law school. He set me up with this job."

"Is it okay?"

"The job?" She grabbed her glass of tequila with two dainty fingers and spoke while staring at the clear liquid. "It's a job. It pays well. And I'm learning."

"Saving for law school?"

She chuckled. "Not nearly enough."

"It ain't easy," I said.

She grinned. "No, it sure isn't." Then she took a long sip of the tequila, grimaced, her eyes slightly glassy, and laughed. "That's much better."

This was all terrific—but the warning lights were flashing all over inside my head. Everyone's a suspect. *Think clearly, Dexter, think clearly.*

"Tell me something," I said seriously. "Do you have any idea who might've wanted to hurt Liam?"

She stared at me for a moment, her eyes going far away and coming back. "No."

"Not from the college days?"

She shook her head. "Not that I can think of."

I leaned back on my stool, draped my arm over the backrest so I could get a better look at her. "And what about Jay—I mean Terrence Oliver?"

She smiled. "Terrence and Liam went to boarding school together. They both grew up hating their fathers. I know Liam did for sure. But I think with Terrence it was worse. He basically ran away, came to Sarasota. He's the one who convinced Liam to move down here."

"And Liam convinced you to move here."

She looked to the side; her eyes seemed to go far away. "I moved here when Mr. Pearlman offered me a job."

I sighed. "What can you tell me about Mrs. Fleming?"

"I never met her."

"Really?"

"I never met Mr. Fleming either. All I know about him is what Liam told me. He made him sound like a tyrant. But I guess I could also see Liam's prejudice because of the way Mr. Fleming treated him."

"And how was that?"

"Like property," she said quickly as if she'd been prepared to answer that question for a long time. "Did you know when Liam's mother died, he just told him over the phone. He didn't even fly him home for the funeral."

"Fleming told me."

Vivian glanced down at her drink. I studied the bottles lined along the back of the bar. Vivian coming here and talking about the case didn't seem like the natural progression of things. Even if she'd been a friend of Liam's. I glanced at my watch. It was just past six. Sure, maybe she'd just gotten off work and wanted a drink. But she'd walked straight up to where I sat. Too clean. She wanted to know what I knew.

I didn't have time to waste so I just came out with it. "Why are you here?"

"What?"

"Why are you here? Did Pearlman send you down here to see what I knew?"

"What? No. I just got off work. I wanted a drink."

"I'm serious, Vivian. All this secrecy is making me sick."

"I told you. I wanted a drink."

"Bullshit. You came right here and sat next to me—on purpose."

She drew back. "And what's wrong with that?"

"Something's going on that you're not telling me. You started on the subject of Liam. Why?"

"I thought we were having a conversation."

"Fine," I said and turned back to face the bar. I grabbed my little glass of tequila and took a long sip. I set it down, licked a wedge of lime. I could feel her eyes staring at me.

After a moment she said, "I'm sorry."

I took another short sip. No lime.

"Okay, you're right," she said. "You're absolutely right. I came down here because I wanted to know how things were going."

"Go on."

"Liam was a good friend. I cared deeply for him."

"You're not helping me, Vivian. I need to know everything."

She stared at me, her eyes a little wider. Her lower lip trembled slightly. She bit it, held it steady under her teeth.

"You can trust me," I said.

She sighed, looked past me. "About four months before Liam drowned, he met me outside the office and asked me to help him buy a house on Siesta Key."

"He needed money?"

She shook her head. "He wanted me to negotiate with the owner."

"Please," I said, "from the beginning. And in detail."

"This man inherited the house from his uncle. He was getting ready to sell—"

"Where? What man? Details, Vivian. Please."

She stopped, took a deep breath. "His name was George something. I forget. Liam approached him about buying his house on Beach Road. But there was another interested party."

"Who?"

"I don't know. All Liam told me was to keep in touch with this guy and keep offering more money."

"No limit?"

"Liam didn't say. He just wanted me to be in touch with the guy and if at any time he said he had a better offer, to take it up by a hundred grand."

"You meet the guy?"

"Once. We had lunch at the Old Salty Dog on the key. He was in his fifties. Nice guy but not from here. Apparently, his uncle died and left him the house and he was cleaning the place out, had a garage sale and was going to sell the house and go back to whatever town he'd come from in Massachusetts."

"And Liam won the bidding war."

Vivian chuckled. "He had unlimited funds."

"Courtesy of his father's guilt."

She nodded.

"What did he pay for it?"

"Three point three."

"Million?"

Vivian didn't seem fazed.

I said, "I could live on that for the rest of my life."

"He overpaid. But it's a beachfront house, around the corner from the Village. If he hadn't died, he'd make the money back eventually."

"But he died. Or was killed. And so was his business partner."

She shook her head. "When I heard he drowned, I just . . . I was in shock, in a total daze for days. I just couldn't believe it."

"And?"

"A week after Liam drowned, Mr. Pearlman asked me to get him information on three private detectives."

"What for?"

"I don't know. Or at least I didn't know it then. I gave him the information on three people."

"What came out of it?"

"I don't know."

"Did any of them come for an interview or look at the police report?"

"No. A couple of days later, you showed up. That's all I know."

"So you're just curious about what happened to your friend."

"Is that so hard to believe?"

"What happens to the company now that both Liam and Terrence are dead?"

"I don't know."

"Vivian . . ."

"I swear. I don't know anything about his company. He handled all that through a lawyer. Bidding on that house on Beach Road was the only time he asked me to do anything to help. And all I ever did was answer the phone and tell that guy we'd go a hundred grand higher."

"That guy. You didn't like him?"

She shrugged. "I felt he was taking advantage of Liam."

"You think maybe there wasn't another bidder?"

"I don't know. Maybe at first. But then he was just calling and saying the other interested party had made a better offer."

"And you did what Liam instructed."

She nodded. "I offered a hundred grand more. No questions."

I took a drink of tequila. I didn't see exactly how this could motivate someone to kill. I said, "And this was four months ago."

"About. Yeah, early April."

"I don't know," I said, "but it might be worth looking into."

Vivian nodded. "What about his so-called friends?"

I shook my head. "I've met most of them."

"That entourage of freaks that hung out at his house drinking and smoking dope. Some of those people looked pretty sketchy. Maybe he got in a fight with one of them."

"I don't see it," I said and took a sip of tequila, touched a lime wedge to my tongue. "When people lash out in anger, it's immediate. These murders had to be premeditated."

"What about Tessa Davidson?"

"What about her?"

"She was obsessed with him. Maybe—"

"No. She could never do it—" I caught myself being too quick to defend her. I added, "She would've needed help. And she seems pretty distraught over it."

Then my phone rang. John Blake.

"Okay," he said getting right down to business. "I got the goods you asked for."

"Talk to me."

"Terrence Oliver . . . wasn't he the guy that was just found off Blackburn Point?"

"The one and only," I said.

"Well, he's clean. Has a prior for possession of marijuana about seven years ago up in Gainesville. Pleaded no contest. Did community service."

"Sounds pretty innocent."

"Yeah, he does. But Keith Peterson doesn't come across as a guy you'd wanna hang out with. Guy's got two possessions with intent to sell."

"Pot?"

"Yeah. Got probation and community service."

"Not so bad," I said.

"Well, he also has a couple of domestic abuse calls, but no charges. Then three months ago his wife, who is now his ex-wife, took out a restraining order against him."

"Shit."

"He can't get near her. Or their kids."

"What?"

"They've got two boys, nine and twelve. Can't get within five hundred feet from them."

The hairs on the back of my neck stood up as the scene outside Liam's house played out inside my head: Keith telling me he'd been kayaking with his kids in Ten Thousand Islands. And he'd brought back the kayak. The missing kayak.

"Thanks, John. I owe you one."

"You don't want to hear about the other one?"

"Tessa?"

"Tessa Davidson: assault and battery in Longmont, Colorado, six years ago. Assault and battery in Sarasota."

"When in Sarasota?"

"November 9th of last year."

"What did she get?"

"Probation in Colorado. The one here was dismissed by the judge."

"Who was the plaintiff in Sarasota?"

"Guy named Lewis Stevenson."

"Who the fuck is that?"

"Don't know," John said. "You good?"

"Yeah. Thanks."

I hung up, stared at my drink, my mind reeling. At that moment, I had erased the fact that Keith had lied. I was just thinking of Tessa. What the hell?

Vivian laid her hand on my arm. "You okay?"

I blinked, came out of the trance. I took a generous last sip of tequila and waved my credit card at the bartender. "I gotta run."

CHAPTER 30

IT WAS GETTING late. Dark storm clouds moved from east to west. Another day, another storm. It all seemed to be moving toward Siesta Key.

My instinct was to go straight to the Old Salty Dog and face Tessa, see what she had to say about her obsession with Liam. Her jealousy. The two assault charges against her. Damn it all. She knew all the players. She was knee deep in it. And I was a fool for being blind to it.

But I convinced myself that my primary target was Keith Peterson. He lied to me. And he'd had the kayak. He was up to something, and I was going to get to the bottom of it once and for all.

On my way down to Turtle Beach, I called Detective Kendel, left a message: "I'm on my way to Turtle Beach. Keith Peterson gave me a false alibi when I asked him about Liam's death. And I'm pretty damn sure he's having an affair with Mrs. Fleming. And just in case you haven't figured this out yet, Liam Fleming and Terrence Oliver were partners in a real estate corporation called Beach City Holdings. They'd been buying distressed properties around the key and out in East County. Now they're both dead."

I skipped crossing on the north bridge to Siesta because I was way too tempted to stop by and face Tessa. Instead, I raced down the Trail and drove Tessa's Fiat over to the south bridge. My gut told me Keith killed Liam. And Terrence either knew this or was a part of it.

Then it went bad between Terrence and Keith. Or Keith and Tessa were in it together. It was a stretch, but I do have a paranoid mind when it comes to these things. Tessa was angry at Liam for using his friendships and acting like a beach bum when he was buying up property to develop the key. That could've been Keith's motive as well.

The parking lot at Turtle Beach was half empty. In the area reserved for trucks with trailers where the boat ramp was, I saw Keith's cream Toyota Land Cruiser, a trailer hitched to the back with two kayaks, two stand-up paddleboards, and a small surfboard.

I parked on the beach side, crossed the street and over the wood barricade to the Land Cruiser. The front windows were open. Keith wasn't around. I walked to the back of the truck, to the small boat trailer with a weird aluminum homemade rack welded on so a dozen kayaks or boards could be stacked one over the other.

The kayaks on the rack were simple plastic ones, nothing like the fancy one he'd dropped off at Liam's house the day I met him. The paddleboards were at the top of the rack—unattached. Two long paddles rested on top. The surfboard was at the bottom. It was dirty, like maybe it hadn't been used in a while.

I ran my hand over the surfboard and looked across the parking lot to the boat ramp. Maybe Keith was out on the lagoon or the Intracoastal, paddleboarding or leading a group on kayaks. When my hand reached to the back of the surfboard, I felt a bump. It was the place to attach the leash. It didn't have one.

I glanced at the paddleboard. It had a long coiled leash that looked like one of those old telephone chords. I walked slowly to the side of the SUV, peeked in the window. No leashes.

My heart raced. No. I told myself to chill. Anyone could have a surfboard without a leash. And if Liam and Jaybird had been killed by the same guy, there would have to be two leashes missing.

If—and that's a big if—Liam had been drowned in the same way as Jaybird. Besides, Keith, young and strong as he was, could not have managed it alone.

The rain was getting close. I could smell it coming from the south. I crossed the street, walked over to the beach side. It was almost empty. A few families with their colorful umbrellas were still holding out, getting the last few minutes of beach before the late afternoon downpour.

To my right, near the trailer park, a few couples were taking in the sunset, drinks in their hands. A man blew into a conch like a native calling his warriors. To my left, by the south end of Turtle Beach, a man was fishing alone. Another man was reeling in his gear trying to beat the rain that was now coming fast like a huge gray sheet, stretching south and west.

I made my way back to the Fiat, sat in the driver's seat, my eyes staring across the road at Keith's Land Cruiser. I told myself to be patient, not to jump the gun and go to the Old Salty Dog. Tessa was not going anywhere. And Keith had lied. Tessa had just kept her own secrets a secret. I couldn't blame her for that. We all had them.

The rain started with a drizzle, then intensified in a flash. In less than a minute, Turtle Beach was awash. It came down gray and hard, causing a racket on the roof of the little car.

The rain made me think of Zoe. She was born in late August. That month it rained more than it had rained all year. When Nancy went into labor, the drive to Sarasota Memorial was slow and difficult because of the flooded roads. It wasn't apocalyptic floods, the kind that washed away cars and inundated houses, but it caused huge problems: power outages, closed roads, events canceled, constant tornado warnings. And I was called in to work to help cover the storm.

I missed the birth.

I got to the hospital hours after the fact. And it was still raining when we brought that little peanut of a girl home the following evening. She was seven and a half pounds and all reddish and wrinkled. I'll never forget how she felt in my arms, light and soft, her head still covered in the hospital cap, her squinty eyes. And when I held her up to my face, I swear she smiled at me.

I took my phone out and dialed Zoe's mother in Texas. But she said Zoe was at her piano lessons, wouldn't be home for at least another hour. "And when she comes home, we're having dinner. I would rather you didn't call her then," she said in that rancorous tone that irritated me more than anything in the world.

I ended the call. The windows of the Fiat had fogged up. I wiped the windshield with my hand and looked out my side window. I wrote her name: Zoe: a big Z like Zorro and then an O with a happy face, a lowercase E.

After twenty minutes, the rain let up some. There was no movement out on the parking lot. All I could think of was that Keith was out there somewhere getting soaked. I adjusted my seat a little and thought of starting the engine and cranking the AC for a few minutes so I could cool off and defrost the windshield, when a white Maserati drove up.

It stopped in the middle of the road between the place where I was parked and Keith's truck. It just sat there idling for maybe a minute. Then the passenger door opened and Keith stepped out into the rain. The Maserati moved forward. Keith ran to his truck.

The Maserati did a U-turn outside my line of vision and drove past me on its way out, taking a left out of the parking lot and heading north on Midnight Pass Road.

Keith moved around his truck, rolling up all the windows. Then he paused, hopped over the wooden fence, and ran diagonally to my left.

I couldn't see where he went. Parked cars blocked my view. I stepped out of the Fiat. I could see the top of Keith's head. He was about twenty yards away, facing the passenger side of a red SUV or truck that was backed up into a parking spot.

I started walking slowly toward him.

Keith nodded, stepped back from the truck, and turned. He saw me, smiled, started toward me.

The truck started its engine, pulled out of the parking spot. It was a red pickup, right side scratched and dented from the front wheel passenger door—the truck that ran me off the road.

The passenger saw me—probably recognized me, because a second later, the truck spun its wheels on the wet asphalt toward the exit.

I ran back to the Fiat, got in. I sped out, the little tires spinning, the car fishtailing almost all the way across the road to the other parking lot.

I stabilized the car, sped forward. But Keith stood in the middle of the road with his arms out. I slammed on the brakes. The car skidded a few feet, stopped inches from him.

I hopped out. "What the fuck, Keith?"

"What's going on, brah?"

I waved toward Midnight Pass Road. "That asshole crashed my car the other night. Almost got me killed."

He turned to look, but the truck was gone.

"What's going on?" I said.

Keith pointed at me, smiled like a clown, forced a laugh. "They're cool."

"Why'd you lie, Keith?"

The rain kept coming down, only lighter. He licked his lips and looked left and right like he was lost. "What're you talking about, brah?"

"You weren't in Ten Thousand Islands with your kids."

"What the fuck?"

"I know about the restraining order."

His face tensed, jaw clenched. The rain pelted down, lightning flashed north of us. He turned quickly and started toward his truck.

I followed. "And that was Mrs. Fleming dropping you off—"

He hopped over the low barricade and got into his Land Cruiser.

"Keith, don't. The cops are on their way."

He started the engine and gave me a look, his eyes wide and wild with panic. Then he sped in a circle, the back of the truck skidding, the trailer fishtailing. The two paddleboards flew off as he raced out of the parking lot.

I ran to the Fiat and followed.

He took the stop sign and turned, screeching and skidding—north on Midnight Pass.

I floored it.

Within seconds we hit seventy on that narrow road. I kept on his tail. The trailer bounced around up and down, left to right, the tires picking up a cloud of rainwater from the road, blinding me.

I fell back a little, putting some space between us as we approached the Crescent business district near Stickney Point.

Keith's Land Cruiser swerved left, passed a Hyundai going the speed limit on the right. He bumped the curb at the median as he came to the intersection. The Land Cruiser skidded left. Then right. The trailer hit the curb hard, went airborne. The Land Cruiser made a one-eighty. The trailer fell over.

I slowed down.

Keith never stopped. He kept the wheels spinning, turned the Land Cruiser around, and took a right onto Stickney Point—the south bridge—dragging the trailer on its side. Traffic on the opposite side of Midnight Pass stopped despite the green light.

I followed. The lights of the drawbridge were flashing. The traffic barrier was down. The bridge was going up. Two cars were stopped in the right lane. The left lane was free.

Keith gunned it, dragging the trailer on its side.

I thought he was going to try and jump the opening of the bridge like in the movies. Crazy. But he slammed on the brakes, skidded. The Land Cruiser hydroplaned sideways, hit the median and bounced back and smashed against a car in the right lane.

I pulled over, hopped out, and ran. Keith stepped out, glanced back in my direction, sprinted to the side of the bridge—stopped—looked down the bridge. It wasn't a long fall. He could jump, swim to shore. Run. We'd catch him eventually.

"Keith!" I was about thirty feet away. An older man who had been driving the car Keith hit had stepped out of his car, dazed.

"Why'd you kill them?" I yelled. I was twenty yards away, walking fast, my phone at my ear, telling the 911 dispatcher what was happening.

At ten feet, I stopped.

"What're you talking about?" he yelled.

"Liam and Terrence—Jaybird. Why'd you kill them?"

He forced a laugh, shook his head. "I didn't kill anyone."

"Was it because of Mrs. Fleming?"

"I didn't kill them," he cried. "They were my friends."

"Who are those guys in the pickup? I saw you talking to them."

He looked to the side. The bridge was up all the way. The mast of a tall sailboat was just starting to pass under the bridge.

"Talk to me, Keith."

His face was twisted, his shoulders folded forward. "I swear I didn't kill them."

I took two steps forward. "What happened?"

"I don't know." His surfer drawl was gone. A small crowd had gathered behind me and to the side.

"If you talk to the cops, they'll go easy on you. They'll be cool. I'll help you in any way I can."

He tilted his head to the side. The rain that had been falling lightly came back harder. Keith looked up and raised his hands, palms up like Jesus. He chuckled. "What a bitch, huh?"

The sailboat passed. The bridge was starting to come down. I took another step.

"My kids," he cried. "I was doing it for them."

"Doing what?"

He turned and sat on the rail, stared at the ground. "They're my kids, too," he said, his voice low, angry. "I know I have problems. But it's not right. I love my boys."

"I know how you feel," I said, my voice quivering as I thought of Zoe. "I have a seven-year-old. I only get to see her a couple of weeks in the summer. But it's better than nothing."

The clinking bell of the bridge broke the moment as the bridge closed and the barriers began to rise.

Keith looked away at the other side of the bridge. The blue and red flash of the cops came and went with the sheets of rain. "I was doing it for the money." His tone was steady. "So I could pay a lawyer and fix it. Get my kids back."

"What about Mrs. Fleming?"

He turned to look at me and pursed his lips. "That just happened."

"What just happened?"

"The affair." The cars moved slowly, crossing the bridge heading west to the beach. Our lane, heading east, was blocked by the accident. Someone at the very back honked. "We met at the beach one day and kinda hit it off, just kinda happened. I didn't know who she was."

"What about those men in the truck?" I said.

Keith shook his head. The rain let up some. I came to his side.

"Keith, they tried to run me off the road," I said quietly. "Who are they?"

"Dealers," he said flatly.

"Weed?"

"Pills. Oxycodone, Fentanyl."

"But why?"

He dropped his head in hands and wept, shook his head. "They weren't for her. She said they were for a friend with a back problem."

"Who said that?"

"Brandy."

The Sheriff's deputies reached us. One placed his hand on Keith's shoulder. "You hurt? Do you need an ambulance?"

Another one stood back, talking into his radio on his shoulder. I stood. "Call Detective Kendel. He has to be in on this."

"Who was driving the Land Cruiser?"

CHAPTER 31

KEITH HAD CONFESSED nothing. But the Sheriff's deputies cuffed him and put him in the back seat of a cruiser. I got back in Tessa's little Fiat and went straight to the Old Salty Dog.

The usual crowd of scruffy drunks and sunburnt tourists who sipped Bud Lites and tall fruity drinks with fancy garnishes stared at me as I marched up the steps to the bar. Everyone—except the older man with the messy gray hair and long goatee, a pint of Guinness in front of him. Cap'n Cody.

"Dexter!" Tessa cried and covered her mouth. "You're soaked."

I took a stool next to Cap'n Cody. Tessa grabbed a stack of paper towels and set them on the bar in front of me. "You look like shit."

"The cops busted Keith," I said point blank. I wanted to see her reaction, see if she was in on whatever Keith was in on. Pills. Affairs. Murder?

She just stepped back and looked a little stunned. "What for?"

"I think he killed Liam," I said.

Her expression didn't change.

Cap'n Cody leaned forward, touched my arm. "Did you know Jaybird was Terrence Oliver?"

"I found out this morning," I said.

"Unbelievable shit," he said and shook his head. "All these years. Little guy goes around like a bum. I just can't . . ."

"You're not playing tonight?" I asked.

He dismissed me with a wave. "They're filming that damn reality show at the Oyster Bar. Brought their own musicians."

Tessa forced a chuckle. "Cap'n Cody's music isn't hip enough."

He slapped his chest. "MTV ain't even about music no more."

I dismissed him and looked at Tessa. "Keith wasn't acting alone."

Her mouth twitched just slightly. "Who else?"

"I don't know," I said. "But it's in the hands of the authorities now."

She came out from around the bar and put her arms around me, held me. I could feel her heart beating hard against my chest. Cap'n Cody and the two drunks were staring at our little soap opera.

When she released me, she held me at arm's length, studied me, her eyes traveling from my chest to the top of my head and back. She had tears in her eyes but she didn't let them out.

"I'm off," Cap'n Cody said and set a ten-dollar bill on the counter. He slid off his stool and walked out.

Tessa smiled at him. Then she looked back at me, her lower lip trembling. "You're soaked."

"Yeah, it's pouring outside."

She went behind the bar and came back to where I was and handed me her house keys. "Why don't you go to my place and dry up?"

I looked past her at the taps. Handed her the keys to her Fiat. "Can I have a pint of that JDub's IPA first?"

She cracked a smile. "You'll never change, Dexter Vega."

After I downed a pint to settle my nerves, I took Tessa up on her invitation and walked out of the Old Salty Dog and headed toward the beach. I was confused about Keith. So he was having an affair with Brandy Fleming. Fine. But he was dealing drugs— or just getting them for Brandy. Still, I couldn't see her as a pill popper. She was too . . . uptight, angry. Fentanyl and oxycodone.

Opioids knocked you out, numbed your body, mind, and soul. They were addictive and dangerous. The piece didn't fit the puzzle. I didn't see how it could get Liam and Jaybird murdered.

Outside it had stopped raining. The key was back in party mode. Tourists dressed in bright t-shirts, shorts, thin minidresses and flip-flops made their way along the sidewalks, shuffling out of one bar and going into another.

Across Ocean Boulevard I could see the lights of the MTV crew filming the Siesta Key reality series. I kept going, curious to see the spectacle. The crew's truck blocked my view. A large crowd packed Siesta Key Oyster Bar. A band was playing an older U2 song. People stopped to watch, but the cops working security moved them on. Just past the trucks, outside the Daiquiri Deck, I saw Cap'n Cody walking with a man in a beige suit. Cap'n Cody was waving his hands in front of him, probably complaining about his gig being canceled because of the MTV guys.

When I got to Tessa's apartment, I took a hot shower and dried off. I found a pink and yellow terrycloth robe that was a little too small for me and put it on. I went into the kitchen, made myself a sandwich, and grabbed a cold Corona from the fridge. I sat in the living room and ate and drank and tried to put the pieces of the puzzle together.

But it wasn't easy. I kept thinking of Keith and his kids. I had a good idea of what he was going through. Maybe he was being screwed in the divorce, didn't deserve to lose his kids. But maybe he was an abusive husband, a bad father. Shit. He was sleeping with Brandy Fleming and buying drugs.

People dig their own damn graves.

So why did I feel so guilty about his arrest?

Divorce. When Nancy told me she wanted a divorce, it didn't come as a real surprise. We had lost the connection we'd once had.

We'd become different people. I was obsessed with work and she was trying to build a family. I understood that now. But when it's happening, when the world you love crumbles before your eyes, you don't see it. I couldn't see it then. Instead I felt attacked, pounced upon by her accusations and her complaints. Then came the lawyers. And with them came the poison that still lingered in our bloodstream.

But in the end, she was right. I was selfish. All I cared about was my stories, the newspaper. Only now I wished we could reconcile enough to be civil to each other for Zoe's sake.

Maybe I saw that in Keith. His world had been turned upside down with the divorce and the loss of his boys. He needed money for a lawyer to fight the restraining order, get partial custody. But what did any of that have to do with killing Liam and Jaybird?

* * *

I woke up to the sound of a door closing. I sat up. The room was bright. In my hand was an empty Corona bottle. Across from the coffee table was the reflection of the lights of Siesta Village against the dark buildings that blocked the view of the ocean.

"Hey." Tessa's sweet voice sailed gently across the room. She looked tired, her hair a little disheveled but still holding shape, her lips moist. I could tell from the redness of her eyes and the slight puffiness around them that she'd been crying.

"You okay?" I said.

She nodded and sat beside me. Then she grabbed the empty from my hand and held it up. "Really?"

"I was thirsty."

"Did you eat something?"

"I made a sandwich."

She placed the bottle on the side table and leaned back on the sofa, flipped off her shoes, and crossed her legs, her feet up on the coffee table. "I can't seem to wrap my brain around this."

"Neither can I."

She dropped her hand and took the cord of the bathrobe between her fingers and twisted it, coiling and uncoiling it over and over.

"Did you get a chance to make that list?" I said after a while.

"Yup." She bounced back up and went into her bedroom, took a while coming out. She'd changed into a pair of pajama pants and a t-shirt, wore her hair down. Her laptop was in her hands. She sat next to me again and set the computer on her lap. We both leaned forward as she clicked open a Word doc.

She pointed to the screen. "So these are the three latest properties."

Two small parcels in East County and the house on Beach Road at the end of April.

"Vivian said Liam hired her to bid on this property."

Tessa recoiled in her seat. "Vivian McCutcheon?"

"Yeah, Pearlman's assistant."

"That woman was obsessed with Liam."

I smiled. "That's what she said about you."

Tessa set the computer on the coffee table, leaned back, looking at me. "What else did she say?"

"That's all. But she said Liam asked her to outbid whoever was trying to buy that house." I pointed at the computer.

"Whatever." Tessa waved. "I guess it doesn't matter."

"What?"

"Nothing."

"Tessa . . ."

"She was Liam's ex from college. She was jealous of me. Until I broke it off with Liam."

"Jealous enough to be violent?" I said. I hadn't even considered Vivian as a suspect. But . . .

"I don't think so," Tessa said with a short smile. "Besides, I know how to take care of myself."

I was thinking of the assault and battery charges, but I had to be careful. I said, "Do tell."

"There's nothing to tell."

"You like a karate expert?"

She tilted her head to the side. "I've been in a couple of bad relationships. With . . . abusive guys."

"Liam wasn't like that, was he?"

"No! Absolutely not. He was perfect."

"Yet you broke it off."

"I told you. He lied to me. I couldn't trust him. He was a hypocrite. Said one thing and did the other. I can't stand that."

"And Vivian?"

Tessa shrugged. "She used to come to the beach and hang out with us. But it was obvious it wasn't her scene. She didn't like the whole Bohemian lifestyle. She used to lecture Liam about it. I used to think his father had put her up to it, you know? To get him away from us."

"You think he did?"

She shook her head, picked up the computer, and tapped the space bar to wake it up. "She's just a sad, lonely girl."

"And you don't think she could've killed Liam and Jaybird?"

"No, she wasn't a psycho. She was just . . . alone."

We sat quietly for a long time, just the bass coming from a speaker somewhere far away—the MTV show.

"This town is growing too fast," I said.

"Why do you say that?"

"The building boom, the TV show, Number One Beach. All this attention is killing paradise."

"It's not so bad."

"But it's starting," I said. "And this business of closing Beach Road. I don't know what Liam and Jaybird were planning, but they were probably going to build something big and expensive and get very rich."

"You can't stop progress," she said.

I wasn't so sure. I glanced at the computer screen. "So who owns the third house on Beach Road?"

Tessa scrolled down. Stopped, pointed at the information: *Dieter & Waxler.*

CHAPTER 32

MY CELL PHONE woke me up. I was lying in Tessa's bed. The place smelled of perfume, something nice and slightly sweet. I was naked. I wrapped the sheet around my waist and followed the ringing to the table by the closet.

Too late.

A few seconds later, the voice mail sound chimed. *Mr. Vega, this is Joaquin del Pino returning your call regarding Beach City Holdings. I'm about to walk into court and should be out in a couple of hours. I'll try you back then.*

I dialed him right back. It went to voice mail. I hung up.

I heard movement in the apartment, glass against glass, flatware against flatware, steps. In the alley, a trash truck was backing up and the intermittent beeping sound bounced all over the apartment. *Siesta Key,* I thought. *A nice, peaceful little island.*

The robe I had worn the previous night was on the floor. I put it on and went to the bathroom and focused on last night. I had not been able to determine who was lying, Vivian or Tessa. Or maybe both women were right. They both loved Liam Fleming. But Tessa had pretty much fallen off my suspect list. In her own way, she had confessed that she'd defended herself against a couple of creeps. It explained the assault and battery charges. Vivian, I knew nothing about. But if she was involved, someone else had to be, too. I couldn't see her killing two grown men, especially Liam, who was athletic. She would've needed help.

Then there was the third property on Beach Road owned by Dieter & Waxler. It was just coincidence that the same company that was building a nine-story condo next to my little cracker house downtown owned the house on Beach Road.

When Tessa and I looked at a map, the layout on Beach Road was this: Dieter & Waxler owned the first house on the corner. Beach City Holdings owned the other two. The property Vivian had been in charge of bidding on—and the one with the most recent transaction date—was the one in the center.

I had a very strong hunch the other bidder had been Dieter & Waxler.

We looked up Dieter & Waxler on both Corporationwiki, a website with a ton of corporate information, as well as in the State of Florida Division of Corporations website. But we came up empty. We figured the company was not incorporated in Florida—nothing wrong with that.

What we did find was an office for The Majestic and Alex Trainor. They were conveniently located at One Sarasota Tower, that glass monstrosity across from the new Westin.

I walked out to the living room and found Tessa in the kitchen. She wore a very sexy purple nightgown that hung on her shoulders and breasts and came halfway down her thighs.

"Good morning," she said with a quick smile. "Coffee?"

I nodded and stood leaning against the counter across from her.

"Cream and sugar?"

"Black, thanks."

She placed the cup on the counter in front of me, grabbed her own cup, and brought it to her lips, never taking her eyes off me.

I took a sip and set the cup down. "So," I said. "Did we?"

She shook her head and hid her smile. "No, but we fell asleep in each other's arms."

"For real?"

"What, you find that difficult to believe?"

"No, I just . . . I didn't know."

"It was a pretty intense night," she said.

"And we were both very tired, right?"

* * *

After an amazing breakfast of pancakes and eggs and freshly squeezed orange juice, I got dressed. Tessa had thrown my clothes in the dryer for me. They smelled nice, too. I had to get my car out of the pound, but the case took priority. I left in Tessa's Fiat for the mainland and the offices of Alex Trainor.

I parked on the street at the end of Palm Avenue behind One Sarasota Tower and took the elevator to the fifth floor. The offices were in a suite at the very end of the hall. A sign with the fancy cursive logo for The Majestic was glued to the wall. The door was locked.

I knocked, looked around. There were three other doors in that part of the hall, but they each had their own signs. One was for a financial advisor, the other for an estate attorney, and the other said, *Agency Travel*, whatever that meant.

I knocked again. Didn't even hear a sound. I turned to go. Then the elevator at the end of the hallway dinged and a crew of four men in jeans, work shirts with name patches, and boots came marching toward me.

One of them used a key to open the door to Trainor's office. He let the others in, then looked at me. "Can I help you?"

"I was looking for Mr. Trainor," I said.

"Canceled his lease," the man said and walked into the office.

I followed. The place was nice: small waiting room with an Eames-style faux-leather couch and a small reception desk. The walls had large architectural renderings of what I assumed were future projects—including the ugly modern nine-story tower that was re-placing the small 1920 bungalow in my neighborhood downtown.

Other than that, the place was empty. No receptionist or secre-tary. I picked up a *Sarasota City Magazine* from a side table. It was four months old. The men had gone into a different office. I peeked inside. It was empty. No furniture, no papers, nothing on the walls.

"Any of you guys know Dieter and Waxler?" I asked.

They ignored me, but the man with the keys shook his head. "Not in this building."

"How long has Trainor been here?" I said.

"Who's Trainor?"

"The guy that rented this office. You just told me he canceled his lease."

The man with the keys glanced at one of his friends and they both shrugged. "Didn't know the guy's name," he said and nodded at his friend. "What was it, like ten months?"

"Something like that."

"You know where they're moving?" I asked.

"Beats the hell out of me. We just clear the space for the next tenant."

I gave the place another look-over, but there was nothing in the office or in the reception that gave me any ideas or leads. The recep-tion looked legit. Like the kind of place people came to be treated well while they were being sold a million-dollar condo.

I left the office and walked a couple of blocks to Main Street and went up to Mr. Pearlman's office in the Orange Blossom building.

"Dexter!" Vivian seemed genuinely surprised to see me. "What are you doing here?"

"I need your help."

"You mean Mr. Pearlman's?"

"No," I said. "I need to get in touch with the man who sold Liam the property on Beach Road."

"I don't have his contact information."

"You can get his name from the County Appraisers website. Look up the property address. There's a record for previous owners. I need you to find his phone number."

"But I have work and—"

"Take twenty minutes off your busy schedule and do this for me," I said and wrote my number down on a Post-It on her desk. "I need to know who was doing the bidding for the other side."

"Does this have to do with Liam's death?"

"I'm not one hundred percent," I said quickly. "I have a feeling it was Dieter & Waxler. And I think they might be in cahoots with one of our county commissioners."

CHAPTER 33

I HEADED BACK to Siesta Key. Bob Fleming hadn't hired me to spy on Brandy Fleming. And whatever was going on between her and Keith Peterson was really none of my business. It was the pills. True, I didn't like Brandy Fleming. She seemed like a real opportunist. And she was aggressive enough that she was probably pulling Keith's strings. She certainly wielded her power around like the world owed her a favor. I could see her manipulating Keith into killing Liam. But why?

The pills. Opioids were highly addictive. And addicts would do anything for a fix—even kill.

The guard at the gate of the Sanderling let me through without calling it in. Maybe my name was on a list. Maybe he was busy watching TV. I passed a nanny pushing a stroller and an elderly couple walking together in matching exercise suits and neon-colored tennis shoes. I made the curve. From here I could see the ocean in its infinite blue. The people of Sanderling had what the county was trying to take away from the rest of us: a nice stretch of beach and an unobstructed view of the ocean. They would never have to deal with condos or county commissioners stealing their slice of paradise.

I pulled up beside the white Maserati. The car was sparkling clean. As I walked past, I touched the rear of the car. It had just been waxed.

I rang the doorbell. Mrs. Fleming answered immediately—opened the door a quarter of the way and stepped out, pushing me back with her perfectly manicured hand and shutting the door behind her.

"Now you listen to me," she said quickly, her voice low, the tone just this side of aggressive, "my husband is not well. I don't want you riling him up in any way. You understand me?"

I stared at her dark almond eyes. Somewhere in there lurked a deadly poison. It angered me. "Don't sweat it, lady. I'm here to talk about Liam, which is what he hired me to do."

She grabbed my arm, her artificial fingernails digging into my skin. "I'm warning you. One word about me and Keith and you're gone."

I smiled, teeth clenched. I imagined her conversation with Keith. I could see them sitting in the cockpit of the Maserati in the pouring rain, barking at each other like a pair of desperate teenagers caught in the act. Keith freaking out about me knowing what was going on between them. Brandy Fleming ordering him to be cool, act it out. Only she didn't know Keith came clean about the pills. He'd said she said they were for a friend—the oldest lie in the book.

Mrs. Fleming held my stare for a moment. Then she released my arm, turned on her heels, and opened the door.

She walked ahead of me into the living room. She sauntered around a chair, glared at me as she opened one of the French doors that led to the covered patio. "Darling," she sang out in a friendly Donna Reed tone, "your detective's here."

Bob Fleming was sitting in a teak Adirondack chair facing the pool and the Gulf of Mexico.

Mrs. Fleming didn't wait for me. She shifted her weight to one leg for just a second, like a model striking a pose, then walked away, disappearing somewhere in the house.

I stepped out and closed the door behind me to keep the AC from escaping out of the house—force of habit.

Fleming leaned his head back a little to face me, but his eyes seemed far away. "Vega," he mumbled, "come in. Tom Pearlman called last night . . . said that . . . said you stopped by his place."

I came around, offered him my hand. He didn't take it. He just gave a tired nod to the matching Adirondack chair to his left. "Sit down."

I pulled the chair and turned it at an angle so we could see each other.

Bob Fleming looked at me and raised his glass. "Like a drink?"

"I'm fine, thank you."

He turned and faced the Gulf again, pointed at it with his glass. "Is a nice view, isn't it?" He slurred. I figured the man had probably been drinking all morning.

"Indeed. A real money view."

He chuckled. "Whattaya mean by that?"

"A view of the ocean doesn't come cheap."

He laughed and it turned into a cough. He wiped his mouth with the back of his hand and nodded. "That's the truth alright."

"I wanted to tell you about Liam," I said.

"I was hoping for that. Tom said you were full of questions."

"Well, your suspicions were correct."

He didn't flinch or change expression. He just stared out at the ocean as if all was fine with the world. Then he raised his glass and twirled it over the armrest and set it back down without taking a drink. His eyes narrowed to a squint. "What happened?"

"He was drowned. Someone also drowned his partner, Terrence Oliver."

"Terr . . . Oliver . . . I saw that in the news. That was his partner?"

"Yes. The two of them owned Beach City Holdings."

"You have any idea who . . . did it?"

"I'm not sure," I said. "But there is something I think you need to know."

His head bobbed and he turned, his squinty eyes trying to focus on me. He seemed wasted. Like he was there but not there.

"Are you okay?" I said.

"Tell me about Liam."

"I think I better tell you about Keith."

"Who's that?"

"He's one of Liam's beach friends. And . . . he seems to be involved with your wife . . ."

"Tom told me last night," he said and stared out at the Gulf. I figured that's why he was so drunk.

"Yes," I said. "I'm sorry. But it appears Keith is also supplying pills to your wife."

"What does it have to do with Liam?" he said half mumbling but in a loud voice, his face turning crimson.

"I'm sorry."

Fleming drew in a long, deep breath. "Why?"

"Why what?" I said.

"Why did he kill Liam?"

"No." I shook my head. "I don't know that he did. I just think there's more going on between Keith and your wife than you think."

"I don't think so," he barked, then he huffed and took a long sip of his drink. He set the glass back down on the armrest and opened his mouth to say something when the doorbell rang.

He turned slightly as if to look behind him, but he couldn't turn all the way. I did the same. Across the living room in the foyer, Brandy Fleming stood with the door slightly ajar.

"Who's it?" Fleming slurred.

My phone vibrated with a text. I pulled it out and glanced at it. It was from Vivian: *Guy's name is George Finney,* followed by the number.

The front door opened wider. Brandy Fleming turned and stormed across the living room. "Bob!" she yelled, her arms swinging. "Bob, call Pearlman this instant!"

Detective Fenton Kendel and two Sheriff's deputies walked slowly into the house looking around like they were admiring the decorations.

Kendel's eyes followed Brandy Fleming to the patio. Then his eyes fell on me. He pushed the front of his pork pie hat up on his brow and frowned.

I smiled.

He made a quick gesture with his right hand to the two deputies and the three of them followed Brandy Fleming to the patio where she was holding a portable telephone receiver out to Bob Fleming.

"It's the police," she snarled in that nasty tone of hers. "Do something, Bob. For God's sake!"

Bob Fleming pushed himself up off the chair with difficulty. He shifted as if he might fall, then regained his balance just as Detective Kendel joined us on the patio. The two deputies stayed behind him like a couple of well-trained dogs, hands resting on their belts.

"What's this," Bob Fleming barked with surprising authority. His face was crimson, his jowls shaking as he jerked his head at Kendel. "What's the meaning of this . . . this . . .?"

Kendel ran his hand over his handlebar mustache and offered a folded paper to Mr. Fleming. "We have a warrant for the arrest of Brandy Fleming."

For a moment, Fleming seemed suspended in air, frozen like he hadn't understood Kendel's words. Then he blinked. The red color drained from his face. He shook his head and his hands trembled. I thought he was going to fall back, but instead he stepped forward and ripped the paper away from Kendel's hand.

Brandy Fleming took cover behind her husband, perched her hands on his shoulders, looked over him as he unfolded the paper and read the warrant.

"I don't understand," he muttered and grabbed the phone from his wife. "What's the charge here?"

It was as if he'd said it without expecting an answer. He was already dialing the phone when Kendel said, "Trafficking in illegal drugs."

"You're crazy!" Brandy screamed at Kendel. "I don't do drugs."

"Keith Peterson says otherwise," Kendel said. "We also have a search warrant and—"

"You go to hell!" Brandy spat.

Fleming didn't look up. I couldn't tell if he'd even heard what Kendel had said. He finished dialing and placed the phone to the side of his face. "Tom. I have the police here with a warrant for Brandy's arrest."

Kendel looked past the Flemings and locked eyes with me. "What the hell are you doing here, Vega?"

That's when it hit me about Bob Fleming and that mighty powerful vodka he offered me the other day. That's why he was so out of his head. Maybe even why he drank.

"Check the Grey Goose," I said.

"What goose?" Kendel said.

"The vodka," I said and pointed at Bob Fleming's drink. "She's putting it in his vodka."

For an instant, all we could hear were the waves lapping in the ocean. A seagull. All eyes focused on the drink sitting on the armrest of the Adirondack chair. Then Brandy swung her arm and flicked the glass off the chair. It sailed between Fleming and Kendel and crashed into pieces against the pool deck.

Fleming lowered the phone from his ear and turned to his wife. "Brandy . . ."

"What?" Brandy Fleming screamed and waved a finger violently at Fleming, at Kendel. "I had nothing to do with it. It was Keith. I never—I never."

"Mr. Peterson says different," Kendel said.

Brandy Fleming grabbed her husband's arm with both hands and spoke over his shoulder. "It's a lie, Bob. I swear, it's a lie. I didn't do anything. Please make them go away."

Bob Fleming's whole face seemed to sag. Color came back to his flesh. But he looked different, older. "Tom said you better go with them."

"What the fuck?" she cried, the Jerry Springer coming out of her like spit. "This is bullshit, Bob. I didn't do anything."

"Tom's on his way downtown," Fleming said, his tone steady. "We'll sort it out there."

"No!" Brandy Fleming yelled and stepped back but still held on to her husband's arm like a lifeline. "Don't let them do this, Bob. Help me. Stop them!"

Fleming stepped to the side. One of the deputies moved past Kendel and Fleming and grabbed Brandy by the arm.

She flailed and slapped at him, her manicured nails scratching. "Get the fuck away from me, you creep. I'll fucking sue your ass. Get off me!"

But the officer managed her like a pro, twisted her arm so she was forced to turn her back to him, held both her wrists, staying in control as he gave her the Miranda rights.

Bob Fleming hung his head and watched his wife lose whatever little dignity she had left.

"No!" She shoved shoulders, tried kicking the officer. "No, no. Bob, do something, you impotent fool. Stop them!"

I tapped Kendel's arm. "You got anything on Terrence Oliver's murder?"

Kendel pushed his glasses up on his nose. "Why should I tell you?"

"Hey," I said. "I told you about the laced vodka."

"Yeah, thanks."

"Come on, Kendel."

He didn't answer but motioned for the other detective to move back into the living room.

The deputy that had cuffed Brandy turned her around. She spat at his face. He held her with one hand while he wiped the side of his face on his shoulder. Bob Fleming watched the whole thing without expression—just blank like when he was looking out at the Gulf—stoned on fentanyl or oxycodone.

The officer led Brandy Fleming past us, through the door, where he joined the other deputy in the living room.

Kendel nodded at me and Mr. Fleming. "Let's take a look at that vodka."

The two deputies made their way across the living room and out of the house with Brandy Fleming in handcuffs. Kendel and I went to the bar in the small section between the living room and the dining room. I pointed to the big bottle of Grey Goose.

Kendel opened the bottle and sniffed it. "How'd you know about the vodka?"

"He gave me a drink the other day," I said. "I took two sips and it knocked the hell out of me."

"Really?"

"I just now figured it out." I looked back at the patio. Bob Fleming was back in his chair, his head resting on his hand. Alone.

"You got any idea why she was doping the old guy?" Kendel asked.

"No idea," I said, but I did have a suspicion that what Brandy Fleming was after was control. Keeping Bob Fleming addicted and under the influence would give her the run of the house—and the finances. But that was me. And I had no proof of any of it. And it wasn't my job. I was fishing for a different criminal.

I said, "You gonna give me something on Terrence Oliver or what?"

Kendel took a deep breath. "We ain't got much. But I did reopen Liam Fleming's case. Both men owned a company that invested in real estate. They lived in the same house. Both were drowned less than a couple miles from each other."

"That's what I've been trying to tell you."

He grinned. "Oliver had a serious contusion on the side of the head. Obviously knocked out, then drowned. I've got the medical examiner goin' over Liam's case again, see if there was anything we missed."

"Any chance Mrs. Fleming and Keith Peterson were involved?"

Kendel shrugged. "We'll find out soon enough." Then he waved to a group of deputies who'd come in with a couple Pelican cases full of gear. Kendel offered the bottle of Grey Goose to the crime scene investigators. "Bag this one and any others like it. And check the inside of that little sports car out front."

CHAPTER 34

KENDEL MADE IT obvious he wanted me out of the way. And I was of no use to him or anyone there. The way I saw it, the question was whether Brandy Fleming was drugging her husband before or after Liam's death. If it was before, I figured Liam could've found out and threatened her with going to the cops. If it was after, all I could imagine was that she was trying to take over.

I knew I was grabbing for straws. Brandy could've been jealous of Liam, or maybe she was so greedy she didn't want Bob Fleming bankrolling his kid's business. I just hoped Kendel would figure it out. I was hired by Fleming to find out if his son's death was an accident or a murder. Nowhere in our conversation did we agree that I was to find the murderer. He wanted closure. He was going to get it now. My job there was done.

I got in Tessa's Fiat. But before leaving the Sanderling for the Village, I had one final errand. I dialed the number for George Finney in Massachusetts. But before the call went through, I had another call coming in. It was a Sarasota number. Joaquin del Pino.

"Whatta you got?" I said. I knew lawyers. They hated wasting time unless they were getting paid.

"The properties are going into a trust," he said quickly. "With one exception."

"Don't tell me," I said. "The houses on Beach Road."

"No. A two-story, twelve-unit apartment on Calle Menorca."

"You serious?"

"Stamped and notarized," he said.

"Who's getting it?"

"Tessa Davidson."

I almost dropped the phone. I told myself I was jumping the gun. Yes, it gave Tessa motive. But she'd said she didn't know Beach City Holdings was Liam's company. If she was lying, she wouldn't be the first one.

When I got to the light at Midnight Pass and Beach Boulevard, just before the public beach, I dialed the Massachusetts number.

A kid answered the phone and told me to hold on. A moment later George Finney announced himself over the line.

"My name's Dexter Vega," I said. "I'm looking into the transactions of a company on Siesta Key that purchased a property from you in April."

"What are you talking about?" he said, getting defensive. "Everything was legal. Talk to my lawyer."

"Absolutely," I said quickly. I could feel he wanted to hang up. "There's nothing wrong. I'm just trying to find out who you negotiated with."

"The lawyer for Beach City Holdings."

"Joaquin del Pino?"

"Yeah, I think that's who. My lawyer handled all that."

"My understanding is there were two interested parties, is that right?"

"Yeah, that's right. Nothing wrong with that."

"Absolutely. I just wanted to know who was on the other side of the bidding war with Beach City Holdings?"

He chuckled. "I don't recall the name. Something with a W. Wesley or Wesleyan."

"Waxler?"

"Yeah, that's it. Something and Waxler."

"Dieter and Waxler," I said.

"That's them. The scruffy fella kept nagging me. Said he'd been friends with Uncle Frank. But that young lady with Beach City Holdings—"

"Vivian McCutcheon."

"Yeah, her. She was all class. Every time Waxler raised his offer, she countered with an even hundred K. No small talk."

"What about Waxler?"

"I'm sorry, not Waxler. The scruffy guy. Sings at one of the bars around the corner from the house."

"You mean Cap'n Cody?"

"Yeah." He laughed. "Cap'n Cody. He was all over the place. Like a character out of *Glengarry Glen Ross*. You know the play?"

"I know the movie."

"David Mamet," he said. "Guy's a freakin' genius."

"What do you mean by all over the place?"

"Desperate, you know? What happened was that the real estate guy, young man, what's his name, Trainor—"

"Alex Trainor."

"Yeah, yeah. I was getting ready to list the house, right? And that Cap'n Cody fella says he's got an interested party and says how I could save on paying commission to a real estate agent. Six percent on a two-three-million-dollar house ain't chump change, you know what I'm saying? So he introduces me to Trainor who made the original offer for Waxler."

"But there was Vivian."

"That's right." He laughed. "We had dinner at one of the places there and she said the company she worked for was interested in Frank's house. When I told her I was already talking to someone else, she said she wanted the opportunity to counteroffer. I hadn't signed a contract with Waxler, so we spent a couple of days going back and forth."

"Where did Cap'n Cody come in?"

"When Vivian countered with two point seven, Trainor went AWOL, and Cap'n Cody took over. But I could tell that wasn't his game."

"Why's that?"

"Too desperate. Kept giving me stories about how he grew up there, how I should make a moral decision and not be blinded by money, wanted to know who the other party was. Honestly, I didn't think he and Waxler could get the funds."

"Did you tell him?"

"Tell him what?"

"Who the other party was?"

"Yeah, why not?" he said. "You know, Uncle Frank bought that house a few years after the war. Paid like eleven grand for it. Who would've thought one day a couple of companies would be fighting to pay millions for it, hey?"

Those last words stayed with me like an ominous echo: *fighting to pay millions.*

There was no parking in front of the Old Salty Dog, and I had to circle around the block a few times. On my second pass, I found a tiny spot across the alley from the restaurant and tucked the Fiat into it without much difficulty. Nice little car.

I heard someone cuss across the alley, "Where the fuck are they?"

A silver Range Rover was parked on the other side of the dumpster. I made my way slowly across the street.

The driver's-side door of the Range Rover was open. A man was pulling at the driver's arm, cussing like a sailor.

The driver leaned back on the seat and kicked the man on the chest, throwing him back. His back hit the dumpster. It was Cap'n Cody.

I ran over to him just as the Range Rover pulled out, almost hitting me. Then I saw the bumper sticker: *Coexist*.

It was the same SUV I'd seen at Liam's place. I glanced at the driver. He was staring at me. I knew those eyes. But this time I recognized the face from the real estate ads: Alex J. Trainor.

The Range Rover spun its wheels on the gravel and took off away from Ocean Boulevard into the dark streets of the key.

I turned to go back to the Fiat then heard a noise, fabric moving. I stopped and turned, scanned the alley. Cap'n Cody was gone. I started again toward the Fiat when a violent blow smashed against the side of my head. My knees buckled. I dropped to the ground, body flat against the asphalt. I tried to push up, got a kick on my side, fell back down.

Before I could take another breath, Cap'n Cody was on top of me, pummeling my face and head with his fists. I covered my face with my arms but it didn't do any good. I got it hard all over—stars and more stars.

Then Cap'n Cody flew off me, fell to the side, landed beside me on his back, his eyes dazed, then shut, arms stretched out like Sonny Liston at the Central Maine Youth Center in 1965.

I turned to the side. At Cap'n Cody's feet, Felipe stood like Ali—only he was wearing an apron and holding a shovel in both hands. "You okay?" he said softly.

I shook my head, trying to pull out of the daze.

He dropped the shovel and knelt by my side.

"Thanks," I said and forced a smile. My head was pounding.

Felipe helped me up. I looked down at Cap'n Cody. He lay flat on his back on the asphalt, a small cut on his cheek. But I knew he'd come around soon. I fumbled in my pocket for my phone and called 911.

Felipe led me a few steps to the back door of the restaurant and sat me on the cinderblock that held the door open. "I get you some water," he said.

Before Felipe made it back, the blue and red of the Sheriff's deputy cruiser flashed all over the back alley. Two of them. Cap'n Cody was already moving, slowly, dazed. The deputies went to him.

Felipe came back with a glass of water. Tessa was behind him, her hand over her mouth. "Dexter, what happened?" Then she looked past me at the street. "Oh, my God, Cap'n Cody."

One of the deputies walked over to us. "What happened here?"

"Guy attacked me," I said and pointed to Cap'n Cody.

"Ambulance is on its way," he said and gestured to my face. I touched my cheek. Blood. I felt Tessa's hand on my shoulder.

"Call Detective Kendel," I said. "I think he needs to be in on this. And tell him Alex Trainor is involved."

"Who's that?" Tessa asked.

"Real estate guy. He was at Liam's place when I went there the first time. I'm pretty sure it was him who knocked me out that day." Then I nodded toward the road where the other deputy had Cap'n Cody sitting up. The ambulance was honking its horn a block or two away in the traffic of the Village. "I think these two killed Liam and Jaybird."

CHAPTER 35

THE FOLLOWING MORNING, I was woken from a deep sleep by an aggressive knock on the door. It was eight thirty a.m. I sat up in bed. My head and back ached. I touched my face, my cheek, felt the scar.

Then it came back to me: Cap'n Cody, the Range Rover, Alex Trainor, Felipe, the cops.

Kendel never showed up. We gave our statement to the deputies. Tessa didn't ask me to come home to her place. I didn't ask either. I gave her the keys to her Fiat and took an Uber back home.

Now I walked out in my pajama pants and no shirt to see who was trying to break down my door. I got a glimpse of dark green through one of the windows.

Still, I had to ask. "Who is it?"

"Mr. Vega?"

I stood at the door waiting, my hand on the latch. "Yeah, who is it?"

"The Sarasota Sheriff's Office."

I paused a moment, then threw the latch and pulled the door open. A Sheriff's deputy stood behind the screened door. He gave me a short grin. "Mr. Dexter Vega?"

I nodded and stepped aside. "Come in."

He stepped inside the house, didn't look around but turned to face me from inside the living room. "We need you to come downtown."

"What for?"

"We got the driver of the hit-and-run you were involved in—"

"I told you guys I was never on Fruitville Road that night."

"No, sir. I'm talking about the incident on Siesta Drive just before the bridge."

"The red pickup?"

"Yessir."

I made some coffee and the good deputy waited for me to put some clothes on and we drove to the station. For once I was in the front seat of a squad car. Nice.

I was escorted by the deputy right through the lobby and up the elevator to a small office that reminded me of the principal's office at my high school: puke-yellow walls, fat industrial desk, a short and uncomfortable vinyl couch, and an old map of Sarasota on the wall. On the desk was a big ceramic cup with the slogan: *World's Greatest Grandpa*.

The deputy left me alone in the office, and for a moment, I thought maybe it was a trick, that they were going to arrest me for something I didn't do—the fracas with Cap'n Cody. Or Brandy Fleming turned on me with her poison and convinced the authorities I was the one drugging Bob Fleming.

Detective Kendel walked in, gave me one of those smiles where only one side of his mouth turns up—a kind of you're-okay-but-not-really type of grin. Either way, I knew it couldn't be that bad.

"Vega," he said and tossed a couple of folders on the desk. He pushed his hat up and didn't offer his hand. Instead he went around to the other side of the desk and sat, leaned forward, gave me another half smile, and added, "You seem to be everywhere, son."

"That's how I roll," I said. "What's going on?"

Kendel leaned back and took a deep breath, ran his hand over his mustache. "This guy Peterson . . ."

"Yeah, Keith."

He nodded. "Guy's a real piece of work. Took a plea deal from the DA before we could even charge him."

"For his kids," I said.

"Apparently so."

"What's the deal with the guys in the pickup?" I asked.

"Dealers," he said. "Both of those jokers have records as long as my arm. Seems they were supplying Peterson and a whole lot of other people with pills and heroin."

"And Keith was supplying Mrs. Fleming who was doping her husband."

Kendel nodded, touched his glasses, and opened the folder on the top of the stack. "I guess them two thought you knew what was going on because of some conversation you had with Peterson at the beach a couple days back. So, they followed you that night and tried knocking you off. DA's talking attempted murder."

"Damn."

He raised his eyes from the papers and looked at me. "You deny they tried to kill you?"

"I can't assume their intentions."

"They ran you off the damn road," he huffed. "Right before the bridge on a rainy night. Ain't that right?"

"I guess it is . . ."

"Good," he said somewhat satisfied. "Now, Mrs. Fleming's probably gonna end up with a slap on the hand. But Peterson's another story. He's got priors. He's gonna see some time."

I felt bad for Keith. I didn't know him, but it just felt as if he'd been given a raw deal from the start. I latched onto the idea that he abused his wife and kids, that he was selling drugs. So he deserved it.

Still, I didn't like it.

Kendel looked at me and shuffled his papers, opened another folder, scanned it up and down, tossed it to the side. Then he leaned back on his chair and set his hands on the armrests. "Now, about last night at the Old Salty Dog. Care to tell me about it?"

"Do I need my lawyer present?"

He turned his hands palms up and frowned.

"I went there for a drink after I left Fleming's place. I parked in the back and I saw Cap'n Cody and Alex Trainor having an argument—"

"You know these guys?"

I shrugged. "It's a long story."

"I got four months 'til retirement," he said. "Why don't you start at the beginning?"

Against my better judgment, and the advice of Brian Farinas, I figured it was time to come clean. And Kendel was okay in my book. Maybe he was old and lazy because he was eyeing the rest of his life on a green manicured golf course, but he was a straight shooter. And I had nothing to feel guilty about. I'd done nothing.

"The day Fleming hired me to find out what happened to his son, I went to the cottage on Midnight Pass Road. There was a silver Range Rover parked in the driveway—"

"Plates?"

"I don't know. But it had one of those *Coexist* bumper stickers in the back. You know, where they use all the different religious symbols as letters . . ."

He nodded.

"I checked around the house and then this guy comes around the corner and belts me one in the gut and the back of the head. Puts me out."

"You're such an amateur." Kendel chuckled. "Always check the plates. Take notes. Proceed with caution."

"You want the rest of it?"

He gave me a little wave of his hand to proceed.

"So I'm trying to put this thing together when Terrence Oliver gets killed. Now, I've seen Cap'n Cody around—"

"His name's Cody Harkin."

"Okay," I said. "When I saw him behind the Salty Dog, I thought maybe he needed help."

"What were they fighting about?"

"I don't know."

Kendel stared at me. I couldn't read his poker face. But I could tell he wanted to put this case to bed. And so did I.

He took a deep breath and leaned forward on his chair and shuffled his papers, picked one up and looked it over. "We took Alex Trainor into custody late last night. We're getting a warrant to search his place."

"I guess you're not retired yet, huh?"

He didn't find that funny. He pushed himself up from his chair, adjusted his hat, and motioned to me. "I want you to talk to Harkin."

"What for?"

"You know more about this than we do. You'll know what to ask."

I followed Kendel across an open office with a few deputies sitting at computers, the smell of grease from someone's breakfast hanging in the air like Fabreze. Then we went down a hallway and paused by a door.

"You go in alone. He'll talk to you."

I frowned.

He gave me one of those half smiles. "He's cuffed to the table. And I'll be in the other room. We're recording."

What could I say?

He opened the door. The room was small and nothing like the plush digs of the Sarasota PD. County had it bad. If you left me in this room for a few hours—yellow walls, no window, concrete floor, table bolted to the wall—I would confess to anything just to get the hell out.

Cap'n Cody was sitting on the only chair in the room, folded over, his forearms resting on his knees, his right wrist cuffed to the table. When he saw me standing behind Kendel's big frame, he straightened up. Didn't smile.

"Here he is," Kendel said and left the room, shut the door behind him.

Cap'n Cody stared at his shoes, Converse, no shoelaces. After a moment I said, "What's going on, Cap'n Cody?"

He raised his eyes to the little black dome on the corner of the ceiling, then to me. "Christ, man, just call me Cody."

"All right."

He sighed, looked at his hands. "You think they'll gimme the chair?"

"It's an injection. But that's something for a lawyer, not me."

He laughed nervously and looked up at the camera again. "I bet Alex gets off."

"Why do you say that?"

"The rich ones always do."

"What happened, Cody?"

He was quiet, his breathing speeding up. Maybe he was figuring out things in his head. Maybe he was assessing his punishment. Maybe he was trying to figure out how to get out of whatever mess he'd gotten himself into. Or maybe he was just scared.

"You and Alex Trainor were at the cottage the other day, right? He knocked me out."

He nodded.

"What were you doing there?"

"Liam's computer," he mumbled. "We wanted the documents on the properties."

"That's how you learned Liam had a partner. That Jaybird was Terrence Oliver."

He raised his head and his eyes narrowed. "I toured with Jimmy Buffet, man. I played with Petty. Fuck this bullshit—"

"Cody."

He shook his head. "Alex suckered me into the deal. He said it was a sure thing. Then he said if I expected the deal to work, I'd have to get Beach City Holdings outta the damn way."

"Meaning Liam and Jaybird."

"Shit threw me for a goddamn loop, man."

"I'm not—"

"I was just trying to get set up. Make a nice investment. Retire well. You think I dig playin' the bars, same songs over and over like a broken record?"

I raised my hands to stop him. "You're not making any sense, Cody. Can you tell it from the start?"

He let out a sad, broken chuckle. "When the fuck did it all begin?"

"Did you kill Liam and Jaybi—Terrence Oliver?"

He looked at the camera. He opened his mouth to speak, then shut it and bowed his head and nodded. "I fucked up."

CHAPTER 36

IT WAS NOON when I finally left the Sheriff's Office at the County Building on Ringling Boulevard and took an Uber to my place. I made a quick sandwich with stale bread, got a cold Siesta IPA, and sat at my computer to write a brief report for Bob Fleming.

Mimi jumped up on my desk and lay there purring on a swath of sun. Outside, the sky was clear. In the empty lot catty-corner from my house there was still the big sign for Dieter and Waxler's nine-story condo building that would never get built. And across the sign in big block letters it still urged buyers to hurry: *90 Percent Sold!*

A historic bungalow was gone and in its place was a flat square of lies. It had all been for nothing. And if Alex Trainor had had his way, he'd have a few million in the Caymans and there'd be a lot of unsatisfied condo owners standing at the end of my street wondering where their building had gone. I only hoped whoever ended up with the lot would build a nice little house, something quaint that jived with the neighborhood.

I finished my sandwich, took a long sip of my beer, and reread my report:

According to Cody Harkin, the man who has confessed to murdering Liam and his business partner, Terrence Oliver, it all began in April

when Liam's company, Beach City Holdings, purchased a house on
Beach Road in Siesta Key from a man named George Finney.

Mr. Harkin had invested his life savings with a real estate developer,
Alex Trainor, who had purchased the house adjacent to Mr. Finney a
few years earlier. When Beach City Holdings purchased that house,
it foiled Mr. Trainor's development plan to build a condominium in
the double lot he would have otherwise owned, causing Mr. Harkin to
lose—or at least block—his investment.

According to Mr. Harkin, Mr. Trainor said something to the effect
of, "If Beach City Holdings was out of the way, we could proceed."

Mr. Harkin, desperate to turn a profit on his investment, took
those words literally and on the night of July 9th of this year, he suffo-
cated Liam in his sleep using a pillow, then he tossed his body into the
Intracoastal.

Almost two weeks later, and a day after I was hired by you, Mr.
Harkin hit Terrence over the head with a hammer, tied his leg to a
cinderblock, and threw him into the Intracoastal.

It appears as if Mr. Trainor was running a scam, selling fraudulent
real estate. This part of the case is currently being investigated by the
authorities. Both Mr. Harkin and Mr. Trainor are in custody.

I finished the note offering my condolences with a little personal
note wishing Mr. Fleming a quick recovery and that I hoped he
would find happiness in the future.

Maybe it was too thick and syrupy, but I felt like the poor man
didn't deserve such suffering. I didn't know if he'd stay with Brandy.
I certainly wouldn't. But most people cannot stand being alone. And
as someone who had a distant relationship with his own daughter, I
can understand his effort to get close to Liam.

There was a lesson in there somewhere—a bunch of them, actually. Certainly, I knew I did not want to find myself estranged

from Zoe in the future. I didn't want her telling her husband or her children how her father was never there for her. I made a note to put more effort into our relationship, even if Nancy protested. I just needed to talk with her, listen and give her support—everything Bob Fleming did not do for his son.

I set up a spreadsheet with my expenses for the job and included the automobile damage my poor Subaru had suffered thanks to Brandy Fleming's pill pushers, all of which happened during the course of the investigation. It was a legitimate expense. But I knew a guy who knew a guy in Bradenton who did pretty good bodywork on the cheap. I guestimated the damage at about two grand. Then I printed out the report and my expense sheet and drove over to the corner of Palm Avenue and Main Street to see Pearlman.

"He's not in," Vivian said and invited me to sit.

"I guess he's got his work cut out for him," I said.

"He always does."

"Is Mr. Fleming okay?"

"He's at the Betty Ford Clinic in California," she said with a wave of her hand. "He'll be fine, I'm sure."

I handed her the envelope with my report and expenses. "It's all in there. Explains the murders."

She set it on the side table next to her chair and locked eyes with me. "Thank you," she said. Both of us like old friends sitting in the two cushy high-back chairs. All we were lacking were martinis and cigars.

"It's my job."

"You think they'll also charge Alex Trainor with the murders?"

"I hope so," I said. "I can't excuse Cody Harkin—Cap'n Cody. I mean, he did kill Liam and Jaybird, right? But Trainor was pulling the strings. Cody was just a sucker, thought he was making an investment, then worked himself into a corner. His life savings were gone. Trainor, on the other hand . . . That son of a bitch deserves some kind of punishment."

"All for a little piece of the beach," Vivian said, shaking her head.

"It's more than that," I said. "Trainor was a real piece of work. He convinced Cap'n Cody to invest with him. The old guy sold his guitar collection, whatever investments he had for retirement. Everything. He used the money for a down payment on the first house at the start of that stretch of Beach Road a couple years back."

"Why did Harkin go for it?"

"He's a fixture in the Village. I guess he's been there for years. He knew Frank Finney. He knew the old guy was sick. He knew he was going to either sell or die. I guess he figured it was a done deal. It was just a matter of waiting."

"That's where Liam came in," she said.

"Yeah, when Liam bought that house, it stopped their plans."

Vivian crossed her legs, leaned forward on her chair. "Why didn't Trainor just sell the house and split the profit with Harkin?"

"'Cause he's a slimeball. The son of a bitch had a bigger scam going. He borrowed on the house."

"So it was underwater."

I nodded. "He set up this shell corporation, Dieter and Waxler, bought an old bungalow, which so happened to be in my neighborhood. He flattened it and put up a sign for a future luxury condo and started selling pre-construction."

"He never intended to build it?"

I shook my head. "But I think the cops will have a hard time proving that."

"Wow." She sat back on her chair and touched her chin with the tip of her fingers. "The whole beachfront property was never really going to be developed?"

"I have no idea," I said. "Maybe if he'd bought the Finney house, he might've run another scam."

"Or maybe he would've built it. I mean with the county commission talking about closing Beach Road . . ."

"Well, that's another thing," I said. "Apparently our good county commissioner Troy Varnel is now being investigated for fraud."

"He was in on it with Trainor?"

I nodded. "Took a nice little bribe to get behind the closing of Beach Road."

"Well, someone else'll build something there," she said.

"In the downtown lot?"

"Sure, and on the Beach Road properties."

Sadly, Vivian was right. That was how it was going to be. That was how it always was. Del Pino had said a trust had been set up for the properties. I had no doubt they would eventually sell out to a developer. Or maybe they would buy Trainor's house on the corner and develop the last piece of unobstructed ocean view in Siesta Key. Except now they probably wouldn't close Beach Road.

"You can't beat progress," I said.

"That's what they say."

CHAPTER 37

ON SUNDAY AT sunset I went to the beach for Jaybird's celebration of life. It was probably the nicest day we'd had all year. The clouds weren't threatening rain and there was a breeze that kept the temperature at a tolerable level. The drum circle was bigger than I'd ever seen it—even for a Sunday. The huge crowd extended from the sea oats almost all the way to the lifeguard station.

And forget somber. This was a party. The drumming, as disrupting and out of rhythm as always, made some kind of sense this time. It seemed to jive in some place where order and disorder meet and people simply live by emotions and good vibes.

I sat on the sand and closed my eyes and listened, felt the vibrations against my ribs and the breeze against my face. I could hear the laughter of the children and the song of the ocean behind me as small waves lapped against the sugary sands of the Siesta Beach. And for a moment I felt this immense sense of peace, something I'd never felt before or since.

When I opened my eyes, I saw Tessa inside the drum circle tapping Jaybird's old ratty djembe drum. After a moment, she passed it to the young man sitting next to her. He began tapping it and shaking his head left and right to the rhythm of the circle. Tessa wiped the tears from her eyes and stood. The young man with the drum passed it to the person next to him. Like that, Jaybird's drum went around in a circle until the older lady sitting next to me passed it to me. I placed it between my legs and tapped with my eyes closed. I could see Jaybird on the day I met him for the first time. He was smiling up at me, staring at my scarred ear. He was as real as life. Maybe he'd really had the key to happiness. Unlike Bob Fleming who'd pursued a career and money, Jaybird had pursued a lifestyle, one of friends and nature and personal freedom—and of a place he loved.

After a moment, I had this strange feeling that he was nodding at me. That he understood that I understood. And that I'd said good-bye. I stopped drumming and caressed the drum once over the tight skin and passed it to the person sitting next to me.

The sun went down in a spectacular sunset. The array of clouds splashed in warm hues of orange and the sky took on this light iridescent blue. Willow, the hippie girl who'd pointed out Jaybird to me almost two weeks ago, walked to the center of the circle and gestured for everyone to quiet down.

"This is a great day for Jaybird," she said. "We're gathered to celebrate the life of a man who brought us together as human beings and taught us to protect nature's gift."

The event went on for about twenty minutes with some of Jaybird's friends telling of his antics, or sharing a memory. They spoke of his love of nature and of surfing and of the help he'd given others, or the simplicity of his life as an example of how to live in harmony with Mother Nature. It was very moving to see friends coming together for a friend. But it was also wonderful to feel the kindness that seemed to reverberate through the drum circle at sunset, something I had been too damn cynical to acknowledge when I first came here and met Jaybird. There was a true sense of community among these people. That was exactly what was missing in the world today.

And it was missing in me.

After the speeches and after the ashes had been spread across the beach and in the shallows of Siesta Beach, and the sun had gone down and only a thin stream of crimson lay across the sky like a parting kiss, Willow returned to the center of the circle and raised a few papers up over her head for everyone to see.

"Friends," she announced. "It's a shame and a real bummer that Jaybird isn't here to see this, but here it is. A little good news. We've gathered enough signatures in the petition to place the amendment to save Beach Road on the ballot in November!"

Everyone applauded. The drummers banged on the drums. People hopped up and started dancing again. The party got a new boost.

I stood and started toward the parking lot when a hand grabbed my arm, laced itself under mine.

"Hello, stranger." It was Tessa.

"What's this?" I said. "I thought you were ignoring me."

"I was busy." She turned me around and we started walking north on the beach, our bare feet touching the water whenever a wave broke. "All these friends, so many people I hadn't seen in a while."

"You're a popular girl," I said.

"I've met a lot of good people here on the key."

"You sound like a person who's getting ready to leave."

She shook her head. "On the contrary. I'm digging in."

"Really?"

We were coming up to the north end of the beach where it made a small curve. To our right was that short stretch of Beach Road that had caused so much trouble.

"Jaybird and Liam's company . . ."

"Beach City Holdings."

She brought me closer to her and squeezed my arm. We stopped walking. It was almost dark. The sky was a deep blue and the sea seemed to perform a magic trick reflecting the colors of the sky, which blended with the phosphorescence of the waves.

"Their lawyer called me."

"Joaquin del Pino?"

"In person."

"What'd he say?"

She smiled and turned slightly to the side so the lights of the Village reflected in her beautiful eyes. "It seems Liam and Jaybird put me in their will."

"For real?"

She nodded. "My apartment building."

"I know."

"What?"

"The day I found Cap'n Cody behind the Salty Dog. I was coming to tell you."

She frowned. "You thought it gave me a motive."

"Not really," I said. "Del Pino told me you didn't know. So it couldn't be a motive, now could it?

She smiled. "I'm a landlord."

"You are."

"I was wrong about him," she said sadly.

"Sounds like Liam was very generous."

"Yeah," she said. "But I don't mean about that. It turns out they never wanted to develop the land. They were doing the opposite. They were buying land to protect it. Midnight Pass and Beach Road and the properties out East."

"Del Pino told me they set up a trust."

"That's right. The Nature Conservancy is going to manage the properties and keep the land undeveloped."

"All of it?"

"Yup."

"What about the houses on Beach Road?"

"That will be up to the board of the Conservancy. But del Pino said Jaybird and Liam wanted it to be part of the beach, like a park. They might tear down the houses and leave it vacant, even if the county closes the road."

"Damn."

"I feel like a fool," she said. "All this time I thought he was faking it. I thought he was using all of us to find deals on the island so he could develop the land."

"And he was doing the exact opposite."

She rubbed the side of her face against my shoulder, maybe tears. I didn't see. Then she turned and pointed at the water. "Look, dolphins!"

In the shallow, two dolphins swam back and forth playing in the waves. It was beautiful to see them in the dim light of dusk, their skin reflecting the last of the sunset.

Tessa ran to the edge of the water and raced up and down the beach alongside them. It was almost as if they were all playing together: Tessa laughing and holding her arms up in the air and kicking at the water while the dolphins raced and jumped out of the water where the waves broke.

My phone rang. Zoe.

"Hi, Daddy."

"Hey, whatcha doing, little one?"

"I'm not little," she said.

"I know. It's just a saying."

"Well, I'm not little. I'm growing up. Mommy says too fast. You need to find another nickname for me."

"Fine," I said. "How about peanut?"

"No. That's from when I was a baby."

"Okay, how about *linda*? That's Spanish for pretty."

"I'm not sure," she said seriously. "I'll have to think about it."

I laughed. "You think about it all you want and let me know."

"Guess what? Mommy said I can stay with you an extra week when I come over."

"Really? That's great!" I watched Tessa knee deep in the water, waving at the dolphins. Beyond her the sky was falling and the stars were smiling.

"Listen, Zoe, I was thinking. Maybe instead of going to one of those all-inclusive resorts we talked about, we just stay in Sarasota. Make it a special beach vacation?"

"Really?"

"Sure. We can learn to surf and go kayaking and do all kinds of cool things."

"Can we make a sandcastle?"

"We can make anything you want, baby."

"Daddy!"

"What?"

"I'm. Not. A. Baby!"